KING OF THE UNDERWORLD

EARTHBOUND SERIES
LUCIEN & SCARLETT

BOOK ONE

V L PETERS

Copyright © 2021 by VL Peters

All rights reserved.

No part of this book may be reproduced in any form or by any electronic or mechanical means, including information storage and retrieval systems, without written permission from the author, except for the use of brief quotations in a book review.

PROLOGUE ONE

AS THE YEARS HAVE GONE BY, humans forgot they weren't alone on this planet. Once upon a time, they knew about the others who called Earth their home. They were known as Supernaturals, or just Naturals. Now they are mere villains in the scary stories parents tell their children in order to get them to behave. The monsters lurking in the dark.

As the years turned to centuries, society removed us from their collective memories, believe we were naught but a fictional element in the movies they watched and the books they read. And we let them believe it.

Until it was no longer possible to keep our existence a secret, that is. Until those who thought they knew best decided we should come out of the darkness once more, naively believing it was possible for us to roam the planet with the humans and live together in harmony. It didn't work the first time around. It only stands to reason it wouldn't work this time either.

War broke out. Cities fell, humans and Supernaturals were killed. Some Supernaturals went into hiding, disappearing, never to be seen again. A hundred years after the war began, a group of humans and Supernaturals came together and decided enough was enough. We had to learn to live together.

A treaty was agreed upon and two councils were formed: one for the humans and one for the Supernaturals, twenty-four members in total. As time passed, different threats came and went. Witches gained

They were evil, showing no emotion, no weakness. They didn't think twice before gutting someone, caring not who or what they were. They were wiped out, or so it was believed.

Things are about to change again. Witches are re-emerging, the Supernaturals the world believed extinct will be coming forward once again, and the Troglodytes are clashing with a new enemy, one they haven't fought before. If they don't combine forces, will all be lost?

PROLOGUE TWO

THE DREAMS ARE BACK.

I've had the same ones for so long it's become routine. Some nights I have only one; others the dreams are continuous. The Demon appears, tormenting me, and as the dream unfolds, the Demon turns into a man. He always looks the same way, dark tailored suit, sharp features, jet-black hair, and eyes as dark as the night sky.

The outcome is always the same as well. The Demon and the Man both claiming me as their own. His touch burning, setting my body aflame until it turns into a raging ball of fire. I knew I would be meeting this man, this Demon. Only the fates would decide when and how it would happen, and everyone knows how fickle the fates can be.

Last night, the dream started as it always has, but then it changed. The vision developed into individual figures I couldn't make out. A dark ominous fog emerged, blending and combining the dreams until I couldn't discern one from the other. Megan appeared before me, a smile upon her face and her eyes lit up with laughter. An arm appeared out of the fog, its hand closing around her mouth dragging her back into the darkness. I can still hear the manic laughter over the sound of Megan's muffled cries, her arms reaching toward me, her terrified eyes beseeching me to save her. The panic I saw in her eyes was real. I took it for what it was, a warning.

Megan is in danger. There's no telling when it will happen, but one thing I do know is none of us will be able to stop what is coming, no matter how hard we may try. Whoever is going to take her is powerful enough to do so without interference.

I have no choice in what I have to do. I know who the man was in my dreams. I'd known for a long time. I had chosen not to tell my family. But no matter how much they protest, it has to be me who approaches him when the time arises.

My siblings can't help this time. Mia and Abigail must be left out of this, no matter how powerful they are to become.

Is this what the fates had foreseen? Is this what we have been training for so long? Only time will tell.

All I know is… it has to be me.

CHAPTER ONE

SCARLETT

We all knew this day was coming; it was predicted long ago. Our parents had trained every single one of us for this moment and had made sure my sisters and I never forgot this was all part of our destiny. We thought we'd have a few more years before we had to step out into the open. We've been in hiding for so long, revealing ourselves now will be risky.

We know it's going to be dangerous; it's possible we will be hunted and killed off one-by-one; or even worse, tortured beyond recognition. The latter is far more daunting a prospect than the former.

With Megan's disappearance, it seems the time is finally upon us. Our parents had been the backbone of our community. With them gone, we need to stick together and put the plan we agreed upon into action. We need to get to work finding Megan. Getting her home safely is our number one priority. The stupid bickering has to stop, and it needs to happen now. It isn't helping our situation in the least. We still haven't managed to decide which one of us will go into the lion's den.

I hate sitting here listening to them squabble; we're wasting time. I have no choice and know what needs to happen. I'd known even before we sat down to discuss things. It will be harder to convince them than it was for me to come to terms with the way things were meant to happen.

I stand up and move over to the fireplace, watching and waiting for my opportunity. I can't wait any longer, time is too precious. "I'll do it.

I'll go," I call out, trying to make my voice heard over the deafening noise of their argument. The decibel achieved by my sisters is shocking, but the fact nobody hears me over it is not.

Bloody hell, if they don't stop this bickering, I'm going to pull my hair out. I continue listening to my five sisters speaking over one another, saying who will do that, what is necessary and what isn't. Do they include me in this conversation? Of course not. Being the youngest completely sucks sometimes. They rarely listen to what I have to say, and they consider my opinion far less often than that. I already know this time won't be the exception.

I study each of their faces, watching as they turned more and more crimson, wondering whose temper will reach its boiling point first. Someone is going to blow a gasket, and soon. I must admit, I've never before witnessed any of my sisters lose their cool this way. Sure, they sometimes disagree with one another over stupid shit, but it never reaches this level of rage. One would think that if anyone were going to lose their shit, it would be me, what with my wild red curls and the temperament to match.

As usual, my sister Pamela is gesturing wildly with her arms. If she's not careful, she's going to smack someone in their face with one of them. She's arguing with Ava, one of my other sisters, who is standing there with her hands on her hips, her eyes scrunched up as though she's trying to block the sound of Pamela's voice. My other sisters Mia, Abigail, and Emma are arguing amongst themselves, their voices rising higher and higher, as if they're trying to compete with one another. Their combined voices are causing my head to throb. I cannot stand idly by and listen to their nonsense for even a moment longer.

"STOOOOOPPPP!" I scream, my voice growing hoarse from the effort, but I'm pleased when I achieve my desired result. They all stop speaking at once, turning their attention towards me. Eyes open wide in shock, it's almost as though they just realized that I've been in the room with them this whole time.

"I said I will go," I repeat, raising my voice to get them to take notice of what I'm about to say. I need them to listen.

It takes exactly two seconds before all hell breaks loose. I'm forced to listen to all the reasons I couldn't, shouldn't, and wouldn't do it. In my eyes, none of them come up with even one solid reason against it, though. Megan has disappeared. It's been three days since anyone has seen her. The last sighting was at The Fallen Angel, a notorious nightclub.

Rumor had it that if you wanted to find a certain type of pleasure, The Fallen Angel was the place to go. It is said that as one ascends the floors, the experience becomes more and more extreme. Everything from dancing to sex, even blood feedings if one so desires. There is a price to pay for your pleasure, and the more perverse the desire, the higher the price. But that doesn't always mean money.

The club is owned by none other than Lucien Sinclair. Sexy as hell, trouble with a capital T, and if the rumors are to be believed, a Demon. Sources say he isn't fond of humans and despises witches even more. If he finds out a witch visits The Fallen Angel, they're fucked, and not in a way they'll enjoy. He is a force to be reckoned with, someone nobody wishes to cross. We've all heard the rumors about what happens to the people who cross him. They're damn lucky if they get out with all their limbs intact. Anyone with a lick of sense stays far away from him and his clubs. He rules with an iron fist and staying off his radar is the only way to be safe. The other thing to note about Lucien; he rules over this city and its surrounding regions.

Why Megan and her friends would have gone there is all our comprehension. We questioned her friends already, demanding that they explain why on earth they'd chosen that particular nightclub. Their answers had been vague and unhelpful. It seemed their memories of that night were hazy. They could remember Megan going to the bar for a round of drinks before heading to the bathroom, but after that, nothing.

Each of them thought Megan had told the other she was going home, but she hadn't. She was there one minute, gone the next. I wasn't the only one who wanted to slap them silly for their foolishness.

The human police were useless, and they'd done nothing but waste our time. They stayed away from all things Supernatural, even if humans were involved. They preferred to leave things in the hands of The Enforcement, which is the Supernatural's police force. A group of the most powerful Supernaturals, or Naturals as they prefer to be called, maintains The Enforcement.

Then you have the Councils, a mixture of human and Naturals, and they're rarely much help. They prefer to leave matters they consider beneath them to The Enforcement or the human police force to deal with.

We had reluctantly approached The Enforcement, hoping that they would help us. It was a wasted effort. Even though Megan was on a Supernatural's property when she was last seen, they refused help, no matter how much we pleaded with them. They claimed it was a human matter and told us to go to the human police force for help. So, with no help in sight, we realized we had no choice but to deal with her disappearance ourselves.

I've never seen Lucien Sinclair in the flesh, and I know the next 48 hours will mean that fact is going to change. Everything is going to change; I feel it in my bones. But I am absolutely certain that I am the only person for the job. I've never gone against my sister's wishes before, but I don't feel I have much choice this time, no matter what they say to convince me otherwise. I know, without a single doubt, that I need to be the one to infiltrate The Fallen Angel.

I feel like screaming. Don't they realize how much time they're wasting? Or that time is a commodity we have precious little of? Megan is missing, and we need to find her quickly, no matter the cost. She is the one who anchors us all when we need it.

I've already spoken to our cousin Melissa, and with some persuading, she's agreed to give me some of her herbs, along with a spell of protection. She didn't want to put her family in danger by helping me, but she understood the importance. Before this heated discussion began, I'd given the spell and herbs to Pamela, briefly explaining why I'd gotten them. As the eldest, she preferred to be the one in charge, so she wasn't the least bit pleased I'd gone behind her back to Melissa.

Pamela steps forward, eyebrows knitting together as she takes my hand in her own. "Scarlett, why do you feel it must be you who goes rather than one of us?"

I realize Pamela already knows the answer as soon as she asks her next question. "Have you been dreaming again?"

I know the reaction I'll receive if I tell them the whole truth. I'm not going to lie, but I need to watch what I say and how I say it. Placing a smile across my lips, hoping they don't realize how forced it is, I give a quick nod. "I know she was there. We all do," I sighed. I know them too well; I can tell by the look on their faces that they're about to protest. To tell me I can't go. I know why, too. It's because of my age.

"Stop," I order, shaking my head, halting their arguments before they can voice them. "Hear me out. It must be me. You are correct, Pamela. My dreams…. I just know I have to go," I pause, trying to find the right words to express my emotions without frightening them and freaking them out further.

Admitting to them what my dreams truly comprise of is difficult and it will cause them to go off the deep end. I know I need to tell a little white lie. I'm going to hold back a bit of the truth, namely the part about Lucien Sinclair. I know by going into his nightclub that I will end up meeting him. I saw it in my dreams. If I even mention his name, my sisters will flip. They'll lock me away, telling me it's for my own good and they wouldn't let me out until they decided I'd come to my senses.

If they stop me, it will not only put Megan in even more danger, but it will endanger the rest of us as well. Something is coming, something that will change everything; changes that were already in motion long before Megan went missing. With her disappearance, *they* had upped the ante. Dangerous times are on the horizon, and it frightens the fuck out of me. They all know it too; they can sense it. Maybe not as strongly as I can, but it's there just the same.

"None of you can go. It must be me." I tell them. I know each of them can see the fear in my eyes, but I also know they hear the clear determination in my voice. Even if they don't like what they're seeing and hearing, they all know that if they don't help me, I will just find another way, and they know I'll be far safer with their help. They just have to trust me and let me be the one to find out what happened to Megan.

They know my dreams always come to pass. The ones I'd been having lately are different, though. They're more intense and feel more vivid. It's as though I'm truly there, not just seeing, but experiencing the events of my dreams. The dread that has been materializing within all of us for weeks is threatening to overwhelm us.

PAMELA

WHEN SCARLETT CAME TO ME EARLIER and handed me the herbs along with the spell from Melissa, I didn't fully realize what her intentions were. In shock, I abruptly sit on the nearest available chair and watch as my sisters do the same. I study their faces for their reactions to Scarlett's announcement.

I notice Mia's and Abigail's eyes have glazed over, their faces devoid of expression. They are likely communicating with each other via their own personal link. Ava and Emma are just sitting there, looking between me and Scarlett. I watch as Ava frowns, her face filled with worry as she rubs the back of her neck. Emma starts twiddling her thumbs, a habit she uses when she's upset or uncertain about something. I watch as she opens her mouth as if to say something, only to immediately shut it again.

I know Scarlett feels she must be the one, just as I know we're going to agree to let her go. I just hope none of us will end up regretting it. The feeling of our combined guilt travels down our mental link, but I also feel relief swelling inside the room. It may sound selfish that most of us feel relieved to know Scarlett wants to go, but none of us have any desire to set foot in The Fallen Angel.

We especially don't want to set eyes on Lucien Sinclair. I pray she won't have to see him, but there's always that slight chance. Just the thought of it sends shivers down my spine. He is bad news in more ways than one. Everything we know about him shows how dangerous he is. I would even go as far as saying he is downright deadly.

With none of us there to cover her back, Scarlett will have to be on her guard the entire time. We've all received self-defense training over the years, so we know how to protect ourselves. Thankfully, Megan and I carried that tradition on after our parents died.

We understand that being witches doesn't mean we can't get hurt or killed. We are just as mortal as the humans of the world, we just have a little... extra inside of us. Every normal witch possesses powers, but those powers can be quite different. The thing is though, we are not normal witches. Scarlett and the rest of us, including our cousins Melissa, Evelyn, and their own families, are unique. Scarlett differs slightly from the rest of us, as she possesses a wider range of powers.

She can see both the past and the future. It is one hell of a burden; one I know she carries heavily on her shoulders. She has seen many gruesome deaths from the past, and I know she's aware there are only more to come. She also has the power of psychometry. Sometimes, all she has to do is touch an object and she will see the memories and feelings of the people who possessed it. This can be uncomfortable because she has no control over when or what she sees.

She once told me the one power she has never considered a burden, the only one she genuinely thinks of as a gift, is her ability to heal. Scarlett learned from an early age that she not only has the ability to heal the earth's soil with a touch of her hands, but she can also heal the wounded.

Megan also has the power of psychometry and is gifted with the same healing powers as Scarlett. When the two of them combine their powers, they are impressive and potent beyond belief.

I can feel the fear coming off my sisters in waves. It's palpable, overwhelming. Fear, not just for Megan and Scarlett, but for ourselves as well. As we sit there listening to her reasons for putting herself in danger, we understand where she was coming from and we are relieved not to have to do it ourselves, but that doesn't mean we're happy about it. None of us want to step foot in that nightclub, but we plan to be there for Scarlett if she needs us. We have no intention of losing another sister.

I can feel that Mia and Abigail are unhappy with this turn of events. They feel they should be the ones going into the nightclub to find out what had happened to Megan, rather than Scarlett. Being twins, their powers combine, and they are the strongest out of all of us. However, they are still training and mastering their skills, so they aren't quite ready to handle a situation of this magnitude.

"If you're so determined to go, then we will support you," I tell Scarlett before turning my attention to our other sisters. "We have to make sure Scarlett is protected."

I turn back to Scarlett. "None of us will be able to go with you. It's too risky." I want to make sure she knows what she's walking into, that she will be alone.

"I know," Scarlett replies, meeting my gaze. I can see the determination in her eyes as well as her acceptance of her fate. If we hadn't agreed, I know she would have gone there alone, likely with nobody knowing she had gone, and with no one to help her.

Tapping her chin as though deep in thought and tilting her head to one side as she narrows her eyes, Mia says, "We will have to combine several spells to protect her. It needs to be powerful enough, not only to hide any markings, but also to provide her with a concealment spell and a protection spell. Melissa can help with that."

We all know our cousin Melissa is our best bet. She won't have any problem conjuring up another spell or two. I must inform them that Scarlett has already taken care of contacting our cousin. "Scarlett already contacted Melissa and got the protection spell from her, so part of it is done."

I turn my attention to Ava. "Ava, get ahold of Melissa, explain what else we need, and thank her for her help." I know our best option is to combine all our powers together, fitting them together as if they're pieces of a gigantic jigsaw puzzle sliding into place. That, along with our cousin Melissa's spells, will give us the best odds of success.

"Will do," Ava replies with a nod of her head, giving Scarlett a small smile as she gets up from her seat and walks into the other room.

Placing a protective shield around someone can be difficult enough on its own, combining the shield with different spells will be even more so. The primary problem being that we have no way of knowing how long it will last, or if it will even work at all. Even if the spells can stop one person from seeing the truth, it doesn't mean it will work on the next person. It's an enormous risk. We stay up talking well into the night until we finally come to an agreement. We have little choice but to take a chance and trust that Scarlett can handle this. There is just no other option.

CHAPTER TWO

SCARLETT

THE FOLLOWING EVENING: WINTERS' HOUSEHOLD

"ARE YOU READY FOR THIS?" EMMA asks with a slight smile, worry shining in her blue eyes.

"Ready," I let out a light laugh as I feel Emma take a seat next to me. I stayed awake the rest of the night last night, wondering what the hell I'd done and regretting everything.

"Nope, I am nowhere near ready. I'm so nervous, I think I'm going to be sick," I tell her as we watch Pamela and Ava rearrange the furniture.

"We are one-hundred percent behind you, Scarlett, but if you want to change your mind, we will understand. One of us can go instead," she tries to reassure me, placing her hand upon my own and gripping it tightly.

I know she means it. Any of them would step into my shoes with just one word from me. They wouldn't want to do it, but they would. But even if one of them came forward now, at this precise minute, to announce they wanted to go in my place, it just wouldn't work. I would not allow it; I could not allow it. I'm the only one who can do this. Too much is at risk. They don't know what's at stake and what is waiting in the shadows.

"I know," I whisper, placing my head on her shoulder. "I know every single one of you would take my place, but I can't let you." Sighing, I lift my head and turn to face her, "What's happening is bigger than any of us realize; bigger than any of you realize! We must stay strong because if we don't, the consequences…"

I look over at Pamela and Ava, trying to think of a way to put this without frightening her. There just isn't any other way, I have to be brutally honest. I turn my attention back to her. "It will not only bring devastation to us, but to everyone we love and know. Even to those we don't! To everyone."

She sighs, her eyes downcast and a frown appearing as if she is really absorbing what I'm saying. "I'm terrified, Scarlett," *she confesses, raising her eyes to meet mine.* "Truth be told, we all are. We're worried Megan isn't going to come home in one piece, or at all. It terrifies us thinking you might end up the same way," *she admits with tear-filled eyes.*

I squeeze the hand that's tightly holding onto my own and with my other, I gently push aside the white-blonde hair that had fallen and is hiding one side of her tanned face. Even though I'm the younger one, at that moment, for the very first time, I feel a reversal in our roles.

"I have to go," *I tell her, resolutely. I place my hand on my chest, trying to get my point across. She has to understand. To make this work, they all have to understand and accept that it must be me and that nobody can take my place.* "There isn't any other option, Emma. It. Has. To. Be. Me." *She shakes her head, opening her mouth to protest. Before she can speak, Pamela walks over and stands over us, looking down with concern. She places one of her hands over our joined ones and we both know from her face that she overheard our conversation.*

"Emma's right, all of us are more than willing to go in your place. All you have to do is say the word."

"Pamela, we had this discussion last night. You all know it must be me who goes. It's the only way we all make it through this," *I insist. This is ridiculous. I know they're petrified, more scared than they've ever been. I know they fear something bad happening to me, but I thought we sorted this all out last night. Apparently, that wasn't the case.*

"She's right," *states an unknown voice from the corner of the room.* "It has to be her."

The sound of a stranger's voice coming from inside our home makes us all jump and turn in the direction it came from. Seeing nothing, we frantically look around at each other.

Suddenly, a beautiful woman appears in front of us. Her long silver hair appears like a halo around her head, and she has a small dark mole on her right cheek. Her skin is smooth, except around her eyes, which has fine lines around them, telling us she is older than she appears. Her figure is wavering slightly, as if she's an apparition and is trying to establish a stronger connection. She turns her head, appearing to look at someone or something behind her and then frowns, saying something we cannot hear, and I realize she is an apparition.

She swings back to face us again, "I haven't much time," she tells us, annoyance written across her face. "Scarlett must be the one to go. If she doesn't, then everything you know will cease to exist. You will all have to learn to trust one another, put your trust in ..." her voice fades but we can see her mouth still moving, even as her figure gradually disappears until it's as if she was never there at all.

All hell breaks loose, as each of us begins talking over one another. The thing all of us seem to want to know, but none seem to have the answer to, is who the hell that woman was. None of us recognized her, though I feel as though I should have. I have a strong feeling we should know exactly who she is.

Realizing we aren't going to be able to answer that question, we start discussing how she could have gotten in here. It's obvious she used some kind of projection ability, but she shouldn't have been able to get through our spells. The room is silent for several long minutes, and I know we're all wondering the same thing. What the fuck just happened and how the hell are we going to deal with it?

"Whoever our mystery guest was, it seems she, and some person she must have been talking to wherever she actually was, they really want Scarlett to be the one to go," Mia says, breaking the silence. "She was quite persistent about that."

"We need to find out who she was. I don't know about any of you, but I feel as if we should know her?" Emma questions, and we all nod our heads in agreement. All except Pamela, who looks lost in thought.

We look over at her and she notices us staring. "I don't like it," she mutters under her breath, chewing on her lower lip and shaking her head. She crosses her arms over her chest and stares back at us defiantly, as though she's decided on a path, one we have no say about.

"We're about to do a confinement, protection, and binding spell, and some strange woman somehow manages to get inside our own home! How can we move forward with our plan knowing the rigorous spells we've kept in place over our home for so many years have somehow failed? We need to start over, work out a new plan."

I hate that she isn't entirely wrong, but it doesn't matter. "There isn't time. We can't afford to wait any longer to take action," I protest, shaking my head. "Megan disappeared and now she's missing. How or why, we haven't a bloody clue. But whoever that woman was? She's right about one thing. It. Has. To. Be. Me." I tell them, emphasizing each word with a slap to my chest.

Sighing, I run my hand though my long hair, mentally cursing when my hand gets snagged in the curls. I don't want to argue with any of them. I can't handle a repeat of last night. We discussed it, and we all agreed. The decision has been made and we can't change our course now. It doesn't matter how much they argue or plead; I am going to continue as planned. "Deep down, every single one of you know this is the way it has to be."

I see the distress in their eyes, they all know I'm right. They will have to push their misgivings aside if they wish to be of any assistance to me.

Pamela gives a miserable looking smile, and I know what it means. She isn't overjoyed, but she has come to accept what is going to happen. She knows I'm right; they all do. Now they just have to come to terms with it as well.

She moves to Ava and takes the bag she's holding in her hands. It contains the new herbs, along with the new spell Melissa brought to us late last night. Our cousin rigorously drilled us on the spell, making us practice over and over, until we all knew it by heart. Seeing us all united with a common goal, she wanted to stay and help, but she knew, and so did we, that it simply wasn't an option. Her own family needed her.

I watch as my sisters form a circle around me. Opening the bag, Pamela sprinkles the herbs around the circle. I can hear her muttering to herself the entire time, as if praying under her breath. She finishes and places the remaining herbs in a bowl, lights them on fire, and places it inside the sealed circle.

The sweet fragrance weaves together, the scent rising into the air and flowing around us. My sisters tighten their circle around me, and I position myself directly in front of the bowl. I watch as they join hands, and we all bend our heads. We begin to chant, and I know my sisters have the same silent prayer running through their minds as I: that this will protect me long enough for me to get in and back out again.

CHAPTER THREE

SCARLETT

OUTSIDE THE FALLEN ANGEL

I STAND, AS IF ROOTED TO the ground, staring at the building in front of me. I know the concealment spell is working. The memory of my sister's reactions takes me back to the moment they first saw my transformation; I knew something was wrong, their jaws had dropped open, eyes bulging in shock.

As if coming out of a daze. Abigail remarks with a smirk on her face, "Do you think Melissa has done it on purpose?"

Mia sniggers, eyes wide open, while trying to hold in her laughter by placing her hand over her mouth. Ava elbows her sharply, but can't help her own giggle as she whispers, "Stop it!"

Pamela and Emma are speechless, they just stare at me.

"What's wrong?" I cry out and, not getting a reply, I rush to the full-length mirror. Gone are my wild red hair, green eyes, and milky skin. Where normally I have loads of curves, tits for days, and am of average height, I see I've been transformed into a six-foot tall, willowy blonde, blue-eyed woman. As a child and teenager, I always wished for the body of a runway model. I'd come to terms with the fact it was never going to happen, but now it seems that wish has come true.

"I can't go out like this," I scream, appalled at the reflection of the stranger looking back at me.

"I know it's a shock. Not only for you, but for all of us," Pamela tries to soothe me. "However, we don't have time to get more herbs or to perform another spell. You'll just have to grin and bear it."

Bloody hell, I think. *She's right. Whether or not I'm happy about this, I must suck it up. I have no other choice.*

"Fine, but when I see Melissa, I have a bone to pick with her!" I retort, glaring at myself in the mirror and trying to come to terms with my new appearance.

ONCE THE INITIAL SHOCK FADED, MY sisters were visibly excited to see how well the spell worked. I just had to hope it would hold up until I was finished doing what we'd planned. We decided that the safest plan was for me to head out before first light, hoping it would give me enough time to figure out where Megan had gone inside the club, what had happened to her, and get the hell out before anyone knew I was there.

The thought that I might have to open myself up to the feelings of those around me made my stomach churn. That gift always left me shaky and uncomfortable, and I wasn't pleased when the power had suddenly hit me, not all that long ago. Witch powers tend to manifest at different points in their lives, but they usually appear over decades. My ever-growing list of powers has been expanding at such a rapid rate, I'm struggling to keep up with them. For example, I recently discovered that I can now use telekinesis, the ability to move small objects with my mind. I haven't told any of my sisters yet because I haven't had an opportunity to gain full control over it, and I want it to be an effortless task when I announce this new gift.

THE CLUB IN FRONT OF ME is massive; tall as it was long. Floodlights are placed around the roof, reflecting down onto the ground. Five, maybe six stories high, with the words The Fallen Angel lit up in neon lights across the entrance door as if beckoning, daring you to enter. How the hell am I going to find out what happened to Megan? It's going to take me forever just to search, and we've all been operating under the assumption that I will be able to find her. What if I fail?

As I begin to panic, I will myself to take deep breaths and calm down. Ever since I announced my decision to my sisters, I've been an absolute wreck. My stomach has been a tangled knot of queasiness, and I keep experiencing uncontrollable tremors in my legs. The pep talks I've tried giving myself haven't worked, I just can't seem to settle my nerves. I call upon every ounce of my strength and push my anxiety to the side, knowing I must do so in order to get through this.

Standing in the shadows, I observe the various women entering the nightclub. More than half of them are wearing skimpy lingerie, leaving nothing to the imagination. I know I'm going to stick out like a sore thumb. My black skinny jeans, ankle-boots, light green blouse, and gray jacket will bring undue attention, but I'll have to find a way around it. No matter the outcome, I have no choice but to go inside. Everyone is depending on me, especially Megan. Thinking of her and what she's likely going through washes away my remaining tendrils of anxiety, leaving nothing but relief. I can do this, and I will.

Taking a deep breath, I stride to the back of the line, near the entrance. Standing with a handful of others, I try to ignore the funny looks I'm getting. When I get to the front of the line, a large, dark-haired man dressed in black is guarding the entrance to the club. His eyebrow lifts as he looks me up and down, his eyes lingering on my breasts before giving me a nod to enter. I manage to hold off an uncomfortable shudder, not liking his focus and attention.

Once inside, I look around the nightclub, trying to find the staircase that will lead me upstairs to the other levels. Scanning the room, I feel my eyes widening. I'd heard the rumors, everyone has, but seeing it with my own eyes is a uniquely scandalous experience. Bodies are everywhere, undulating against one another to the beat of the music. Naked pole dancers are performing remarkable acrobatics with bodies that look like they've been covered in stardust. To my left, fully visible from the club entrance, is a VIP area where men and women are receiving lap dances, the dancers rolling their naked bodies over the prone forms of their customers.

From the corner of my eye, I see a man holding a woman, her legs are wrapped around his hips. The woman is writhing in ecstasy as he sucks her nipples with enthusiasm. I watch, in disbelief, as she rides his jean-covered leg to completion. I'm so far out of my depth. The urge to run is overwhelming.

I close my eyes and think of Megan. Bringing up her image, I manage to calm down and repress the urge to bolt. When I gain the courage to open my eyes, I see the couple is still at it. The woman appears to be enjoying his *attention; her head thrown back, eyes closed, mouth wide open, and it looks as though she's moaning, but they're too far away and the music is too loud to be certain.*

I can't tear my eyes away from them. I continue to watch her grind her pelvis against the man's hard thigh, the look on her face one of rapture. I'm mortified to find myself getting turned on by the scene, feeling a tingle develop between my thighs. Oh god, I really shouldn't be watching this. What the hell is wrong with me?

Anyone who is paying attention could see how intently focused I am on the couple. But no man has ever made me feel the way the woman is clearly feeling right now. I've never experienced the level of wanton lust I see written across her face. Ha, who am I kidding? There are no men in my life, unless you count family, and in this situation, family is definitely off the table.

I give myself a mental shake, dragging my gaze away from the couple. I must focus. I need to shut out the distractions around me and concentrate on the reason I came here.

I'm not usually one to drink, but I could really use some liquid courage right about now.

TEN MINUTES LATER

I SIT, GLASS IN HAND, GAZING across the crowded dance floor and watching as multiple couples walk up the staircase. I haven't taken my eyes off it since I sat down with my drink. I need to find a way to go up that staircase. I take in the huge bugger standing at the bottom, guarding it like a Rottweiler. I know he isn't going to let just anybody walk up those carpeted stairs.

There must be a way to get up there. But how? I've thought of a distraction, but there's no guarantee it will work. No, my best option is to find someone to get me up there. So far, nobody, human or Natural, has approached me. The thought has crossed my mind that the spell of protection placed on me might be working a bit too well. If that's the case, I'm fucked. I wonder if maybe all the men in this place just find me unattractive. That doesn't make sense, though, not with this supermodel glamour I've got going on.

My primary concern, for now, is how to gain access to the floors above. I have to get up there somehow. If no one approaches me soon, I will have to come up with another plan. I've noticed that none of the staff has used the staircase. They've all been using a door with a sign in bold black letters, declaring Staff Only. If the staff members don't use the public stairs, there must be another access point for the higher levels. Maybe an elevator or another staircase.

I frown, deep in thought. Walking through the Staff Only door would be a bold move but, if I'm caught, I would draw much less attention than if I'm stopped trying to go up the stairs in the middle of the club.

Recognizing the lack of choices before me, I swiftly gulp down the last mouthful of my drink, barely managing not to cough from the burn as it slides down my throat. With determination, my head held high as if I belonged there, I stride purposefully to the Staff Only door and walk through it as though I've done it many times before.

Perhaps it is sheer luck or perhaps my new look makes me look like someone who would work here, but when I get through the door a woman shoves a black and red uniform into my arms. With a high-pitched voice, she snaps, "It's about time you got here. I'm Ms. Burns. I hope your tardiness isn't going to be a regular thing. Mr. Sinclair expects all staff to show up on time, dressed in their uniforms. As this is your first shift, I will give you a pass. But only this once," she says, making it sound as though she's doing me a favor.

The woman, some kind of manager I assume, is very tall. If it weren't for the spell, she would tower over me by at least five inches. She's rail-thin, with enormous breasts sitting high on her narrow chest, and I can't help but think how artificial they look. Her blonde hair hangs down her back, and her dark brown eyes emit a certain animalistic rage, and I can tell she isn't human. She's looking at me as though I'm an unwelcome rodent at a dinner party. I have the feeling she's taken an instant dislike to me. Probably because she assumes I'm an employee with a tardiness problem, but perhaps because I'm human. Most Naturals look down their noses at humans, and there's no way she can sense I'm anything more than that. Whatever the cause of her hostility, I don't intend to hang around long enough to find out.

The sooner I do what I came here to do, the better. I'm not here to make friends or start a new career. I'm here to, hopefully, pick up some kind of vibration or vision of what happened to Megan. Once I complete that task, I plan to get the hell out of here as quickly as possible. I sure as shit don't want to end up running into Lucien Sinclair or any of his minions, even if my visions and dreams have been showing that exact thing happening. If I'm being honest with myself, it scares the fuck out of me and it's the thing I'm most worried about. I know, the second I lay eyes on him, my life will be forever changed.

I half-listen as she drones on and on. She's really starting to irritate me. I note my surroundings, trying to get my bearings. I have no clue where we are. This place is far more extensive than it looks from the outside.

I follow along behind her as she takes me deeper into the staff area and I nearly collide with her when she abruptly spins around to face me.

"Are you listening to me, girl?" She snaps out in an annoyed tone, looking at me with narrowed eyes.

"Yes! Yes, of course!" I reply nervously.

I hear the huff fall from her mouth and I can tell from her demeanor that she knows I wasn't. Rolling her eyes at me, she says, "At the end of this hallway is the changing room. Here's your key. Change into those straight away," she commands, pointing with the key at the uniform I'm holding in my arms and dropping it on top of it. "I will be back for you in fifteen minutes to do something with your hair and makeup. You look like a harlot," she sniffs, before turning on her heel and walking back the way we'd come. I watch as she opens a door further down and goes inside, the door closing behind her with a click.

What a bloody nerve! I have never in my life looked like a harlot. Cheeky bitch! Clutching the uniform tightly in my hands, I hurry down the hallway to the room she told me to use to change, paranoid that at any moment someone will spot me and know I don't belong here. To my relief, I manage to get the door unlocked, opened, and closed behind me without seeing another person.

I step inside the room and look around. It looks like a large dressing room straight out of a department store. I place the uniform on one of the chairs and start stripping off my clothes. I change in record time and look down at the uniform. The top is covered in a delicate, deep red lace and has laces up the front keeping it closed. It's paired with the tiniest set of black silk shorts I've ever seen in my life. I don't have to look in a mirror to see my breasts spilling out of the top or my ass cheeks hanging from the bottom of the shorts… or to know that all my assets are on full display for anyone wanting an eyeful. I've never in my life gone without knickers but, not having a thong available to me, I have no other choice. The shorts are smaller than the knickers I'd worn with my jeans. I just have to hope nobody can tell. I'd also been given black fishnet stockings along with a pair of red-soled, six-inch high-heeled shoes to complement my outfit.

Taking a deep breath, I turn to face the mirror. I stand there, staring in disbelief at the person looking back at me. Seeing myself in a different body, with a different face, wearing this outfit, the likes of which I'd never dreamt of wearing, this all feels so surreal. My God, I look like a tart! How on earth can I leave this room for every person I come across to see me dressed this way?

By pulling up your big girl panties and getting on with it. I hear in my head and the supercilious voice continues, Megan must be found, and your entire family is relying on you to not mess this up.

Ugh. Be quiet. I didn't ask for your opinion, I think. But the voice is right, I admit, much as I hate when that happens. I need to think of what I came here to do. I need to keep reminding myself that the six-foot blonde woman I'm looking at in the mirror isn't really me and that nobody here knows who I am or what I look like in my natural form. Otherwise, I might start to panic.

I twist one way then the other. In my natural form, I'm not what anyone would consider a small-busted woman, but in this form, my bust is even larger. The top pushes my breasts up and together. I know that if I try to take anything more than the shallowest of breaths, they will likely spill out completely.

The slip of cloth these people consider shorts is hardly more than a thong for all they cover of my ass. The only part of the entire outfit I don't have a problem with is the shoes. They're absolutely stunning and I know they cost a bomb to buy. Walking in them will be a challenge, the highest heel I've ever worn was only two inches. I will just have to try my best and pray I don't look like an idiot and draw too much attention to myself. Or, even worse, fall flat on my ass and alert the entire club to the fact that I don't belong here.

If there is one upside to this madness, it is that this outfit will allow me to blend in and give me a better chance of finding out what happened to Megan. I just need to find out where all she went in the club before she went missing and, dressed the way I am, I shouldn't have any trouble moving around the club.

Loud banging on the door interrupts my thoughts. "Have you changed yet?" comes through the wooden door in that irritating high-pitched voice from before. "I hope I don't have to remind you how much Mr. Sinclair despises tardiness."

Her voice is like nails on a chalkboard, causing me to shudder. Just hearing it makes me want to hit her. I roll my eyes, thinking to myself, no, I don't need to be reminded, you sour-faced cow.

"Yes, I'm dressed. I'm coming out now," I call out sweetly, hurrying over to the door, nearly falling flat on my face. Thank heavens I never have to see this woman again after today. She seems to be a right dragon.

I open the door to find her standing directly in front of me. She looks me up and down and says, "Well.... I suppose you'll have to do. Just make sure you're on time tomorrow and that your hair and makeup are perfect."

Is she for real? I didn't have time to do anything with it, and she said that she was going to fix it when she came back for me. Oh well, I shrug. She can kiss my ass. I see her wrinkling her nose in distaste as her gaze flickers up and down my body once more. She turns abruptly, her narrow nose up in the air as if she's smelled something distasteful as she walks back the way we came earlier.

I realize with a start that she wants me to follow. I hurry to catch up on wobbly legs, praying I don't slip and fall over. When I catch up to her and attempt to match her stride, I realize she's giving me instructions. "You're being placed on the second floor tonight. No one will make any inappropriate advances towards you if you have this choker on." She stops and turns to face me. "Lose it...." She pauses, a smirk twisting her lips as she pulls her hand out of her pocket and hands me what I assume is a choker. I hold it up and examine it. The thin velvet is black and red and there are five diamonds in a single row in the middle. "Let's just say... you might not like the outcome." She threatens with an evil laugh.

My whole body freezes at her sinister tone. What the hell does she mean by that? The smirk she's giving me isn't the least bit reassuring, either. Trying my hardest not to show how much she's rattled me, I deliberately meet her gaze while putting the choker around my neck and clasping it. I have a strong suspicion she's doing everything she can to frighten me, and I refuse to give her the satisfaction of knowing it's working. What a dirty bitch.

With a fake smile and a sickly-sweet voice, I reply, "Don't worry. I have no intentions of losing it," all the while maintaining eye contact with her calculating stare.

There is certainly more to this woman than meets the eye and she's giving me the creeps. There's just something... not quite right about her. Maybe it's the fact I know she isn't human. I just hope I don't run into her again once we part ways.

"Suzette is waiting for you, and she will take you to your floor," she says, indicating a young woman that seems to have appeared from thin air. "Unless you're told to do so by myself or Mr. Sinclair, do not, under any circumstance, go to any floor other than the one you're assigned to. Suzette will explain your job duties and show you how to complete them, as well as go into more detail of what is expected of you as an employee of The Fallen Angel." She gives me one last disapproving look before swiftly turning and walking away. Now, more than ever, I want to know about the floors that have been deemed out of bounds. I already know certain… depraved pleasures are available for a price, but it must be worse than I thought if even employees are kept out of the loop.

Is Lucien Sinclair hiding something else? While I genuinely don't wish to be caught snooping around while looking for clues about Megan, I am struggling to temper my urge to dig deeper than strictly necessary. I can feel the two sides of myself warring over the issue, with one side prompting me to throw caution to the wind and the other warning me of the potential consequences of doing so.

I look at the young woman standing beside me, Suzette, I believe Ms. Burns said. Suzette's hair is cropped tight to her head and dyed a deep purple. She's petite, probably under five-feet tall.

Together, we both turn and watch Ms. Burns disappear down the hallway and she whispers to me, "Avoid her as much as you can, and for heaven's sake, whatever you do, do NOT get on her bad side," she pauses, a frown appearing upon her face as I can see her debating whether she should say more. I see her shrug and assume she's decided against sharing whatever thought she just had.

"Come on, I'll show you what your duties are," she says in a louder tone, moving over to a wall and pushing a button to summon the lift. "By the way, my name is Suzette. What is yours?"

"I'm Scarlett," I answer, looking at her curiously. "Why are you warning me?" I ask. She doesn't know me from Adam, so why would she help me? Why should she care if I piss of the bitchy gargoyle?

She chuckles, shrugging her shoulders. "You're new. It only seemed fair to give you a heads-up. She's a right bitch seeing as she's Mr. Sinclair's… special friend…"

She trails off, appearing to think about her words before continuing, "They are very friendly, if you get my meaning," she says with a wink right as the lift doors open in front of us. We step inside and she goes on, "She doesn't like anyone paying too much attention to him. Then there's Aria. At least she comes and goes and isn't here all the time. She's been with Mr. Sinclair way longer than Ms. Burns. Though the way Ms. Burns acts, you would think it's the other way around. Just watch out for both and if you see Mr. Sinclair, it's best to limit your contact with him. If you want to keep your job... and your head... just don't cross either one of them. They're both nasty bitches,"

Oh great, I think, just what I need. Two jealous, crazy-ass women who think every other female is trying to get with their man. There's no way in hell I will ever seek out Lucien Sinclair. I want to avoid him at all costs. Besides, I have no intentions of coming back here after tonight. Waving my hands in front of my chest, attempting to assure her I have zero interest in our boss, I laugh lightly and say, "They have nothing to worry about with me. I'm here to do my job and get paid, not to get involved with anyone, especially not Mr. Sinclair."

"Then you should be fine," Suzette replies with a smile. "Come on, I'll show you the ropes," she tells me as we walk out of the lift and down another long hallway. On one side, the walls are painted in a deep red; the other in black and gold. There are five wooden doors, two on one side, three on the other. I can see from here that the furthest one has black writing on it.

"The job isn't exactly rocket science, it's actually pretty simple. Once a room becomes vacant, you will go in and get it ready for the next couple. You will shadow me for the first couple of hours, and then you'll be on your own. Always keep your choker on, but if you lose it, leave the floor straight away and report to Len. That's who oversees the security around here; I will introduce you to him later." She pauses and studies me for a moment.

Appearing to reach some kind of conclusion about me, she continues, "I will warn you now. You will see vampires feeding off people, both Naturals and humans. I assure you, they are all willing. If you ever have to go up to any of the other levels, you will see stuff that's even more extreme; the higher the floor level, the more extreme the pleasure. Remember, this is a sex club where people get to act out their darkest, dirtiest desires and pleasures. Nothing's forbidden or off-limits, so long as all parties consent. If anyone breaks the rules, they are swiftly dealt with." She said all this over her shoulder as we're walking down the hall, but now she stops and looks at me.

"There will likely be instances, albeit rare, when you will come across someone who is overly friendly. If anyone gets out of hand, make sure they know their advances are unwelcome and you feel uncomfortable. If they continue, let Len know and he will deal with it." She starts walking again and I follow, until we reach the door at the end of the hall. The black letters I'd seen before say 'PRIVATE' and underneath 'STAFF ONLY'.

As she opens the door, I think of everything I've just learned. Bloody hell, what have I gotten myself into? I feel like a helpless sheep going into a den of hungry wolves. It doesn't matter that I know self-defense and have my magic to protect me. I can't allow myself to be put in a position to use either because I need to stay under the radar as much as possible. I can't have anyone here find out I'm anything other than human; It would put me and my entire family in danger. She did say it was rare for the customers to, how did she put it? Oh right, it's rare for them to be 'overly friendly.' So, there's no reason to freak out. Right?

The door opens into a large room with bare, off-white walls. The center of the room is mostly empty, except for a large wooden table with wooden chairs placed around it. Along one wall is a kitchenette with a long countertop that has a coffee and tea maker along with a selection of different sandwiches. There's also a large refrigerator and several cabinets.

"This is where we keep the cleaning supplies and where we take our breaks. The food and drinks are available to staff. Mr. Sinclair employs both humans and Naturals, so don't freak out if you see a vampire or any other Supernatural feeding in here," she warns.

I already knew Lucien employed Naturals, but I'm shocked to learn he has so many humans working for him. Why would he do that? It doesn't make sense. Everyone knows how much he hates humans. Schooling my expression, I say, "Thanks for the heads-up," and casually look around the room, hoping my face isn't mirroring any of my thoughts.

Trying to keep my face clear of expression is far more difficult than I would have thought. The rest of my body isn't doing such a good job of cooperating with me, either. My stomach is rolling as if I'm riding a roller-coaster. I actually feel so sick, I'm concerned I might throw up all over myself and the floor in front of me. I'm out of my depth. Something is going to happen; I feel overwhelming dread building inside of me. The sense of impending doom is so strong, I have to fight to stop myself from running from the club as though the hounds of hell are *chasing me. I close my eyes and breathe deeply, feeling my corset top strain against my breasts.*

I manage to calm down and open my eyes to see Suzette opening a cabinet and grabbing a caddy filled with an assortment of cleaning supplies. She hands the caddy over to me and grabs another. Oh, great, I'm a cleaning lady, I think to myself. The cleaning part isn't going to be the problem; it's the kind of cleaning I'm going to be doing.

"The main doors to this level will open in thirty minutes. All the clients who have pre-booked a room will be allowed to enter first, while the others wait in private booths placed discreetly around each chamber until their room becomes available. Please try not to panic if you see something shocking. You will get used to things once you've been here for a while. We give each room a quick look-over before the punters roll in. Oh! Before I completely forget. Mr. Sinclair's private residence is on the top floor. He has his own private team that deals with his needs and his office is on the floor below that. Rarely will we have to do anything on his floors, but we do occasionally get called in to clean up there."

I feel myself nodding, feeling like one of those bobble head dolls people like to keep on their car dashboard. My poor brain is whirling, trying to take everything in. I remember being shocked downstairs, but if I had known what awaited me up here, I may never have gotten this far.

Coming into the club, I'd known I would be seeing things I could never even imagine, but now that I'm faced with actually seeing them, I realize that I wasn't nearly as prepared as I'd thought. I just had to hope I won't be unlucky enough to get called to Lucien's private quarters and that my glamour will hold on long enough for me to get what I came for.

While I don't know exactly how long the glamour will hold, I know it won't last forever. Not knowing exactly how long she spell will hold is a really big problem. My sisters and I had agreed that I had to be out in under five hours. I look at my watch; four hours left.

I need to get my bloody ass in gear and start searching for any sign of what happened to Megan, but I can't until I'm left alone. While I haven't noticed any cameras, that doesn't mean there aren't any. I know they wouldn't be placed in plain sight for everyone to see. I'll just have to do my best to make sure I don't get caught.

If Lucien or his security team does catch me, I will likely have to use my powers. Staying any longer than we discussed could spell disaster.

CHAPTER FOUR

LUCIEN

I'M SITTING AT MY DESK, WONDERING what the fuck is wrong with me. I feel ... Off. Fuck, even my demon feels unsettled. Lately, he's been getting too close to the surface, and it's getting harder to hold him back. If he breaks free, shit will hit the fan, and I'll have a hard time gaining back control. No matter what I've tried to do, the feelings just won't disappear.

I told Xena to meet me in my office and I fucked her until she couldn't do anything else but lie there, exhausted. I had let her rest for an hour before waking her up and sending her on her way. She wasn't happy. Did I give a shit? No. I hoped she'd take some of the edge off, but she hadn't.

The feeling is still there, and as each day passes, it only continues to grow. I always listen to my gut, and it's telling me danger is on the horizon. So many changes coming. Then there are the fucking crazy dreams, all featuring the same woman. In some, she beckons to me, asking for my help. In others, it's obvious we have carnal knowledge of one another. Whoever she is, I already know she is going to be my downfall. The dreams are so bloody fuzzy I can't even make out her features. I know her body is curvy and busty, and she wouldn't quite meet my shoulder if she were standing next to me. The only way I'd be able to recognize her is by a small birthmark that looks like a crescent moon on the inside of her left thigh. The woman will become vital to me, and I know I'm going to do everything in my power to protect her. She's going to be the weakness I can't afford, but I know there's little I can do to stop the hands of fate, no matter how hard I try.

When the time comes, if necessary, I will kill to protect her.

With my reputation, people think twice before crossing me. I give little thought to taking lives. If they don't betray me, they will go on to live happy, fulfilling lives. If they request my help, I'm more than happy to do what I can. I am feared throughout my territory and beyond. Any debts people have with me must be paid either in weekly payments, or in full, with interest.

No matter the outcome, everyone realizes that my help comes with a cost. I'm not a charity! How many times this has to be said borders on lunacy. I made sure everyone fully understands what they're getting into, what they're signing, before I allow them to sign on the dotted line. Some just never listen. There's no excuse, they choose not to heed my warnings. That, in my eyes, is their downfall.

My thoughts shift to what I was told earlier. A human woman went missing from The Fallen Angel. It appears as though she simply vanished. As it happened in my territory, I know the human police won't get involved. They no doubt consider it the job of the Natural police to deal with, but neither one would dare step foot on any of my properties without my say-so.

I instructed Damien, my second in command and the closest thing I have to a friend, to get one of the other men to investigate. When I find out someone was taken while in one of my clubs or on my turf, I deal with it. It's a well-known fact that I'm not overly fond of humans. There are a few I can tolerate, but other than those select few, they just aren't worth the fucking hassle. I have enough problems.

A loud banging comes from behind the wooden door, interrupting my thoughts. I'd know that knock anywhere. Damien.

I growl. Shit, I don't need this. The door swings open and he nods. "Lucien," he says in his gravelly voice, and his bald, toffee-colored head reflects the light as he enters the room.

Shit.

EARLIER

DAMIEN

THE CRAZY BITCH IS BACK, WALKING around as if she owns the damn place. She's always liked to get her way, no matter the cost. I left her in Lucien's living quarters because that was my only option. I came to inform Lucien that she was back because I just can't deal with her shit. I'd end up killing her. My demon shares my feelings, my hatred for her runs that deep. She's always been dangerous.

I left two men from my squad outside the entrance, giving them strict instructions that she wasn't to leave. If they disobey me, they know they'll be punished. She's one of the most beautiful females I've ever seen, but she makes my flesh crawl. I almost think they must have come up with the phrase 'beauty is only skin-deep' with her in mind. I know it grates on her that she can't sink her fingers into me. She's tried more than once to seduce me, and even though she belongs to Lucien, it pisses her off to know that it won't work, no matter how many times she tries. She forgets I know what and who she is. Lucien tolerates her and gives into her whims, and as long as he doesn't expect me to do the same, I don't give a shit. Lucien knows I have no love for the woman.

Lucien gave her one of the smaller regions on the outskirts of his territory many years ago, but never told me why. Not that he needed to. At the time, he was so infatuated with her, he would have given her the world if she'd asked him. To this day, I don't understand it, and I don't think I ever will.

Now I have to go tell Lucien that she's back and demanding to see him. I just hope he's in a better mood than he has been the last few weeks. I have two matters for him to deal with. Aria and our other uninvited guest. It's up to Lucien to decide which one to deal with first.

I pause in front of the heavy wooden door before knocking. Lucien is in there and will not be happy to be disturbed.

"Lucien," I call out as I push open the door and enter the room.

I'm relieved to find Lucien alone. It doesn't bother me to walk in and see him fucking a woman. On the odd occasion we've even shared a female or two. But right now, we have more important matters to deal with. Lucien watches me as I walk into the room and let the door click shut behind me. I walk over to the front of his desk.

"What is it?" Lucien asks, his eyes locking onto me as I move closer.

I meet his black gaze. "Aria's here and, as usual, she's demanding to see you." I tell him with distaste, curling my lip as I pull the chair out and ease my enormous frame into it.

Lucien hums, cocking his head back and shifting in his seat. "Fuck," he grunts to himself, running one of his hands over his face. Looking at me, he asks, "Did she say what she wanted?"

Raising an eyebrow, I reply. "You. You know that's the only reason Aria ever comes here."

"I don't have time for her shit," he growls, shaking his head. "Make sure she's put in my living quarters. I'll deal with her later. Is there any update on the human female who went missing?"

"Already done, and she wasn't too happy about it," I give him the heads up on what kind of mood she's going to be in by the time he gets to her. "Nothing on the human woman. I have a man looking through the recordings from that night and so far, nothing has come up."

"Fucking hell! People don't just disappear. When I find the fucker who took her, he'll wish he never set foot on my property. The sooner we can find out what happened to her, the better." Shifting in his chair, he adds, "I don't want anyone to think it's okay to take an unwilling woman from one of my businesses, whether they're human or Natural. I won't tolerate it. I want this sorted. Put out a reward and see if that brings anyone forward."

I nod in agreement before clearing my throat. "Security caught a woman wandering in an area she shouldn't be in."

Lucien shrugs. "That's happened before. We scare the fuck out of them and send them on their way. Why are you telling me about this?" He questions with a raised eyebrow.

"She's in one of our uniforms," I inform him, "and she's a human."

"Why didn't you tell Xena? She's the one who hires and fires!"

"There's something about this woman. My gut tells me she's hiding something." I always go with my gut; it hasn't let me down yet.

"Where is she now?" Lucien asks, sitting back in his chair.

"I put her in the back room, the one that overlooks the lake."

"Put the camera on," Lucien instructs me, "I want to see this woman myself."

I turn until I'm facing away from him and switch on the monitor behind me.

It flickers before a figure appears on the monitor before us. She sits, then gets back up to walk around the room before sitting down on the chair again. She's nothing special. She looks like every other woman that Lucien employs. Tall with long slim legs, tits as big as two softballs and look like they are just barely balancing on top of her chest, with long blonde hair hanging down to her waist. She's Lucien's typical woman.

I hear Lucien muttering something behind me, but I don't catch what he's saying. I hear the scraping of a chair as he gets to his feet and walks through the door I recently came through. What the fuck is going on?

"Lucien?"

He pauses, not saying anything for the longest time.

Finally, he turns his head slightly until I can see his profile and asks, "What do you see when you look at her?"

"A blonde woman with large tits," I answer. "Why?" I stand up and start to move towards the door.

He walks over to the monitor and looks at me. With one finger, he taps the monitor, his head cocked to the side, his black eyes narrowed to slits. "I see someone entirely different," he growls angrily.

"Well, fuck," I mutter, following him out. I know what that means. Only one kind of woman can hide themselves in such a manner and Lucien can spot them from a mile away.

Fucking witch.

CHAPTER FIVE

SCARLETT

How the hell did I land myself in this position? Oh yes, I remember. I scoff at myself. They caught me bloody red-handed, that's how. I'm in a shitload of trouble, and it's only going to get worse. I have to think fast about what I will say, I can't be caught without a good excuse. It has to appear genuine; I can't sound like I'm lying.

Not only that, but I know the glamour isn't going to last much longer. Nor will the protection spells. I can already feel them wavering and know I have an hour, at most. If I'm really lucky, I might get a bit more than that, but my luck hasn't exactly served me well tonight. I just have to hope I can get out of this predicament before the spells wear off. I think my best bet is to play dumb. I'll just say that I got lost and didn't realize I'd entered a part of the club that was off-limits.

I know *he* is coming. I can feel him reaching out. The feeling is so intense, I can sense the energy pouring in through the building walls, his power radiating to my very core. I look down and see the concealment spell flicker, my body briefly appearing before turning back to my disguise.

Shit, the spells are wearing off. Is it because of the power he holds or are the spells not as powerful as we thought? No matter which way I look at it, I'm about to be in deep trouble, and if I'm being honest with myself, there's no way out at the moment.

Megan has been here; I saw her in a vision. She was with somebody else—a man - but I couldn't make out who it was. His face was in shadow. That's the only vision I've had in the two hours I've been in the club. I now know, without a doubt, that somebody took her. But how? Why? I don't know. My vision didn't show me anything.

The only feeling I'd gotten from her was that she'd been happy. So happy. It was as if she had not a care in the world and was floating on fluffy white clouds. Had someone drugged her? It was possible, but with what or by whom I hadn't a clue. Not yet anyway. It is so frustrating not knowing who the hell had taken her. Though she hadn't been frightened in the man's company, I couldn't shake the feeling that she'd been in danger.

My thoughts pause, my gaze turning to where I hear footsteps just behind the door. Two deep male voices penetrate through the dark wood, and I try to listen to what they're saying, but all I can make out are a few random words here and there. No matter how hard I try, I can't make out their conversation. I sit with bated breath, waiting for the door to open.

Without a doubt, I know Lucien Sinclair is behind that door. I don't like the thoughts that keep popping into my mind, a mix of dark and sexual musings. The way my body is reacting to him when he isn't even in the room is beyond frightening.

I know from the pictures I've seen of him that he's a raw sexual being. I've never been one to frighten easily. I generally know what is coming and have learned to accept it to a certain extent. This is something entirely different. *He* is something entirely different. I've never met the man, but I know there is a deep well of darkness inside of him. He is the dark to my light

I can feel that darkness pouring into the room and sinking into the surrounding walls, and I hate to admit it, even to myself… but it scares the shit out of me.

I continue to wait for my fate to walk through the door. I've decided to fight whatever it is the visions in my dreams are trying to show me. It just cannot happen.

I choke back a laugh. Who the fuck do I think I'm kidding? Even if I fight with everything I have, I know I'm incapable of stopping the outcome. The fates must be having a grand laugh at my expense. If I could get my hands on even one of them, I'd give them a piece of my mind. No. I would ring their bloody necks! I don't give a damn that they're supposed to be friends to the witches.

I force myself to get out of the chair and move over to the large window on the other side of the room and gaze out at the inky darkness of night. Taking a deep breath, I let out a low laugh. I want to yank the damn door open and demand what the holdup is; just get it over and done with.

I bite back a scream of frustration. I've never been one to wait patiently. It just isn't in my nature. It's one of my many flaws, or so my family likes to inform me.

My breath catches and I stand deadly still when I hear the door swing open and I'm shocked to see only one figure enter the room. He doesn't need to introduce himself. I knew who it was going to be long before he arrived, and my deepest fears are confirmed once I see him come through the heavy wooden door. Lucien Sinclair.

I can see his reflection staring back at me from the glass window, causing me to gasp for air. It feels as though someone has sucked all the oxygen out of the room and it's making it hard for me to breathe.

The door closes with a loud click, and I find myself utterly alone with the man of my dreams. No. The man of my nightmares. I can feel his dark gaze boring into the back of my head as if he's attempting to worm his way into my mind so he can read my thoughts. I can feel those same eyes running down my body, inspecting me in the red and black uniform. I pray the enchantment holds just a little bit longer. Long enough for me to get out without anyone seeing my true form.

I stand utterly still, my feet rooted to the floor. An air of danger sweeps over me, seemingly oozing from his pores and swirling around me, as if it could trap me and swallow me whole.

He's huge; much bigger in the flesh than in any of the photos I've seen of him. He must stand at least 6'4", maybe even taller. His body appears more muscled than it did in my visions and dreams. His eyes are penetrating past my skin, through my bones, burning a hole down to my very soul. His gaze feels like hands touching me, stroking me, holding me in place. He moves closer, scrutinizing me with those bottomless black eyes like he's a menacing predator and I'm his wary prey.

Does he expect me to make a run for it? Hell, where would I even go? The door is now tightly shut, and he's standing directly in the path of any hope of freedom I could have harbored. My survival instinct tells me to try anyway, to get the hell out of here. This is Hell and the flames will lick at my skin until they burn me alive. I take a steadying breath, attempting to regain control over my thoughts and emotions. This man is far more dangerous than my sisters and I ever could have prepared for.

He stops a few feet away from me, standing half in the shadows, the other half bathed in light. It makes him look like a phantom, a hallucination, and makes it harder for me to get a read on him. He stands there quietly, staring at me. Is he waiting to see if I will say something? It almost feels like he's daring me to attempt escape. I remain silent and so does he, neither of us speaking as our eyes lock on one another.

For the briefest moment, his head moves out of the shadows, and I catch a glimpse of his reflection. His face is a mask, devoid of any emotion. I realize I won't be able to read him. I gather what courage I can muster up, swallow down my fears, and slowly turn around. The room suddenly feels sweltering, as though the heat has been jacked way up.

His eyes pierce through me, threatening to snatch my soul and devour it. I feel like a cute little bunny left alone with a starving feral wolf. For what seems like eternity, but can only be mere minutes, he stares at me wordlessly. His silence speaks volumes. The man in front of me is unlike any I've known before and is more calculating, more dangerous, more *everything*, than I possibly could have understood.

My heart is racing with the realization that I've put myself and my loved ones in an unsafe situation. Coming here to figure out what happened to Megan wasn't the smartest decision I've ever made, but it was the only thing my sisters and I could think of, and the man standing in front of me might be the only person who can give us any answers. Unfortunately, my visions only allow me to see so much.

"I'm Lucien Sinclair," he finally speaks, his head now cocked to one side, his gaze locked on my face. "You are…" he doesn't phrase it like a question, as if he knows the answer already and wants to see if I'll give him the truth.

I stare at the TV monitors situated across one wall, where an array of shots of the interior and exterior of the club have appeared. A sickening realization dawns on me and settles in the pit of my stomach. He's seen everything I've done. He had eyes on me the entire time I was sneaking around and snooping. The possibility that he might have evidence of what happened to Megan also occurs to me. He likely has a recording of the night she visited with her friends and might even have video of the person who took her.

"You've been watching me?" I whisper, my gaze flying from the monitors to the man standing before me.

"Nothing gets by me. I have eyes and ears everywhere," he replies, with no remorse or shame. "Your name? Do not make me ask again," he demands as he takes a seat in the oversized jade green leather chair, his back to the monitors. His eyes bore into me, watching me like a hawk about to strike.

I'm ashamed of how afraid I am in his presence; I'm scared shitless. The other feelings flooding my body are ones I'd rather not scrutinize too closely. He's formidable, his power flowing out around him, filling the room and seeping under my skin. I think I need help, the way I'm feeling can't possibly be normal. If I'm not careful, I may find myself on my knees, begging for his attention like a puppy to her master.

I shake those thoughts from my mind and focus on the matter at hand. While I know the best course of action at this point is to ask him for help, I'm also aware that my sisters will be livid that I didn't tell them what I intended all along. It was the reason I was so insistent that I be the one to come here. Though I'd tried my damnedest to avoid him, I'd known all along that fate would bring us to this moment. Now I need to ask him the question; one simple question that shouldn't be so difficult to ask.

Can I really ask this man, this demon, for help? We need to find Megan, and he might be the only one who can help us. He has enough power in the palms of his hands to find her, but I can't help but wonder what he may ask in return. The very thought terrifies me. I don't doubt his demands will be high. I could end up in a situation far worse than the one I'm currently in.

Looking into the darkness of his fathomless eyes, I can see how accustomed he is to being in control. People bow down to him without hesitation. Asking Lucien Sinclair for help will be making a deal with the devil. Am I prepared for that?

I remain still, incapable of speaking, of answering his question. I feel myself staring at him, my eyes wide open in fear. My tongue feels glued to the roof of my mouth, making it impossible for me to say anything.

The loud slap of his large hand against the top of the desk makes me jolt in surprise and jerks me out of my fog-filled trance. Should I give him my real name? Before I can think it through fully, I hear the words leave my mouth.

"Scarlett Winters," I whisper, feeling like my throat is closing up. The words are thick and heavy, and my heart is racing. My hands tremble, so I make a fist with each hand in an effort to control my reaction. I feel as though I've been drugged and have lost control over my body. I offer up a silent prayer that he can't sense how nervous he's made me. I fight the urge to run, knowing that staying is the only way I will get the help my sisters and I need.

"Scarlett," my name rolls around his mouth as though he's tasting it. Savoring it. "And what were you doing, snooping in areas you shouldn't have been?" he asks softly, raising a dark eyebrow.

I have to make a decision, quickly. It's obvious he knows or suspects that I'm here under false pretenses. How much he knows is impossible to ascertain. I need to give him as much of the truth as possible so I can gain his trust and his help in finding Megan.

The thought occurs to me that whatever we agree on will be nullified once my glamour wears off and I decide I'll just have to make him an offer he can't refuse. What could that be, though? What could he want from me? And will I be able to handle it? I have no experience with sex, though it's unlikely he would ask for it. If the rumors of his distaste of humans hold any truth, he won't ask for sex. I can handle anything else he throws my way. I hope.

So, I'll just tell him why I'm here. If I have to, I'll offer a little while lie and claim we bought the spells from one of those old shops downtown. What could go wrong?

"I'm looking for someone," the words gush from my mouth like water from a busted pipe. "My sister. She was last seen at your club a few nights ago when she was out with a group of her friends." I don't hesitate long enough for him to say anything. "I have no one else to ask for help," I breathe out slowly, trying to appear calm and failing miserably.

He watches me silently with a glare that says I've intruded on his time and space, which is precisely what I've done. I wait for his response, but nothing happens. We stare at each other silently for what feels like forever. His focus is calculating, intimidating. I'm terrified but proud that I found the courage to ask him for help.

He isn't human. Oh, he looks the part, and if it weren't for his soulless, bottomless eyes, and if I didn't know any better, I might believe he was human. But he isn't. He is one of the most dangerous, most feared beings known to any human or Natural. He's someone you do not want to cross.

"Why do you think I'd be interested in helping you?" he asks softly as he leans back in his chair, his face giving nothing away.

I swallow, buying time to think of a reason. "Well, it's not good for business to have innocent people go missing from your establishment. It would be bad news for anyone, but especially for Lucien Sinclair." I swallow hard. I'm nervous and despite my best efforts, I'm certain those nerves are showing. "I will do anything you want if you help us find our sister." Shit! Did those words really just leave my mouth? Please, no. *How could you have been so stupid, Scarlett?* If it were possible, I would kick my own ass. I just admitted that I'm not the only person looking for Megan and outed my family's involvement. I hold my breath, hoping he didn't catch my slip-up.

"So, you will do anything? Does that include your family?" His voice is like ice; emotionless, brutal, and unforgiving as he stands up and moves closer until his body is almost touching mine. I call upon my will to remain still. I steady my feet, unwilling to take a step back or show any sign of weakness. "Or does that offer only include you? Mm, would you let me defile you? Take whatever I want, without question?" His throat releases a rough noise, like a growl, making him sound like a predator on the prowl. The sound causes my body to tense, even more so than the weight of his gaze scouring my body.

Well, he definitely caught my mistake. This isn't good. I wonder if he knows that the façade before him isn't my own. I can't help but look down at myself and feel relief rush through me when I see that the glamour is still in place, though I know it won't remain much longer. The spell has already dwindled significantly over the last few minutes. The thought occurs to me that he can see past the façade in front of him and see my proper form. If that's the case, I'm beyond fucked. I bite back the panic threatening to overwhelm me.

"The offer only includes me," I whisper, biting my bottom lip as I basically admit my family's involvement.

"What makes you think I even want to help?" he eyes me for a long second, reading my reaction to his words and proximity before continuing. "Even with the oh-so-tempting offer you've made."

He begins to circle around me, his eyes raking over my body like hot coals. I sense him behind me just before I feel his hard body press against my own. He bends his head down, and with his mouth right up against my ear, whispers, "You reek of desperation, and that alone makes me rock hard. It makes me want to take you up on your offer."

My entire body is rigid, his fiery breath caressing my skin. His voice is so deep, so heavy, it feels as though it's weighing me down. It's sucking me under, causing me to feel like I need to hold on to something to keep my knees from buckling under the heft of it.

I'm at a loss as to how I should respond. I almost feel like Alice after she's fallen down the rabbit hole, but this isn't a dream I can wake from. This is my reality.

"Tell. Me. Why. I. Should. Help?" he growls softly into my ear, sending shivers down my spine. "And how will it benefit me?"

My mind is a complete blank. I have nothing to offer, no reasonable response to his question. The only thing I have to offer is myself, which isn't a great bargaining chip. He has plenty of women at his beck and call to satisfy his every desire.

I finally force the words past my lips, "I don't know." My words are barely audible, though my desolation screams loudly. He has no reason to help us, but we need him. The fear he inspires, along with the information he could provide would be invaluable in our quest. "I don't know," I repeat, my voice firmer than it was a few seconds before. "But we don't know anyone else who can help us find our sister."

"You're not helping your case, little human. You need to give me something that will make me want to help you," he tells me as he presses his hard body closer to mine.

"Me," I whisper with a murmur, "I can only offer you …Me."

CHAPTER SIX

LUCIEN

THE WORD 'WITCH' ROLLS LIKE THUNDER in my mind. The moment I laid eyes on her, I knew exactly what she was. Once I told Damien my suspicions, he wasted no time finding out who she was. She made a really stupid mistake. By getting into my club using her real name, she made it easy for me to find out everything about her.

I enter the room, not realizing that being in the same room with her would affect me, how seeing her in the flesh with my own eyes would be a kick to the balls. I couldn't have possibly prepared for my demon's reaction to her either.

The air rushes out of my lungs. This is no girl. The creature standing before me is a woman from top to toe. Her uniform hugs her lush body like a second skin and the shorts are so tiny that I can see the cheeks of her luscious ass peeking from the bottom of them. I can't see her tits from this angle, but I have no doubt they're every bit as delicious as the rest of her.

I want to order her to turn around. Something is pulling me towards this human woman, this witch, and I don't like it one bit. The gravitational pull I feel towards her is unlike anything I've ever experienced. A feeling settles deep inside my bones; a feeling that if I don't take what I'm craving from her, my body will combust and burn for eternity.

Yet, no matter how my body seems to respond to hers, my priority needs to be finding out if she's a spy. I have questions that require answers and if that means scaring the shit out of her, so be it. Had one of my enemies sent her? I certainly have enough of those. If that is the case here, I need to find out who *and why.*

The unfamiliar, bizarre gravitation I feel towards her goes against everything I know about myself, every instinct I've ever had. I always maintain absolute control over every emotion, every thought, every feeling. I'm normally an unfeeling bastard. Nobody crosses me and lives to tell the tale. I have zero regrets. In this world, it is kill or be killed. I'm not a psychopath, I don't get off on it. I've never enjoyed hurting anyone, especially not the women I've been forced to hurt or kill.

Damien is what most people would consider my closest friend. He's the one person I trust fully, the only person I would trust and have trusted with my life. There are a handful of others I trust to a certain extent, people who are loyal to me, and they are rewarded handsomely. People who cross me find it to be their undoing. If that makes me sound cold, well, maybe I am. I can't afford to be soft. There are far too many people waiting in the wings for me to fail.

No matter how much my body begs for her, I must remain indifferent. I need to know what the hell she's up to, no matter the cost. I can tell from her posture that she's frightened. Is it because she fears what I may to do her and her loved ones? I feel a hint of pity and ruthlessly shove it down. I cannot allow myself to be swayed by emotion. She entered my club under false pretenses, and I can't let it go without consequence. I will get the answers I require. The more frightened she is, the more likely she is to comply.

As if sensing my presence, she turns towards me, and I feel like I've been kicked in the gut. Her skin is flawless, like whipped cream. Wide green eyes stare back at me, a mass of dark auburn hair is piled on top of her head, and her lips are the color of red roses. Her breasts are large and round, her hips flare out and flow down to her shapely toned legs. She has the perfect hourglass figure. Without the fuck-me shoes, she's tiny, probably only coming to my shoulder. She definitely isn't my usual type; I generally go for taller, slimmer women with bigger tits. However, something about her is calling out to me. I can feel the demon inside of me rise to attention.

"I am Lucien Sinclair," I introduce myself, "you are?" I demand. Though I already have a good idea about who and what she is, I want to see how truthful she will be with me. I see her eyes flick to the TV monitors before coming back to rest on me.

I let her question me, something I wouldn't normally do. I can smell the fear radiating from her and I can't stop myself from relishing in it. I'm a sick fuck. Her terror is like a drug I could feed on forever. I take a deep breath and taste something else in the air. Something that fills me with pleasure. I can smell and taste her desire.

I watch her as she tries in vain to conceal her emotions by keeping her face blank, but I can read every single one of them. I can see that she's feeling overwhelmed and that she's wondering if she should tell me the truth as she worries that I might already know who she is. My demon is delighting in the emotions rolling off of her and he tugs at the reins of my control, wanting to devour them.

I listen as she asks for my help in finding her sister. Apparently, the woman who went missing from my club is her sister and it seems she's willing to beg for my help to find her. Why she thinks I would be interested in helping her, I have no idea. I don't give a fuck about her sister. I know that if the situation weren't dire, she wouldn't be standing before me right now. I can taste the desperation coming off her in waves.

"Why do you think I would be interested in helping you?" *I question, intrigued to learn her answer.*

"Well, it's not good for business to have innocent people go missing from your establishment. It would be bad news for anyone, but especially for Lucien Sinclair." *I watch her swallow, her nerves showing through. She continues,* "I will do anything you want if you help us find our sister."

Oh, this is just too easy. I notice the little slip-up and chuckle to myself. "So, you will do anything? Does that include your family?" *I ask, showing no emotion as I stand up from the leather chair and slowly drift towards her until my body is almost touching hers.* "Or does that offer only include you? Mm, would you let me defile you? Take whatever I want, without question?" *I watch with satisfaction as she fights with herself, trying not to take a step back. She's trying not to show any sign of weakness.*

"The offer only includes me," *she whispers back, unable to meet my eyes.*

"What makes you think I'd even want to help? Even with the oh-so-tempting offer you've made," *I ask, monitoring her reaction as I circle her. Stopping directly behind her, I bend my head slightly towards her neck, taking in the smell of her sweet perfume. Something else, another scent, lies just beneath the surface. WITCH. I can hear my demon shouting out the same –*

naughty little witch.

My demon takes a deeper breath in, sensing more than one spell cloaking her. He identifies a concealment spell. Someone has tried really hard to hide her true self, but it isn't working. Not on me or my demon, anyway. The rest of the spells are for protection, and they were all placed on her simultaneously.

I hold back the growl threatening to leave my throat, fighting to keep my demon buried deep inside of me. I press my body against her softer one, lowering my head further towards hers and pressing my mouth against her ear as I whisper, "You reek of desperation, and that alone makes me rock hard. It makes me want to take you up on your offer." I feel her entire body go rigid as a shiver rips through her body.

"Tell. Me. Why. I. Should. Help?" I growl into her ear, feeling the shivers run down her spine as I demand an answer from her, "And how will it benefit me?"

"I don't know." Her voice is barely a whisper, and she swallows before repeating in a louder tone, "I don't know. We don't know anyone else who can help us find my sister."

"You're not helping your case, little human. You need to give me something that will make me want to help you," I tell her, pressing my body slightly harder against hers.

"Me," I hear her speak in a tremulous whisper, "I can only offer you… Me."

She's offering herself. Oh, this is so good, perhaps too good to be true. No one offers themself as a sacrifice unless they're too stupid to think through the decision or too desperate to care. I can't help but wonder which camp she falls into.

I'm fully aware that she is a human. A witch, in fact. I can smell the witch on her, a scent I haven't caught in a long time. It's coming off her in waves. Standing this close, and with my demon close to the surface, I know she's hiding something else, and she's more successful at concealing whatever it is than she is at hiding the fact that she's a witch. I have the thought that the rest of her family are likely witches as well, but there's something else lingering in her scent. Something neither my demon nor I can get a handle on. I suppose I'll just have to wait for that part to reveal itself.

Then there's the big question. Where did they come from? I remember the witches of old, but I had not seen them for a few generations. Even now, my hatred for them runs deep. The ones I knew in the past had always been fickle, untrustworthy, and you could never turn your back on them. They would think nothing of double-crossing you, and now I had one in my hands, standing here in front of me. Can life get any better? I chuckle to myself. I hate the part of me that wants to fuck and taste her until she screams from the pleasure.

I've done it to many in the past, so many witches. Many witches had tried to kill me or bend me to their will, and I let them believe they had won, let them think they had control over me. I'd given them pleasure so profound; they begged me for more. Even as I plowed into them, relentless in my fucking, before I ripped them to shreds. Many times, I let Aria join in my fun; she was even worse than me. At the time, she was everything I held dear. I hate what she's become, conniving and deceitful. I know the outcome between us won't be a happy one.

"Oh, little witch, I accept your offer," I purr in Scarlett's ear, letting her know I'm aware of what she is. "We're going to have so much fun," I torment her with my words as I slide my fingers down her arm before placing my hand over her stomach. She needs to know that this isn't a fairy tale; she will not be getting her happily ever after with her prince charming. I'm nobody's prince, never have been, and I'm going to love showing her just how bad I really am.

SCARLETT

I hear the words he purrs into my ear, but they don't really connect. His fingers stroke my arm sensuously and it feels as though his fingertips are branding me with fire as he slides them over my bare skin. His hand burns through the material of my top, like he's touching naked flesh.

I need to get out of here before things get any further out of control. My body is craving his touch and I have to press my lips tightly together to stop the moan that's making its way up from my throat to my lips. I bite my tongue to prevent myself from begging him to touch me.

Has he cast a spell on me? That could be the only explanation. I'm still willingly standing here, waiting for his touch. His breath is scorching the skin of my neck, fluttering over my flesh.

He grabs onto my waist, squeezing hard and making me flinch from the pain. I'm certain there will be bruises there tomorrow. He grips my top in his fist and roughly tugs it down until my breasts spill free. He cups each one in his hands and rolls his thumbs over my tightening nipples. I can barely process what is happening, only aware of the fact that they're already hard and peaked before I feel him tightening his grip and pinching them both. I shouldn't be letting him do this, I think, as his tongue licks down the side of my neck.

"Fuck" I scream. My head falls onto his chest as I whimper from pain. Agony, the likes of which I've never before experienced, shoots through me like a bolt of lightning right into my breasts, forcing my back to arch into him as I try my hardest to ease the sensation. He doesn't back off, only continues to twist my nipples. I grab onto his arms, digging my nails in deep, as if begging him to stop. Leaning over me, he bites down on my shoulder, not terribly hard, but still making me scream again from the slight pain.

He releases my tender nipples, slides his hands to my shorts and pops the button free before sliding the zipper down. I want to resist, slap his face for taking such liberties, but I can't. My head is so muddled, it feels as though a cloud has entered my mind and is filling it with fog, causing all common sense to fly out the window. Lust is overlapping all rational thought.

"Don't move," he growls as his hand slides down my stomach and into my shorts, hooking his fingers into my panties and pushing inside them. His touch sends a shot of lust to my heated core, and I can't help but close my eyes, even as I attempt to deny the desperate heat burning inside of me. His fingers find my clit and start to rub the hardened nub. My body instinctually responds, bucking as he hits the perfect spot and sends me into a frenzy.

"That's it," he whispers harshly into my ear, growling as I lift my hips towards his hand while he continues rubbing at my clit. Muffled cries of pleasure escape my lips when he whispers harshly into my ear, "I want to feel your wetness as you come all over my fingers." His hand moves faster as he rubs harder over my nub. "I want to feel your juices running down my fingers and onto my hand."

A thick finger penetrates me, going deeper with every breath. The rapid movement of his rough finger causes me to cry out while he continues to rub at my clit. The friction is too much to bear; it's like a raging fire sweeping through my body, setting my insides aflame.

"I can feel how much you want me, little witch. I can smell your hunger. You're so wet for me," he declares as he slides another finger inside me, stretching my inner muscles. "You're so fucking tight," he growls as I clamp down, my tight walls consuming him. "I can smell your sweetness. Your hunger. I bet you taste just as good as you feel and smell. From this moment on, this body, this pussy, is mine. Everything I demand of you, you're going to give to me willingly. No. Matter. What. It. Is," he punctuates the final words, matching the movement of his fingers that are being pushed harder and faster inside me. A deep, hungry moan escapes me. "Come for me," he demands, his voice deep and sensual, sending a ripple of awareness through me. "Come. Now."

At his command, I scream my pleasure as I explode. My head shakes from side to side from the blinding pleasure he's built up inside me and my nails dig hard into his arms. My entire body is quivering from the aftermath of the orgasm.

He holds me up against his solid body as he waits for me to come down from my high. I've never felt my body respond to anyone as it just did to him. I feel completely out of control, and it scares the hell out of me. This is unbelievably bad. I had known from my dreams how much he would be able to affect me. I just hadn't realized how serious it was until now. I am facing the most difficult challenge of my life and I'm going to have to do everything in my power to protect myself.

Grabbing me by my shoulders, he nudges me away so I'm standing on my own before him. Refusing to meet his gaze, I look down at the floor. I'm embarrassed at the way my body responded to his touch. I've never felt so much desire, never felt such a powerful pull before. I just can't bring my eyes to meet his and I'm mortified at my cowardice. I can feel his fiery gaze burning into my skin.

I need to gather up the courage to look him straight in the eye, as though what just happened was nothing special, an everyday occurrence, even.

I want to run as far away as possible. The way his touch affects me, I know I'm in trouble. Yet I know, no matter how loudly my mind and body are screaming for me to go, I cannot leave. I hear the voice inside my head saying, suck it up, Buttercup. We need his help.

I so want to tell her to shut the hell up, but I can't take a chance that the man in front of me will notice me silently communicating with someone. As much as I hate to admit it, she's right. I need to get a grip. He's yet to tell me what it is he wants in return for his help, but whatever it is, I've already agreed. I've fucked up royally and I know it, but I don't know what else I could have done.

I proudly lift my head while pulling my top back over my breasts and fastening my shorts, as I take a step away from him. I will my body to calm down. I watch him with wide eyes as he lifts the very fingers that had, just moments ago, been deep inside of me and brings them to his mouth, sucking the juices from them.

"Just as I thought," he growls, sounding like a feral tiger about to strike his prey. I watch the tip of his tongue lick along each of his fingers. "You taste like honey… like sweet nectar."

His fingers come out of his mouth with a pop, and he moves toward me with power and confidence, his gaze predatory. His hungry look makes me want to strip myself bare, to stand completely naked before him. It's fucked up, but I want him in a way I've never wanted anything. It scares me to death.

He reaches for me and wraps his arms around my body, molding our chests together. He crushes his lips to mine, and I part them for his fiery tongue. I can taste myself on him and it is beyond erotic. He kisses me with passionate hunger as his dick presses hard against my stomach, the sensation causing my pussy to pulse with desire. His lips trail down my neck to my shoulder and collarbone, nipping in small bites, which I'm certain will leave marks. My body trembles with an unfulfilled need; I want to feel his thickness inside me.

He steps away, releasing me with a mocking twist on his firm lips. I'm startled to find a man standing silently behind him. He's enormous, nearly as big as Lucien, and that's saying something. His head is completely bald, and I have the impression he shaves it. He's one of the most beautiful men I've ever seen. His eyes are a piercing light blue that hold no emotion, and his skin is the color of creamy toffee. I didn't even hear him enter the room and I'm unprepared to hide my shock at the interruption.

I look up at Lucien. I can't read what he's feeling, his face is a total blank. It's as though nothing happened between us. He turns slightly towards the other man, motioning for him to come forward. The man walks over to where we are standing and whispers something into Lucien's ear. I don't have a clue what is being said, but from the look on Lucien's face, I don't think it's anything good. Lucien looks pissed. Turning, he looks at me with narrowed eyes, looking at me as though trying to make some kind of decision.

"Don't think you're free to leave. Someone will be by shortly to escort you to a room," Lucien tells me before turning and walking out of the room without a second glance, the strange, beautiful man following closely behind him.

I watch them leave the room, listening as the door closes with a soft click. Feeling my knees start to buckle under me, I collapse into the nearest chair. Oh my god, what just happened? I can't wrap my head around it. I know the lust and emotions I'm experiencing are completely irrational. The events of the past hour or so fly through my mind. Where was my common sense? It isn't with me now. He has no feelings for me; how could he? I know I'm merely a means to an end for him.

He's more powerful than any of us realized. He somehow knew I was a witch the moment he saw me. I know it's only a matter of time before he concludes that the rest of my family are witches, too.

The concealment spell hadn't worked with him. How could it have failed? I'm almost sure it's because he is such a powerful demon, but that shouldn't have stopped the spells from working on him. Which leads me to another question… Is he something else? If so, what exactly is he? I need to make contact with my family and warn them. I know if I try now, though, I will certainly get caught.

With relief, I realize that he didn't seem to sense what kind of witch I am. It's bad enough he knows I'm a witch, but it would be disastrous if he was aware of the kind of powers I hold. I don't even want to think about what would happen if he were to discover that we are Omega witches. If anyone outside of our family circle were to learn that we're Omega and the powers we wield, it would be catastrophic. If the Natural or human world found out that the Omegas were thriving, and had mated with humans, witches, and Supernaturals, we would be hunted and captured to be used as vessels.

I've never had to use my self-defense training outside of our weekly sessions before. I never really considered that I might have to. My powers give me the strength to defend myself against the average human, and I feel that I have the training to defend myself against most Naturals. However, I'm unsure how effective I would be against someone with great power, and Lucien is one of the most powerful Naturals I've ever met. I will have to build walls around myself and keep him out. I cannot continue to allow him to touch me, not if I'm going *to protect myself and my family from him.*

The only thing to do is get his help to find Megan. And get the hell away from Lucien Sinclair as quickly as possible.

CHAPTER SEVEN

LUCIEN

JUST AFTER LEAVING SCARLETT

AS I WALK BACK TO MY personal quarters with Damien, I half listen to what he's telling me. I hadn't expected Aria to turn up this evening and I don't like the fact that she turned up unexpectedly. I need to know when she's going to be here so I can make sure she is supervised the entire time. I need to be in control of every situation, whether for pleasure or business. Aria knows I won't be happy about her unannounced visit, and she knows she'll have to make it up to me. She usually does give me a heads-up when she's arriving; my gut tells me she somehow found out about the witch in my club.

Someone is feeding Aria inside information and its someone who knows a lot about what goes on here. I will not tolerate someone betraying me, particularly not someone I thought would be loyal. When I find out who it is, they will regret crossing me. They will be dealt with severely. If I allow one person to get away with betrayal, I'll be painted as powerless in the eyes of my enemies.

I will deal with Aria's little spy once I get the proof I need. It pisses me off; did she think that she'd get away with it? She must think I've become weak. She will soon find out how wrong she is.

I swallow down the anger threatening to consume me. My demon puts up a fight; he wants me to embrace the anger so he can come out and play. But if I allow him control, I could end up hurting innocent people. I might be a fucking bastard, but I don't hunt or kill for the thrill of it.

Aria's always been unstable, but I used to have her on a leash. Over the last few years, I've allowed that control to slip and she's become unpredictable. There have been several times I had to stop her from maiming or killing someone for merely looking at her in a way she didn't like. She is nearly unstoppable if she thinks another female is taking too much of an interest in me.

I don't understand her possessive jealousy. We've both taken different lovers over the years. We have what humans would call an open relationship. It works for me; I love to fuck. Since she's gotten so volatile, I have tried to make sure that any of the females I decide to fuck remain out of sight, but she always knows when I'm enjoying the pleasures of another woman and eventually, we end up sharing. At some point, I know she will demand to see my new toy and I don't want Aria anywhere near her. For reasons I don't want to consider too closely, I have no desire to share the witch with anyone. But now I need to feed the hunger the witch has built inside me. I will not call her by her name, it's far too intimate.

Bella is one of the women I recently acquired and she's waiting for me in my pleasure room, which is inside my private quarters. I only met her briefly, so I haven't had a taste yet, but I'm certain Aria will find her most delightful.

I can only hope that fucking both Bella and Aria will sate the hunger burning deep in my gut. Having the witch in the same building as me is going to be a sweet temptation, one I won't be able to resist for long. Having touched and tasted her, I know I will continue to crave her until I work her out of my system. I want another taste. I want her at my disposal. My demon is roaring, and I can't remember the last time he fought so hard to reveal himself.

His need threatens to consume me. He wants to claim her, mark her as his own. He's always lived close to the surface, just under my skin, but I can't remember a time I had to work so hard to remain in control. He's battering at my defenses and if I allow him to come out and take over, he will seal the witch's fate. I don't want or need a bond with anyone, let alone a bloody witch, no matter how much she calls to me. Her smell is more intoxicating than any drug.

I haven't had sex with a witch in over a century, never thought I would again. It is far too dangerous to get mixed up with their kind. But I know that if Damien hadn't interrupted, I would have taken her, fucked her on the floor until she was screaming my name in pleasure, begging me to never stop. I'm irritated at how much she's affecting me. I need to get rid of her. I might play with her some more while I decide what to do. In my time, I've killed plenty of witches and always shared the pleasure of their flesh with Aria. Why am I so hesitant to do the same now? What's different about this one?

I ignore the raging of my demon. He isn't happy with the way my thoughts are turning, the fact that I'm trying to talk myself into getting rid of her and including Aria. I'm disturbed at the direction of his thoughts, vexed by the fact that he wants to bond the witch to us for fucking eternity. He knows I hate witches... hell, he hates them, too. It makes little sense why he would want to bond with her. Centuries ago, witches used his kind, tormented them in ways that twisted even my stomach. I can hear him whispering her name, Scarlett. He keeps repeating it and it's driving me fucking insane. I get it, we both want her, that's glaringly obvious at this point. With just one brief thought of her curvy body, I feel myself getting hard.

I can visualize her on her knees in front of me, her plump red lips wrapped around my dick. Her red hair wrapped around my fingers, moaning as she sucks and tongues my shaft until I blow into her mouth. My cum dripping from those plump lips. The dirty thoughts make me pause on the stairs. Fuck. If I don't get control of myself, I'm going to cum in my fucking trousers.

She is dangerous to my peace of mind. I know she's hiding something else, and I intend to find out everything she's keeping from me. She hadn't denied that they were witches, and I can sense she was telling me the truth about their sister. But there's definitely more, and I will do whatever it takes to figure out what's going on inside that pretty little head of hers.

I finally turn my attention to Damien. "Put the woman in the blue bedroom. Her name is Scarlett Winters, and she is here as my guest. Nobody may touch her without my permission." I instruct him as we continue walking.

"Do you intend to keep her here?" he asks in disbelief, turning his head to look at me with both eyebrows raised in surprise.

"For now."

"I don't think it's the right choice," Damien tells me, shaking his head as he pulls his phone from his jacket. "But then, when have you ever listened to what I think when you've set your mind on something?"

"I listen occasionally," I reply, raising my eyebrow a fraction, waiting for him to go on with correcting me.

I hear the grunt come from his mouth. He knows I'm messing with him.

"I'll get it taken care of immediately. I'd advise stationing someone outside the room."

"Get Adam or Logan." I agree with his suggestion. I would hate to have to hurt her if she found a way to leave her room and ended up wandering in places she doesn't belong again. "Make sure they know she's a witch and is not to be trusted. Tell them why she's here. She mentioned a sister, said she went missing at The Fallen Angel. Other than that, we don't know shit about her or her family."

My men have been trained to never show any signs of emotion, no matter the predicament they may find themselves in. Human and Natural, my men are required to be tough, obedient, stoic, and above all, disciplined. They aren't permitted to question my orders. Ever.

Damien is different. His powers match mine, and he has his own demons to manage. I trust him implicitly. I've repeatedly offered to let him take over a region of his own, but he always turns me down. I've never pressured him or asked why he refuses. I figure he has his reasons and if he wanted to share them with me, he would have.

"Damien, be careful. Don't forget she's a witch," I remind him when we arrive at the door to my personal quarters. "Get hold of Leon. See what he can find out about her and her family. I want to know how they've gone undetected in my territory, right under our fucking noses. There must be someone out there who knows something. How long they've been here, how the fuck they manage to stay hidden. Tell him to get me some fucking answers." My last words are spoken over my shoulder as I open the door to my quarters and step over the threshold. I close the door behind me, not bothering to wait for a response.

I need to deal with Aria. I need to know if my suspicions are correct; if she showed up because she somehow knows about the witch.

LUCIEN

A LITTLE WHILE LATER : PLEASURE ROOM

I HATE HOW MY THOUGHTS keep drifting to my little red-haired witch. No matter how I try to tell myself that she is just a witch, my brain refuses to listen. I can't shake the vision of her. Scarlett. Her name, like music, plays on repeat in my mind. She's fucking with my head and my demon is pissed at me. He's desperate for me to seek her out, but I have no intentions of doing so.

I questioned Aria before we came to the pleasure room together, and my suspicions were correct. Aria had known about the witch in my club. She denied knowing anything, insisted she had no idea I had a witch under my protection, let alone that there had been any in my territory, her face and words showing nothing but shock as I interrogated her. If one didn't know Aria as I do, they would likely believe every word that came from her mouth. Unfortunately for her, I always know when she's lying to me. She often forgets who and what I am, how powerful I am.

How I managed to talk Aria out of going to see the witch tonight is a testament to the hold I once had over her. I may no longer have full control, but I do still have some. The minute I mentioned the word witch, Aria was squirming in her seat, desperate to play. I calmed her down by telling her about Bella and how she was waiting for us. I hate that I had to promise to let her play with Scarlett another time, but I have no intention of keeping it.

It's more difficult to take my mind off Scarlett than I could have anticipated. I can't stop fantasizing about her in every position imaginable. My body tightens, a tingling forming in the pit of my stomach, and my heart jolts as I feel my demon surge against the surface of my skin. My balls tighten and retract. I want to devour her; bite and suck her skin anywhere my mouth can reach. I push hard, forcing my demon back down until he's subdued. If I can't control my hunger, my desires... if I can't control my demon, I'm screwed. Bella and Aria are on the bed in front of me, and I convince my demon that they are enough to feed both our appetites.

I'm not ashamed to satisfy my urges with these two women while craving the taste of another. I push back the thought that if it weren't for Aria showing up unannounced, I would be balls deep, taking my pleasure from Scarlett's sweet body. The urge to leave this room and go to hers instead is like a siren's call I'm barely strong enough to resist. I killed many witches in the past and felt no remorse. Could I kill Scarlett? The thought of harming her causes my stomach to roll with nausea.

Pushing aside my thoughts, I turn my attention to the two women in my bed and I join them. I'm starving and I have to feed that hunger somehow. If I can't have the thing my demon and I are craving most, I will have to make sure

Bella and Aria at least take the edge off that hunger.

Bella lays spread-eagled across the bed, her pussy on display, shimmering with her arousal. I position myself behind her and place her blonde head against my chest, pressing my rock-hard cock against the soft skin on her back. Nerves are rolling off her in waves, and I whisper soothingly in her ear, encouraging her to relax. My hands cup her large breasts, tracing the curves before squeezing them, grabbing a nipple between two fingers of each hand. I start twisting and pulling them, distorting their shape. "These are amazing," I whisper in her ear, giving them a slight slap. "While I play with your tits, Aria's going to eat that pretty little cunt of yours, and then I'm going to fuck it," I growl in her ear as Aria kneels between her legs.

I watch Aria as she rotates her fingers around Bella's clit, "Such a pretty girl," I murmur, as Aria pulls open Bella's cunt. Aria's breath lingers over Bella's wet heat. "Such a pretty pussy. I bet it tastes as delicious as it looks."

I feel Bella's body tense as Aria slides her tongue over her clit, pushing the little nub back and forth. Bella moans helplessly, her hips thrusting upwards as Aria sucks on her clit. Sliding a finger, then another, into her wet slit, Aria closes her mouth over the nub, lightly biting down with her teeth. Aria slides another two fingers into Bella's pussy and starts working them in and out, her movements growing more intense, more aggressive. I watch her closely, not wanting her to hurt the woman lying against me. If I need to demand that she back off, I will.

"Ooooh," Bella's moans fill the room, her hips thrusting up to press her pussy into Aria's face. She continues to eat the treat in front of her, taking long licks as though it's the best dessert she's ever had.

"Lick her pussy," I order Aria, watching as her fingers slide in and out, over and over, her fingers becoming soaked with Bella's juices. "Make her come," I demand. She doesn't like taking orders, but she usually does what I tell her in the bedroom, even if it pisses her off sometimes.

I listen as Bella pants, trying to suck in more air. Aria pushes her thighs wider with a wicked smile, getting better access to Bella's dripping wet cunt. I watch as her back arches toward Aria, trying to spur her on.

"Greedy," I mumble into Bella's ear, watching as she comes apart, writhing and bucking mindlessly, after a final swipe of Aria's tongue.

She turns her head to look up at me. "Please, fuck me," she asks in a broken *whisper.*

"Oh, Bella. I intend to fuck you," I whisper into her ear, nipping playfully on an earlobe. "You'll be screaming in pleasure while I fuck your tight little pussy. I will make you beg for more and not stop until you can't even speak.

Aria continues working her, her hands and face buried in her cunt, causing her to clench the blankets in her fists and arch her back repeatedly. Her head thrashes from side to side as strangled screams rip from her throat.

Aria finally lifts her head, a happy smile written on her mouth, Bella's juices painting her lips. "You taste SOOO sweet," she coos, running a finger around her clit before plunging it inside her dripping hole. "Lucien, you did well finding us this dirty, naughty whore."

I don't give a fuck if she thinks I did well, so I ignore her. I give her a signal, indicating I want to change places. I need to stick my cock inside a tight, wet hole. Kneeling between them, I take in the scene laid out before me.

"Fuck each other," I order in a low-pitched voice, crudely yanking them both back by the hair. I hear their startled gasps and demand, "Don't stop until I tell you. I want to see you both come," I push their faces together, forcing their mouths to touch. Their mouths and tongues dance as they run their hands over one another's body. I watch as they both move their hands to each other's pussies; fingers caressing, stroking, shoving deep inside one another, they do as instructed. I ignore the look of displeasure across Aria's face. She doesn't like how I've taken complete control over the situation, but I don't give a fuck.

I kneel over them and rub my hands over their bodies. Their nipples are rock hard, like little pebbles, as I caress the sides of their breasts. I hear their moans mingling together, their breathing labored. I can tell they're both close to coming undone. I place one hand on each of their hips and rock them harder and harder on each other's fingers.

"Oh fuck," Bella yells into Aria's mouth.

"Let me see you come all over each other's fingers. Aria, do Bella's fingers feel as good as mine? Is her pussy soaking wet?" I taunt her, knowing how much she loves dirty talk. "Fuck Aria with your fingers, Bella. Is that cunt nice and tight? Is my dick going to fit inside it?" They both come apart at the same time, trembling with their release.

Not giving them time to recover, I look at Bella. "Come here, kneel at my feet," I order her, a fire in my eyes as she meets my gaze. Pointing to the floor in front of me, I demand, "And take out my cock." Her small insatiable hands grasp the edge of my underwear and pull them down, my dick springing free as I kick them away. I grip the side of Bella's head and move her down to my cock, shoving it in her mouth until it hits the back of her throat, making her gag. She moans; I can tell how much she fucking loves choking on my cock. I look up and see Aria's eyes light up eagerly, waiting for my next move.

"Show me how much you want to suck my cock and I might give it to you," I instruct Aria, placing my palm in the middle of her chest, making her topple onto her back. I don't care if she wants me to order her around or not. "Put my balls in your mouth," I demand. With a huff, she obeys me. I watch as she takes them into her mouth, sucking one at a time, humming while licking my balls while Bella sucks my cock. Bella's mouth is like a goddamn vacuum. I grab the back of Aria's neck and she sticks out her tongue and licks my balls, moving up to my shaft, while Bella sucks on the tip of my cock. I grab Bella's neck and move them back and forth in sync, forcing them to take turns on my cock.

I let go of Aria and grab the sides of Bella's head once again, plunging my dick into the back of her throat. I push and pull my cock back and forth into her mouth, fucking her face.

"Fuck," I roar in pleasure, shivers rolling through my body, sweat running down my chest. The sound causes Aria to sit back on her knees with an unhappy look crossing her features, her eyes glowing red; I know that look. I've seen it too many times in the past. If I don't get her under control, and quickly, she will do something I will never forgive myself for. Before she can even think about harming Bella, I pull Aria roughly towards me, kissing her as if I can't get enough.

Breaking the kiss, I whisper, "Baby, I fucking love the fact you get so bloody jealous. It turns me the hell on," I bite Aria's ear, sucking the lobe into my mouth. "Best of all, I love the way your suck my cock and fuck me. Nobody is better than you." Hearing my words, she calms down, whimpering in ecstasy while rubbing her soft body against mine like a cat in heat. Taking a fistful of her black hair, I pull her head back. "I want to see Bella's ass nice and red, Aria," I order, with a twisted grin forming on my lips as I gag Bella with my dick, making her eyes water. Aria smirks as she sits up and spanks Bella's ass, one globe at a time, turning the pale flesh a deep red. She fucking loves it. Aria always loves it when she gets to punish the women I fuck.

"That's it, Bella, suck my fucking dick, darling, make me nice and wet," I instruct her before turning my attention back to Aria. "Aria, hit those soft cheeks harder. Get that ass fucking nice and red. I want to see your hand printed on it." I command Aria, watching as she spanks Bella harder, causing her to squeal around my dick on every smack, her ass wobbling with each crack of her palm.

I release Bella's mouth with a pop and watch as she gasps for air while spit and my pre-cum slide down her chin. I reach over and grab Aria by the neck and place her near Bella's mouth. "Lick her clean," I order in a harsh tone, watching as Aria does as she's told. I shove their lips together, and they suck on each other's tongues exactly how they'd done on my cock.

I grab onto Bella's waist, pulling them apart. "Come here," I roughly order, placing Bella on her hands and knees, dragging Aria into the same position beside her. I get behind them and spank Bella then Aria, going back and forth between them. They both moan and shudder with every slap as my hand hits their ass cheeks, making them bounce and jiggle. I rub both of their bright red ass cheeks, loving the sight of the print of my hands on their delicate flesh. They reach behind, and both stroke my cock with their hands, and I growl, spanking them both hard enough to make them fall forward. They look back at me with their eyes dilated, both panting heavily.

"Do you want to come?" I taunt, spanking them again for good measure, loving the whimpers escaping their lips. "Beg me," I cup each of their pussies, one in each hand, rubbing circles around their clits, "and you had better mean it."

"Please, please, Lucien. Make us come," they both beg, making my cock twitch. I groan in a low, rumbling tone.

I grab Aria's hand and place it on Bella's clit. I push two fingers into Bella's tight wet heat, moving them at a rapid speed to make her come hard and fast. Bella's body falls forward, and she convulses around my fingers. I instruct Aria not to let up as she plays with her clit, until she begs her to stop. I order Aria to smack her pussy.

I reach down to Aria's cunt and it's sopping wet. I thrust my cock into her pussy in one swift movement, so hard that she screams out my name. I grab under her ass, tilting her hips up so I can slam her onto my cock, moving her up and down. I let her enjoy the sensation for a few minutes before flipping her over, grabbing Bella, and sitting her on Aria's face, cowboy style.

"I want to see Bella's come dripping down your fucking face. Make her come, Aria. I want to hear Bella scream as you eat her pussy," I goad her, slapping Aria's clit as she goes to town.

Watching Aria eat Bella's pussy while I fuck her is a sight to see and has my balls throbbing and dick aching. I reach down, manipulating Aria's clit while still plunging my dick into her tight pussy. "Stick out that fucking tongue. More!" I hear my demon snarl. My skin ripples as he enjoys the sight before us. Watching them squirm and moan, I must admit, is a turn-on.

I feel Aria come all over my dick as her chest and breasts flush red. She clamps down as her head falls forward, and I carry on fucking her, plunging into her slick pussy harder and faster as she tightens down on my dick even more. I haven't come, yet. Shit, I need more.

I pull out and grab Bella, the sounds of her moaning fill the room. I put her on all fours and thrust into her wet heat, fucking her doggie style. "Please... Please... Harder," she begs, pushing her hips back towards mine. The slapping of flesh fills the room. Aria reaches down and starts playing with my balls. I can feel the muscles contract at the base of my dick, my balls tightening. I know that I'm about to come. Mercilessly pounding into Bella, I crudely grab her hair, pulling her back towards me and slamming into her from a different angle. Fuck. Yeah.

"Play with her clit," I order Aria, my eyes flashing red, my demon close. I hear my voice roughen as it deepens. "I want her tight little pussy to squeeze my cock as I come," my demon growls out.

"Fuck the dirty cunt," Aria screams, her face twisted in excitement, eyes bulging. "Make that tight pussy bleed."

"Fuck... Fuck... Fuck..." Bella screams in pleasure while Aria plays with her clit in a circular motion, pressing the bundle of nerves firmly. I fuck her furiously, thrusting in and out of her tight cunt. I feel the shudder move through her body as I slam in and out of her just before she clamps down around my cock like a vise. I release a loud grunt as I shoot my seed deep inside her tight pussy.

Sweat dripping down our bodies, we lay there panting, each of us needing air and water. Once we recover, I continue to fuck them through the rest of the night until they're too exhausted to take anymore.

CHAPTER EIGHT

SCARLETT

THREE DAYS LATER

After everything that happened between us, Lucien had his grunt Damien escort me to a room in a separate wing from the club. I haven't heard from or seen either one of them since. Turns out Damien is his second in command. I asked him several times when I would be able to talk to Lucien again and he merely said that he would come find me when he had time to speak. It feels like it's been an eternity since that conversation, when in reality, it's only been a few days.

Once Damien left me alone in the room, I immediately took a shower to try and scrub Lucien's touch from my body... and my mind. It didn't work. I can feel his hands on me even now. Part of me feels relieved he hasn't come to see me yet, since I clearly cannot be trusted around him.

Before leaving, Damien told me that there would be a guard outside my door at all times, should I need anything. We both know the real reason they're there is to prevent me from escaping, but I didn't bother correcting him. I tried opening the door once but had been shoved back by one of the guards, a huge shifter who didn't bother speaking before closing the door in my face.

I look around the room and groan. The room I was given is glamorously large and done in tasteful colors. A four-poster bed sits on one side of the room, and the other side has a sofa, chair, and a TV attached to the wall. The other door leads to a gorgeous en-suite. If this room were anywhere else and I were in it for any other reason, I probably wouldn't want to leave. It really is like a five-star hotel. Nothing but the best for Lucien Sinclair, right?

I've searched high and low for a way to escape, but there isn't one. I've seen Lucien from the window several times a day, and I know he sensed me watching him but never even bothered to look up. I would have opened the window and screamed at him, or hell, found a way to climb out of it, but it is bolted shut.

Most of my time has been spent thinking about my predicament. I still can't figure out exactly how Lucien had known I was a witch. The only answer I came up with is that his demon must be far more powerful than any of us realized. It's clear that none of the spells we used to conceal and protect me had worked on him and it's unlikely there are many spells out there that would have any effect on him whatsoever. I just wish we had known that while we were making our plan. We could have requested a meeting with him. I can't imagine that would have worked out favorably for us, but at least I wouldn't be a fucking prisoner in this room, just waiting for him to decide what to do with me.

I know my sisters must be worried about me. Even though they knew where I was headed, the plan was for me to come straight back home. I tried to get a mental link to Pamela, but it hasn't worked. I could barely even feel her. There must be something about this room, or maybe even the building, that's blocking my powers.

Despite my best efforts, my mind drifts back to the other night. I can't seem to stop myself from replaying the sensation of his firm lips, the way they'd felt as they made their way down my throat, leaving feathery kisses in their wake. How his hard body had pressed against mine, making me feel like he was in absolute control of me, body and soul. Just remembering his touch, his taste, sends shivers down my spine. My body still craves him and all my efforts to fight it seem to be in vain. If I'm not careful, I could become addicted to him, and he would destroy me in a way no drug ever could.

I'm grateful to Damien for interrupting us before things could go any further, though at the time, I was just as displeased by the interruption as Lucien. The expression on his face had changed from one of lust to one of silent rage. I never want to be on the receiving end of that look. I saw his eyes flash red for the briefest moment and wonder if I imagined it.

Whatever Damien had whispered in his ear had caused him to turn on his heel and leave the room without a word to me, Damien following behind him. There was the sound of the door closing followed by the loud click of it locking, then total silence surrounded me.

I tried using my powers to get out of the room, but it hadn't worked. The door was obviously spelled to resist magic. Damien came back a while later to escort me to where I am now.

With effort, I shove my unwanted thoughts to the back of my mind and move to the comfortable chair in front of the window, throwing myself down into it. I lean my head back, gaze at the large forecourt below, and study the heavy iron gates and tall surrounding walls. Sensing rather than seeing movement to the left of my gaze, I slowly turn my head and sit up abruptly as the doors swing open, Lucien's tall, muscular figure stepping into view. My gut clenches when a gorgeous woman walks out behind him and moves in front of him.

She's nearly as tall as he is, but willow thin, with black hair hanging down her back, hitting the top of her ass. Her lips are painted a deep blood red and I watch as she presses them to his cheek, leaving a smudge of lipstick behind. My hands clench into fists as their lips meet, her fingers running down his chest. I try but fail to drag my eyes away from the scene.

My chest spasms painfully as his hand strokes the woman's slim waist and pulls her tighter against his hard body, their lips locked together in a passionate kiss. I feel nauseous as I watch them and once again experience the sensation of his hands on my own body. The feeling of betrayal ricocheting through me is completely irrational. What the hell is wrong with me!? We aren't a couple. I don't want to be with him; he terrifies me.

I can't wrap my head around my reaction to witnessing him with another woman. It likely has something to do with the dreams and visions that have become more frequent since I got here. I've somehow been able to sense him every moment of every day. I don't know why I'm so connected to him, why I can sense his emotions. I know when he's pissed off and when he's full of passion. I told myself I was imagining things when I sensed he was having sex several times over the last few days, but seeing him with this woman, I know I was only lying to myself.

Even worse, I can feel something off about the woman from here. My witch and my omega started going crazy the instant I saw her. Darkness is rooted deep inside of her, and I feel a sense of foreboding come over me. Almost as though seeing her is an omen. I know that Lucien has darkness deep inside of him. I felt it the minute he touched me, but it's different than what I'm getting from her. I didn't get the sense that he wanted to hurt me. For some reason, even though I've never even met this raven-haired woman, I get the strong feeling that she wants to destroy me.

Knowing that what I'm experiencing is likely a premonition, I resolve to do everything in my power to avoid her. I know that if we come face to face, I will likely be put in a situation where I am forced to defend myself, therefore revealing my powers, which is something that is far too dangerous for me to even consider.

If anyone ever found out that we're a family of Omegas, shit would really hit the fan. Omegas haven't been seen for over two-hundred years. Everyone thought we had died out, but a small group had gone into hiding and our ancestors were a part of that group.

Omegas could be male or female. For many years humans and Naturals had cherished and protected them. They can breed with both and are born healers.

Legend has it that one such being would be born and be able to control all humans and Supernaturals. Chaos ensued. Humans, out of fear and stupidity, began hunting the Omegas. Supernaturals started capturing them in hopes of breeding the child from the legend. There were a handful of individuals who didn't agree with what was happening, so they came together to help the Omegas escape. They all fled in the night, though some were captured and killed, and only a small number survived.

Witches hadn't fared much better and were hunted around the

same time as the Omegas. There aren't many full-blooded witches left either, and the ones we know about, we avoid. They tend to be dangerous and difficult to get along with. A few have mated with humans, and those are generally slightly less hostile. Even still, outside of the immediate family, there's only one witch we can trust, and that's my distant cousin Astrid, although lately, she's been having a hard time holding her witch back. Astrid is different, though. Her blood is far less diluted than ours.

Our blood has become diluted over the years due to mating with certain humans. What most people don't know is that there were once two different branches of human DNA. One branch was what we would now consider to be 'normal humans,' but the other had certain oddities in their genetic code.

The scientists in our coven realized that in order to keep our ancestors safe and to strengthen their powers, they needed to mate with only those humans who had the special genetic markers. That is what finally allowed us to control both our witches and our omegas.

The leaders of our coven endorsed this strategy, but not everyone agreed. The new laws caused some of the full-blooded witches to rebel and split off from our coven, which is why there are still some full-blooded witches out there.

We try to avoid them as much as possible because they're dangerous. Vicious, even. They're the reason our coven went into hiding. My ancestor's decision to breed with those humans made us stronger and more robust, but it also gave us more human emotions. Like compassion.

My family, being a mix of both witch and omega, must protect our secret at all costs. On top of our powers, we are also stronger and more robust due to our mixed heritage. The first children conceived when my ancestors were in hiding had been bred with a combination of humans, witches, and Naturals. They were incapable of controlling their powers, and there were some dark times. A lot of mistakes were made, but as time passed and each subsequent generation was born, control became easier. When combined, the powers of Omegas mixed with any other race, could turn a child into a being so powerful, they could destroy a city without even lifting a finger.

It's bad enough Lucien knows we are witches. If he, or anyone else for that matter, were to discover what we really are, we would be hunted by humans and Supernaturals alike. The thought of being discovered makes me sick to my stomach.

My gaze drifts back to Lucien and his lover, and I see that they are still at it in front of the house. It's clear they don't care who sees them. There's no way in hell I will let Lucien touch me again. No matter how my body may scream and beg for him, I have no interest in having someone else's sloppy seconds.

I know I'm going to regret what I'm about to do, but I am at the end of my rope and can't seem to stop myself. I reach out for the window with both hands and, using all my unnatural strength, I wrench it open with a loud grunt. It flies up and bangs against the top of the frame. With a satisfied chuckle and zero thought to the consequences of my actions, I stick my head and shoulders out of the window and let out a loud, high-pitched whistle, hoping to gain Lucien's attention. When that fails to work, I begin shouting down at him. Not very ladylike, I know, but I give zero fucks.

"Oi, Casanova," I shout. Lucien looks up at me with a furrowed brow. "Oh, that got your attention, did it? We have a deal; in case you may have forgotten." I snarl down at him, feeling particularly brave. "I want to know what the fuck you've been doing to hold up your end of the bargain!"

Even from this distance, I can tell I've pissed him off. Good. I smile to myself. Maybe now he will get his ass in gear. Curse the witch inside of me, but I can't seem to keep my mouth shut. "Listen here, Lucien 'Bloody Smug' Sinclair. No matter what you say, I'm not staying in this room any longer, and you will either tell me what the hell is going on, or our so-called deal is off, and I will be leaving this bloody dump."

His eyes bore into me like lasers, and if looks could kill, I would perish on the spot. For the first time, I consider the consequences of poking the hornet's nest that is Lucien Sinclair's temper. Staring into the eyes of a pissed off demon is a sensation I will never forget. But I refuse to show him any fear. I roll my eyes and glance at the woman standing next to him. She looks annoyed as well, probably because I interrupted their face-sucking session.

She turns her attention to Lucien, and I see his face get even more pissed off at whatever she's saying to him, something I didn't think possible. I see him reply to her, but I'm too far away to make out their words.

Her face tightens before relaxing into a satisfied smirk. She looks up at me and a smug smile spreads across her lips as she runs her eyes over my face and chest, causing my skin to crawl. I have no doubt that Lucien Sinclair can make my life miserable, but there's something about her, something I can't put my finger on, that causes warning bells to ring in my head. I watch as a triumphant smile lights up her face just before Lucien disappears from view, back into the building, with her following closely behind. My gut tells me I've just gotten myself into a bucket of trouble, more than I've ever been in before, and I'm going to be facing it sooner rather than later.

I have a feeling Lucien is headed up to see me now and that he's bringing her with him. Every part of me, witch and omega included, is screaming at me to get the hell out of this room, whatever it takes. I need to face him on an even playing field, not as his captive. The way I responded to him the other night was terrifying, and I can't allow it to happen again, especially not in her presence.

I have no doubt that whatever that woman asks of him, he will give it to her and if the vibes I was getting off her from a distance were any indication, it would not bode well for me. I'm not a violent person, I would much rather be helping than harming, but if I must hurt someone to protect myself or someone I love, I won't hesitate to do so.

I have a bad feeling that hiding my powers will not be possible for much longer. I can only hope they will assume I am merely an extremely powerful witch and that they will be too ignorant of the past to realize I am also part Omega.

Striding to the door, I wrench it open and am unsurprised to find one of my guards, Adam, I believe his name is, leaning against the opposite wall, typing intently on the phone in his hands. I wonder if I should just carry on down the corridor or wait for him to realize I've left my room. I decide to wait.

It doesn't take him long to sense someone staring at him, and I raise an eyebrow as he slowly raises his head and tucks his phone in the back pocket of his tight black jeans. He scowls at the realization that I've left my room and I give him a mocking smile.

"Get back in your room," He demands, taking a step towards me. A frown appears on his face when I ignore his command.

"Not going to happen, wolf boy," I respond in a deceptively sweet tone. I step further into the hallway and pull the door closed behind me. I will not do his bidding. The complacent little witch is gone; the powerful woman has taken over. Until now, I followed orders without question, only asking to see Lucien.

The human in me is more comfortable cowering in the face of danger, but the witch and omega inside of me will not be held back any longer. Those parts of me could easily overtake the human side of me, making me more powerful. I know I have the ability to make everyone in my path quiver in fear, and at this moment, I need to channel the witch inside of me. My omega wants to come out and join the fun, but that I cannot allow.

As I turn and walk away from him, I feel his enormous hand grab my forearm. I don't want to hurt him, but my patience is wearing thin.

"I suggest you let go of my arm, wolf boy," I warn with a smile, before looking pointedly at the fingers wrapped firmly around my arm. "Either take me to see Lucien, or I am leaving."

"Look lady, I don't want to hurt you. You need to get back in your room. Mr. Sinclair is busy and will see you when he's available." His face is tense and the grip on my arm tightens as he tries to pull me back. He isn't hurting me, but I don't like how he is trying to force me to do his bidding.

I laugh. I know what *Mr. Sinclair* is busy doing... or rather *whom* he's busy doing. He can fuck himself.

"Oh, I know he's *busy*, but I refuse to waste any more of my time here so he can play 'hide the sausage' with his harem." I pull my arm from his hand and walk away.

"Regardless of what you want to do, you will go back to your room." Adam says in a firm voice, catching up to me and grabbing my arm again.

What in bloody hell is wrong with these men? I think angrily, wrenching my arm from his grip.

"Back the fuck off!" I snarl, placing one hand on his huge chest and shoving with all my might. I watch as he staggers a few steps. He gives me a bewildered stare as he regains his balance; I can tell he's confused. He's wondering how a tiny little witch could move him so easily.

"I don't have time for this shit. You will either do what I've asked, or you can bugger off." My temper is being held by the tiniest thread of control, and I know that it isn't going to take much for it to snap. I turn on my heel and walk away. He can follow or stay where he is, I don't care.

"Fucking hell, woman. You're a pain in the ass," he speaks from behind me. "You're going to get me gutted."

I sigh and roll my eyes. "Stop being so dramatic."

"Lady, you don't know the half of it," he drawls, his footsteps sounding closer. "If Lucien finds out I didn't stop you, I'll be in deep shit."

"You can't stop me even if you try," I laugh. "I could have left days ago," I inform him, looking over my shoulder. "Your boss? He made a deal with me. A deal he hasn't held up his end of. You have two choices here. Take me to see him, or I *am* leaving, and you will not stop me. Your choice, wolfy." I give him a blank look and shrug my shoulders. "In fact, I'm sure you can take that fancy phone out of your pocket, you know the one you were so busy playing with when I almost walked out of here without you even noticing? Take it out, call him, and tell him that I. Want. To. See. Him. NOW!"

I see his lips moving and hear him muttering I can't make out the words, but I'm sure it's less than flattering. "Fine. I'll bloody ring him while I take you to wait in the main office." He lets out a deep sigh as he comes to stand beside me and takes the phone from his pocket. "But you owe me one."

Yeah. Right. I don't owe him shit.

CHAPTER NINE

SCARLETT

A FEW MINUTES LATER

I'M BACK IN THE SAME ROOM WHERE I first met Lucien. On the way here, I tried once again to use the mental link to get ahold of my sisters, but it still won't work. There must be something in the walls here that is preventing me from getting a connection. At least I hope that's what it is and not something more sinister.

Another of Lucien's flunkeys is sitting in a chair, watching the security feeds on the monitors. The Fallen Angel is closed tonight, so he's just observing the employees going about their cleaning duties. Adam ordered me to stay here until Lucien arrived. He murmured a few words to the guy watching the monitors and then left me alone with him.

The guy doesn't say a word to me. He's only looked at me once, right after Adam left. He glowered at me for a long moment before turning back around and hasn't looked at me since. It's like I'm not even here. I feel like my current situation is only slightly better than the one I just left.

I get the sense he's not human, but I'm struggling to figure out what kind of Supernatural he is. My aunt once told me about meeting a snake shifter, and I remember her description well. She said they have black beady eyes and pointy noses. She also said they aren't to be trusted, that they will turn on you the second you turn your back on one. This guy is sending off all kinds of signals telling me not to take my eyes off him and I wonder if he's a snake shifter.

"Er, excuse me," I call out to him while waving my hand in his direction, trying to get his attention. He doesn't even glance up. I briefly wonder if he speaks English, but it seems unlikely that Lucien would hire someone to work security who wouldn't be able to monitor the audio feeds. "Hey! Do you know how long until your Lord and Master arrives?" I see his eyes flicker in my direction at my question. Awesome. He's just ignoring me. What a dick.

Whatever. If Lucien doesn't arrive in the next few minutes, I'm out of here. I've wasted enough of my time. Once I get home, we can gather up enough people to help us find Megan. When it first got out that she was missing, we had plenty of volunteers. It was heartwarming to find out there were so many who cared and were willing to help in our time of need. We just hadn't wanted to risk bringing unwanted attention and putting any of our friends or family at risk. We managed to evade scrutiny for so long, it's in our nature to avoid it at all costs. We approached Lucien because we wanted to avoid that exact scenario and because we figured that since she disappeared in his club, he would likely be our best chance to get the answers we needed.

Snaky finally answers me, startling me from my thoughts. "He's on his way, *witch*." He spits the last word at me and gives me a look so caustic, I'm relieved he doesn't have the power to burn me with his eyes. I roll my eyes. Does he really think a dirty look and his disdain for my ancestry is going to intimidate me?

I raise an eyebrow at him. "Do you think I'm insulted from being called what I am? I must admit, I'm not a fan of the way the mainstream depicts my kind. I do prefer enchantress or sorceress, personally." I give him a saccharine smile and am pleased when his face goes blank. I notice the permanent frown lines on his otherwise youthful looking face. If the man ever dared to smile, his skin would likely shatter.

I feel my witch sit up and take notice of what's going on. She's been quiet for a while now, which is odd. She's generally more forceful than my omega. Sometimes I hear the two of them talking to one another and it still feels strange. One would think I would have gotten used to it by now. When I was younger, I really struggled with sharing my mind with two other beings. Having a human, a witch, and an omega inside one brain can be a bit disorienting. As a child, I was too afraid to call attention to myself by asking any of my family members if they had the same problem, and as I've gotten older, I've learned to accept my reality and maintain control most of the time.

The witch and omega often fight my human for dominance, but I'm usually able to hold them back and only bring them forth when needed. My omega is easier to control, but she's remarkably strong and her healing powers are unmatched.

The turning of the door handle grabs my attention. Even before it opens, I sense Lucien on the other side.

My intuition is confirmed when he steps inside, the woman from tonsil-hockey exhibition hour standing next to him. She is beautiful. There is no other word for it. In comparison, I feel dowdy and plain, but I'm well aware that beauty is only skin-deep. I stand up straighter and look her dead in the eye. I refuse to show any weakness around her because I know she will exploit it. From a distance earlier, I hadn't been able to make out details but now, up close, I can see that her eyes are completely devoid of emotion.

I can tell from the disgusted look on her face that she's taken an instant dislike to me, and I wonder if it's because Lucien informed her that I'm a witch. I know she's going to cause problems for me. If I have to show her how powerful I am, I will, but I'd really rather not. I can sense she's a Demon, but I don't know what kind or what level of power she holds. I can tell she isn't as powerful as Lucien, but she's definitely more powerful than snaky sitting over there watching the monitors. There are several factors that contribute to a Demon's power, age being one of them. Unfortunately, knowledge about Demon power is a well-guarded secret that few outside the inner circle will ever learn.

She sneers at me before saying, "You've been causing trouble, *witch*." What is with people using that word as an insult? I merely roll my eyes and turn away from her, looking at Lucien.

He's bigger than I remembered, but his smell is every bit as delectable and it's calling to me. "Do you normally let your lackeys talk for you?" I know I shouldn't have said that, but my petty side has decided to make an appearance. I see his eyes flash red, just the briefest glimpse of his demon, and my witch rejoices. It's strange, but instead of being afraid, my body flushes with lust, the memories of what happened between us in this very room just a few nights ago flooding my mind. I shake it off just as the woman's voice pulls my attention from Lucien.

"Why you little…" She trails off and takes a step in my direction, her stunning face contorting in anger. Her demon makes an appearance, and it confirms my suspicions of her beauty being merely skin deep. Her face is a black pit, as though her skin has been burned beyond recognition at some point. Parts of the flesh look like melted wax, causing her features to distort. I shake my head, trying to banish the horrifying sight, but I know it's one I won't soon forget.

"Watch your mouth, little witch," Lucien growls, his shoulders rigid with anger. He places his muscular arm out to stop the woman's advance. "Aria isn't my lackey." He states plainly, stepping toward me as his dark eyes rake over my body, the same fire I saw in them the other night blazing across my skin.

I now know her name, but I have no intention of using it. I stare at his stern expression before dropping my eyes to take in his muscular frame. A shiver runs down my spine as our gazes lock once again. He isn't the same man who was all over me a few nights ago, despite the similar look in his eyes. He is someone else entirely. I'm facing a man who would take my life as quickly and easily as he would squash a bug beneath his shoe. I school my expression, reminding myself to show no fear.

My witch wants out. She wants to show him where he can shove his intimidation tactics. I can feel her ranting and raging inside of me, making my skin itch. I resist the urge to scratch my arm and use a tiny bit of my power to push her back down. Not far, though. I need her just beneath the surface in case I need to call on her.

I continue staring at him, my face completely blank. I'm over the top pissed off right now, and if he wants a fight, he will get one. Not only did he fail to keep up his end of our agreement, but he brought this *woman,* this she-demon, with him. I feel my skin heat with rage. He can fuck himself. Knowing I'm going to regret what's coming, but unable to stop myself, I stride forward and shout, "Fuck you, Demon! Either you have information about my sister, or you don't. If not, I'm out of here." My green eyes flash in warning.

"Leaving?" the she-demon butts in, looking me up and down with a smirk. "Oh, you aren't going anywhere, witch."

I start laughing the minute the words leave her mouth. She has no idea how powerful I am. "Try. And. Stop. Me." I say in a voice that is deadly quiet, my stance daring her to do something. My witch eggs me on, wanting me to show them both what we're capable of. I fight against her, needing to maintain control for now. But if they try to stop me, I will let her loose, and they will regret it.

Seeing the deadly calm inside of me she pauses a moment before shaking off her surprise. "Oh please," she scoffs, raising an eyebrow as she strides out in front of Lucien, hips swaying. "You don't have a chance against either of us."

"Why don't you try me?" I give her a smile, my rage building to an inferno. I would happily kill the woman standing in front of me and not think twice about it.

She turns to Lucien. "Lucien, I think we need to put this little witch in her place," she says, leaning her body into his and running her hands up his chest. "We could have a lot of fun with her before we drain her of her powers." She gives a maniacal laugh before turning her face towards me and running her tongue over her bottom lip. "Although… to look at her, I don't think there's much to take."

My skin crawls. She-demon is clearly deranged. She might be beautiful, but her mind is broken. If this is the type of woman he finds attractive, I'm insulted he showed interest in me.

I can feel his calculated gaze locked on my face as though burning a hole to try to see my thoughts. I never should have trusted him; dreams and visions be damned. I lock eyes with him, letting him see the betrayal and fury inside of me. He shows no signs of recognition, he merely stares at me, waiting for my next move.

Eyebrow cocked, I warn him, "If you like your little… girlfriend, you may want to control her. I can't be held accountable otherwise. Now.

You either have information about my sister or you don't. Which is it?" I demand.

I can feel the she-demon shredding my flesh with her eyes, but I fight the urge to look at her, even as I see Lucien clamp his hand down on her wrist to stop her from retaliating. I refuse to give her any power over me.

"I do have information on your sister," he says with a smile that sets my teeth on edge. He walks further into the room, his hand still wrapped around her wrist. I can feel in my bones that he's leading up to something. "It's not as much as I was hoping for, but I think it will bring you closer to finding out what happened to her."

"Sister?" She-demon cuts in. "We're doing deals with witches now, are we?" She asks with a sneer.

"Yes," Lucien replies in a clipped, impersonal tone, his hand snagging her wrist to stop her from stroking down his chest to his belt.

"We?" I question, tearing my gaze away. I have no desire to watch her fondle him. I pray that she doesn't mean what it sounds like she means.

"Of course," she purrs, "after all, we are... what you'd call husband and wife, and we do *everything* together." She finishes dropping the bomb and runs her free hand up to cup his neck as she leans in and presses her lips to his cheek, staking her claim. Her eyes are locked on me as though to gauge my reaction to her words.

I stand there in shocked silence, waiting for him to deny it. I'm appalled when he says nothing. I cringe when I realize what she's suggesting. She is in for a nasty surprise if she thinks she can lay one finger on me. I don't care what or *who* they share, I will not be participating in their games. If Lucien wants to share lovers with her, so be it, but I will not be one of them.

"I don't give a damn whether you're his wife, girlfriend, or just his little pet. My deal is with him, not with you," I inform her through clenched teeth, feeling my nails bite into my palms from clenching my fists too tightly. "Lucien and I had an agreement, and you have no part of it."

What a bloody mess. None of our research on Lucien had turned up any indication of a serious relationship. I tell myself that is the reason I feel so shaken, but the truth is, even though I know he has no responsibility to me, I feel betrayed. I take a calming breath, trying to calm the rage building in my chest. I need to corral my emotions, or my witch will take over.

I can feel her, eager to take the wheel and looking for any excuse to do so. She's hoping the she-demon attacks me and gives her the opportunity to strike back. Though I'm terrified of my current situation, because of the witch inside of me, I feel eager, excited even, to take her on. Maybe I've lost my mind. Despite my witch's frenzied state, my omega is just sitting quietly, observing all the action.

Lifting my head and pushing my shoulders back, I lock eyes with Lucien. Taking a deep breath before speaking, I unemotionally state, "We had a deal. If you try to change the terms, the deal will be null and void."

I wonder if I'm imagining the flash of red in his eyes, it is gone so quickly. "I have no intention of changing the terms," he grates out. He's pissed. He clearly isn't accustomed to being questioned. "I don't renege on my deals. It's bad for business."

Her whiny voice rings in my ears and I wince. "Lucien! You will not cut me out of this deal you made. Surely you don't intend to take orders from this… this *witch!*" Her hands desperately grip at him, trying to gain his attention.

He looks down at her and the look on his face is loving but looks insincere. "I'm so sorry, my beloved. I'm not happy about it either, but she's right. I did make a deal with her, and you were not present. I cannot go back on the terms of the deal without sending the message that my word is not to be trusted." He pulls her into his arms and lays a kiss upon her forehead.

My eyes nearly roll back into my head of their own volition. I'm relieved he intends to keep our deal between the two of us but disgusted by their interaction. She seems utterly unhinged. I don't know what exactly is wrong with her, but something is clearly broken inside of her.

I open my up powers slightly, not wanting to draw attention to myself but wanting to view her aura. Her colors are intense, but muddy, showing how unstable she is. My suspicions are confirmed and I'm not happy about it. No, her instability makes her even more dangerous than I could have anticipated.

Tired of witnessing their little scene, I cut in. "If you two lovebirds are quite finished, I would like to get on with finding out what happened to my sister."

Lucien cuts his attention to me and with an emotionless voice he informs me, "A soul keeper took your sister." A shiver runs down my spine and I try to hide it. His black eyes narrow and I know he caught my reaction.

"Soul keeper?" I ask, my voice cracking. A panic unlike any I've ever experienced fills every crevice of my mind. I've heard of soul keepers. While they aren't as bad as soul eaters, they aren't exactly puppies and rainbows, either.

Soul keepers suck out their victim's souls and hold them for their pleasure. I've heard that when they have the soul, the body wanders around lost and in a trance until, if they're lucky, the soul is returned to their body.

"Does that mean they took her soul?" I ask as I begin pacing, my mind whirling with everything I've ever learned about soul keepers. If her soul has been taken, that means all three, human, witch, and omega, are likely inside of this soul keeper. This is bad. So fucking bad.

"From what I've learned so far, no, it doesn't seem her soul has been taken. You're lucky. It seems the soul keeper was some kind of bounty hunter."

I stop pacing and look at him, shocked. "So... they were paid to kidnap her? And how exactly is that lucky?"

"It means that whoever wanted her doesn't want her soul taken from her body. At least not yet. For now, they want her whole. They want her alive." He gives a half laugh before continuing, "And that makes it easier for me and my men to find her. It could have been much worse. If she were already dead or had her soul been taken, we may never have found her. It seems the soul keeper hires himself out to anyone willing to pay his price. He offers all kinds of services. Soul sucking, kidnapping, murder... Kidnapping gives him the least amount of satisfaction, so he charges the most for it. Whoever wanted your sister must have a great deal of money and a great deal of incentive to get their hands on her."

"Do you know who hired him? Or where to find the soul keeper?" I take a step closer to him, hoping he has the answers.

"That's where we are stuck at the moment. It seems he has vanished." A look of frustration crosses his face and I'm surprised that he cares enough for it to show.

"Nobody can just vanish. That's impossible." I mutter to myself, trying to figure this out. The feeling of hope I felt when he told me he knew who took her is gone and has been replaced by cold, hard dread.

He must think I'm talking to him, because he responds. "Nothing is impossible if you want it badly enough. Either this soul keeper got spooked and ran, or whoever hired him made him disappear."

"You think the soul keeper is dead?" I ask, desperately hoping I'm wrong. Finding the creature who took her would be the best lead in finding Megan.

"I don't know." His expression darkens with the words, and I can see that not knowing things is an uncomfortable anomaly for him. "We haven't been able to find him, so that is what I suspect, but I can't say for sure. I was hoping that once I found him, I could get answers as to who wanted your sister so badly. And why." He eyes me curiously, as though he thinks I have the answers to those questions and confirms that with his next question. "Is there something you're not telling me? Why would someone want your sister so badly?"

I shrug. I see no problem giving him the truth. Part of it anyway. "You know we are witches. You knew what I was the moment you saw me. As you likely suspected, my sisters are witches as well. We don't live far from here," I admit, deliberately omitting mention of omegas, desperately hoping that part of our secret hasn't been discovered by anyone.

"A whole family of witches!?" the she-demon screeches, causing me to hunch my shoulders in an effort to protect my ears. Fuck. For a few minutes, I actually forgot she was in the room. She points her bony finger at me and yells, "We have a whole family of witches on our doorstep!

Lucien, you must do something. You cannot help these... these *things*. No matter what deal you've made with this one," she spits in my direction, "you need to get rid of them. All of them."

I look at the woman standing next to the first man I've ever wanted. And yes, despite how stupid and insane it is, I still want him.

"In case you've forgotten, you have no part in any of this," I remind her, staring at Lucien to try and measure his reaction as I direct my next words at him. "And my family has been here a hell of a long time. We chose not to make ourselves known and have never caused any problems for you."

"Don't talk to me like that!! And don't look at him!" She screams at me, her face turning crimson with rage. Does she see my attraction for him? I'm doing everything I can to fight it, but maybe she can sense something. "You. Are. Nothing." She spits at me. Her entire body is quivering with uncontrollable anger. "Remember who you are speaking to, *witch*. I could kill you with just a flick of my finger." She sneers, demonstrating her point by flicking her fingers.

I take a deep breath and push my fear down. I just have to hope Lucien will step in if she tries to attack me. She isn't worth my time or energy, but it's more obvious with each minute that passes in her presence, that she is completely off her rocker. Crazy people are dangerous. I know I will have to watch my back from here on out and that my family will need to be warned as well. If I know anything at all about Lucien, he's peeved that there have been witches under his nose for years and he hadn't a clue. Hopefully he will realize that if we'd meant him harm, it would have come his way long before now. We keep to ourselves and have full control over the witch side of us. Even still, my family will need to be informed that we could have a serious problem on our hands.

Sadly, witches don't have the best history. Our ancestors were unable to control their darker nature, and things had gotten so bad that the entire human and Natural worlds turned against them. It wasn't until they were all nearly wiped out that one coven, the one my family belongs to, decided it was time to learn control in order to save themselves. It took generations of living in total seclusion before we were able to rein in our nature and were finally able to blend into regular society.

This story is unknown outside of my coven, however, and the world would want us gone if they knew of our existence. They wouldn't ask questions or wait to find out the truth. We would be obliterated. Something has to change, but I don't know what.

All I know is that Megan is missing, and I can't bear to think she might no longer be with us. I would know, right? She is my sister, after all. I need to stop my grim thoughts; they will hinder my efforts to find Megan. I pull my focus back to the present and observe Lucien attempting to calm the psycho she-demon. It briefly crosses my mind that she could have witch ancestry. I think back to the stories I've read of my ancestors and her behavior strikes a chord. I can sense her demon, but is it possible she has Pure Witch blood as well?

If so, I may have taken on more than I bargained for.

CHAPTER TEN

LUCIEN

WHEN SCARLETT LOOKS AT ME and says, "I refuse to continue this conversation until she's gone," I know it's time to get Aria the fuck out of here. Not because the witch demands it, but because I know Aria, and she will eviscerate her if given the leeway to do so.

The fire inside of me has been well and truly lit. I'm ready to explode at the slightest provocation and being around Aria is adding fuel to the flames. I have to get a handle on the situation developing around me; it is spiraling out of control. If I'd known how much Scarlett would try to rile Aria, I would have found a way to come talk to the witch without her. But Aria insisted and the more she pushed, the more incensed I became. I finally gave in so that I wouldn't walk into this room without full control of my demon.

The minute Aria set eyes on her, I felt excitement pulsing off her. When Scarlett insulted her, I had to play the part of doting lover in order to calm her down, even if it meant touching her and making her think she had the power. My stomach rolls every time I have to touch her. I need to get a grip. I've never experienced these feelings before, and it's fucking with my head. My demon is grinning like a goddamn loon. He's never liked Aria and is pleased that my feelings are starting to reflect his. It's a shame for both of us that I don't share his joy.

Scarlett recklessly goaded me by sticking her head out of the window and shouting down at me. It was a dare I couldn't back down from. I want to fuck, punish, and protect her all at once and I hate how she is pulling all these feelings to the surface.

Aria's screeching pulls my thoughts back to the room. "Are you going to let her tell me what to do!?" I look at her with a blank expression and don't answer. Her body trembling with rage, she looks back at Scarlett. "Who the fuck do you think you are? You can't demand that I be removed!"

Irritated at Scarlett for pushing the issue, but even more irritated with Aria, I take a deep breath as I feel a muscle twitching in my jaw. I must handle this carefully.

I turn to Aria and pull her into me, our bodies flush against one another. I try to push down my anger and resentment before murmuring softly in her ear. "I know how you feel, and I'm sorry. I made a deal with her, and I can't go back on it. I need you to go now, and I promise I will make it up to you later." I can only hope she listens to my words and doesn't see how insincere they are.

I'm relieved when I feel her body relax and know she will do what I've requested. I escort her from the room, not missing the look she shoots at Scarlett, promising retribution. I take a moment to gather up the reins of my control before going back in the room.

Striding back in, I close the door behind me. "I found out that it isn't just your sister. Several humans and Naturals have been reported missing by their families the past few weeks. My people couldn't get any leads there, but it's an unlikely coincidence."

"You're telling me you think the same people took Megan and these other people? How were they taken? How many have gone missing? Where are they being taken to?" Her last question doesn't seem directed at me, her voice trailing off as she buries her face in her hands.

SCARLETT

"Those are all questions I'm trying to find answers to." Lucien answers the questions I was muttering to myself. I drop my hands and look back up at him, our gazes locking together. "As I said earlier, we know who took your sister, but it seems he's gone. I don't know if he was the only one hired by the person who wanted your sister, or if there are more bounty hunters out there."

I know that if the soul keeper found out that Lucien is involved in tracking Megan down, he would be running scared. The other scenario is just as disheartening; that whoever hired him made sure he wouldn't be able to talk. Either way, it seems the soul keeper is a dead end.

I watch Lucien as he eases his large frame into the sizable green leather chair behind his desk and leans back, causing it to creak from the weight of his muscular body. He nods his head, indicating the chair on the opposite side of his desk as he works the buttons of his navy-blue jacket, causing it to fall open. My eyes fall to his hard chest, mesmerized by the muscles flexing under his shirt. I bite my lip, fighting the overwhelming urge to go to him and rip it open so I can run my hands all over his glorious flesh.

A smirk appears, as though he can read my thoughts, and his eyes wander from my lips down to my breasts. My skin heats and I drop my gaze, my entire body tingling from the weight of his stare. With reluctance, I comply with his request to sit, taking a breath to calm my raging hormones. I need to focus on finding Megan, not on Lucien and how much I want him to take me; to own me.

A shiver works its way from head to toe as his deep voice runs over me like crushed velvet. "I suspect they hired several bounty hunters to do the job. The soul keeper wouldn't have had the resources to pull off that many disappearances. I figure he's just a part of a much bigger picture. We don't know where they're being taken yet."

He leans forward slightly to grab a crystal decanter from the corner of his desk. He removes the lid and pours some of the golden liquid into a glass before tipping it to me in a silent offer. I shake my head. I'm not much of a drinker and besides, I need to keep my wits about me. I can barely trust myself in his presence as it is.

"My plan is to catch one of them in action. I'm working on establishing a pattern in the kidnappings, and once I've done that, I will be able to bait the trap, and once the bait is taken, I'll have someone to question." He swirls his drink, the crystal throwing rainbows of color around the room, before taking a deep sip. His inky stare never once leaves my face, and I try not to react to his intensity. Just looking at him causes my core to heat, burning me from the inside out with lust. I barely resist the urge to rub my thighs together to relieve the pressure as I tear my eyes away from him.

Swallowing, I ask, "How exactly do you intend to do that? Who would be willing to be used as bait?"

"Let's just say I have my ways. One doesn't gain my kind of reputation without being … shall we say… resourceful." It's clear he isn't bragging; his statement is merely matter of fact.

I am aware of his reputation, and I really don't need to know the gory details; I know they aren't pleasant. I don't get off on violence and carnage. I recognize that sometimes violence is a necessary evil, and this happens to be one of those times. But the less I know about it, the better. I have enough trouble sleeping at night.

That's not to say I wouldn't resort to violence myself, should the need arise. Someone I love has been taken and the rest of my loved one's lives are in danger as well. I know there's a very good chance I will need to get my hands dirty before all is said and done.

"I want to know the minute you catch someone, and I want to know everything you learn from questioning them," I demand. I don't feel I'm asking too much. After all, my sister's life is at stake.

"Seeing as you'll be remaining here, I don't think that will be a problem," he steeples his fingers and lays them over his lips, arrogance pouring from him and filling the room.

I shake my head at him, astounded by his temerity. He's clearly used to telling and not asking. I'm sure people rarely, if ever, push back; but he's in for a rude awakening if he thinks I'm going to just sit back and follow orders like a good little girl. I have a life outside these walls, a life I need to get back to. I need to check on my family and assure them that I'm okay and that we're one step closer to finding our sister.

"I'm not staying here," I inform him with determination. "That was never a part of the deal. A man of your means will have no trouble finding me when the time comes."

It feels like the air has been sucked from the room. Even if I weren't looking at Lucien dead-on, I would know that my words have infuriated him. He gives a dry laugh, no humor in it. It sounds like an angry bark. "You're not going anywhere," he says with a twist of his lips. "We have an agreement, as you keep reminding me. You've yet to fulfill your part of it... or have you forgotten?" He questions, a cruel look in his eyes.

No, I hadn't forgotten, but I'd bloody well hoped he had. How could I forget? The deal I struck has been hanging over my head like a writhing mass of dark clouds. I'm still waiting to find out exactly what he will ask of me.

He gives me a smug look. Apparently, he enjoys toying with me and is getting off on making me suffer in apprehension.

"I haven't forgotten," I grate out. "But I refuse to sit around and wait for you to give me information. I have a life I need to get back to and I need to speak with my family." I wait for his reaction. I really don't want to enrage him further, though the urge to needle him is constantly there, under the surface.

I shouldn't be surprised when he repeats himself, "You're not leaving." He shakes his head at me and glares. "We have an agreement, and you owe me. When I'm ready to collect payment, I want you near me."

Despite the fact that I should have expected his response, my mouth drops open in shock and I'm unable to compose myself enough to respond before he continues. "It will be easier to update you on news of your sister if I know exactly where you are at all times. You can call your family anytime you wish; all you have to do is ask. I have no problem with them coming to visit you, so long as they behave themselves." He pauses, a calculating look passing over his face. "Although... I *could* let you go home. Then I could pay you and your sisters a little visit."

My stomach drops at the idea of him visiting my home. Hell no, never going to happen. It's looking more and more like I will not be given a choice on this, so I might as well make a few demands of my own. "Fine. I will stay. But I expect you to keep me up to date. And you'll need to keep your girlfriend away from me."

A look of satisfaction comes across his face and his eyes travel over my body. "Wise decision. I will do everything in my power to keep Aria away from you. You are under my protection while you're in my care.

But you must be careful not to run into her when she's here."

"I have no intention of seeking her out, if that's what you're implying. But rest assured that if she tries to harm me, I will retaliate," I warn him.

He shrugs off my words as though I pose little threat to anyone. *Idiot.* "Stay out of her way when she's here and there shouldn't be a problem," his tone is patronizing, as though he's talking to a two-year-old. I decide to let it go for now. He has no idea of my true power, and it's better for me to keep it that way.

"You'll be staying in the same bedroom you were given a few nights ago. I will make sure to have one of my men remain by your side, for your safety, anytime you're outside of your room."

For my safety, or does he just want someone watching me to make sure I don't snoop around? Doesn't really matter, I'll deal with it. "Fine," I agree.

My mind goes to logistics. I'm going to need clothing and a laptop. Not to mention shampoo, conditioner, lotion… I don't want him or any of his men going to my house to get what I need, though. "Someone is going to have to take me shopping. I need some things if I'm going to be staying here." He raises an eyebrow at me, waiting for me to explain. I huff out a sigh.

"I work from home, and I need a laptop so I can work from here. I need more than two changes of clothing. And I need a way to clean my hair and body." I finish speaking and glare at him, daring him to object.

"That's fine. I will get one of my men to pick up anything you may need. Go ahead and write out a list and I'll take care of it. You'll have your things by this evening," he says, standing up and moving to the door.

Okay, then. I guess our conversation is over. I grab a piece of paper from the side of the desk and jot down a list of everything I need. I hear Lucien call for someone named Alex and assume that must be the name of my new 'bodyguard.' I look up when I hear someone else enter the room. I'm surprised to see how young Alex is. He looks to be about my age and is quite tall, a few inches over six feet. He has light blonde hair and friendly sea-glass green eyes. I can immediately tell that he's a shifter.

"Scarlett, this is Alex," Lucien glances at me briefly. "Alex, Scarlett Winters."

I give Alex a small wave and a slight smile and he nods at me in greeting. He seems reluctant to take his eyes off me, as though I might strike him with a spell if he doesn't maintain eye contact.

Lucien starts speaking and Alex looks at him, listening. "Scarlett is going to be with us for a while. She is my guest; I am helping her find her sister. You are to be her…" Lucien pauses and turns his dark gaze on me, looking me up and down and causing shivers to race up my spine. "…bodyguard. You will remain with her twenty-four-seven, unless I personally tell you differently." Alex nods.

Glancing down at the gold watch on his wrist, Lucien tells me, "I have an appointment I can't miss. Alex will show you back to your room. Go ahead and give me your list and I will make sure it gets done and is delivered to your room later today." I hand the list over to him and he looks it over before turning on his heel and walking from the room without another word.

Apparently, I don't even warrant a goodbye. Things are going to be just *fabulous* staying here. I turn my attention to the young shifter, and we just stand there looking at each other like idiots.

I don't want to go back to my room. I've been cooped up long enough. I need fresh air. "I'm not going back to my room yet," I tell him, "I need some fresh air and a change of scenery."

I hear a huff from the shifter watching the security monitors. I'd forgotten about Snaky.

"Lucien won't like it. You should really just do what you're told," he says, swinging around and facing us. His beady eyes make me shiver in disgust. He gives me the creeps.

Alex shoots him a menacing look, his eyes flashing yellow, causing Snaky to cower. It looks like Alex has a higher level of command in the shifter chain of command than ol' Snaky. A rough, deep growl emanates from Alex's chest, and it's clear that the other shifter has overstepped.

I learned a bit about shifters from my cousin Melissa. She lived with a group of them for a few years, and though she doesn't talk about it much, she did tell us a little about how their command structure works. Every group of shifters has an Alpha, and that's the leader. Then there are lieutenants who take orders from the Alpha and communicate them to everyone else. I don't remember what is in between lieutenant and soldier, but soldiers have the least amount of power. It looks like Snaky is a lowly soldier.

I look at Alex with surprise; I'm sure my mouth is hanging open. His entire demeanor changed in the blink of an eye. The friendly looking guy who walked through the door a few minutes ago has morphed into a menacing, powerful shifter. I'm actually starting to worry he might attack. I need to get his attention back on me before anything else happens.

"Alex, I've been cooped up in my room for days. I will take full responsibility if it causes any trouble, but please, can we just go outside for a little while?" I beg, placing my hand on his arm. I give him a smile as he finally turns his yellow eyes towards me. "Please," I repeat. I ignore the presence of Snaky and hope I haven't made things worse. I know backing down goes against a shifter's nature, but I really don't want to witness whatever was about to happen.

Relief floods through me when his yellow eyes shift back to their human light green. I can see him weighing the pros and cons of what I've asked. Making a decision, he says, "Fine. I'll take you outside." He places his hand on my lower back as he escorts me out of the room, appearing to ignore Snaky, and I resist the urge to shoot back a middle finger as we leave the room.

Letting Alex guide me, I let my mind wander. I will handle Lucien if he tries to get upset that I didn't go straight back to my room. He said I was his guest, not his prisoner. Besides, I need to find a way to make contact with my family, and I would prefer to use a mental link. If it fails, I'll have to call them, but I'd rather do it the old-fashioned way.

We reach the end of the hall and stop in front of an enormous black door. I'm unable to hide my shock when it opens up to reveal a spectacular garden. It's certainly not what I was expecting. There's a large natural lake in the middle, with trees lining its perimeter. One of the trees is a weeping willow, its branches hanging over the water, and at the base of the trunk is an ornate white wooden bench with a padded seat. This is one of the most peaceful places I've ever seen; it feels as though I've stepped into a fairytale.

I take a seat on the bench and lean my head back. Closing my eyes, I allow myself to sink into my surroundings. In the background, I hear birds singing and smell the flowers that are all around me. This is surreal. I feel like I'm in the middle of an enchanted forest rather than a bustling city. There must be magic at work here.

"It's beautiful," I breathe, briefly opening my eyes to glance at Alex who's staring at me as though he's trying to figure me out. I realize I must be a mystery to him, but it doesn't bother me. I wonder if he's ever even seen a witch before.

CHAPTER ELEVEN

SCARLETT

I KNOW WHAT I'M ABOUT TO do will likely shock Alex to his core, especially if he's never seen a witch before.

I sit deadly still, letting my entire body relax and my eyes drift close. It feels as though my very soul has drifted away from my body and is floating around on a fluffy white cloud. I feel the warmth within my body grow, the intensity building and causing my skin to radiate heat. Although I can't see it, I know my hair is flickering like the flames of a burning sun. My mind clears of everything that has happened the last few days and I open the mental link I share with my sisters.

Link open, I can sense each of my sisters right at the edge of my mind. I search until I find the one I need to contact. Relief flows through the line when she senses me, and I breathe out a sigh as it rushes through me too.

"Scarlett!!" Pamela's built-up fear bombards me through the link. "Where the hell have you been!?" Even in my head, her words are loud and I'm glad to be having this conversation mentally rather than in person. She would likely blow out an eardrum with her volume otherwise. "We've been trying for days to contact you." Her concern takes over and I feel as though I'm being pulled into her warm embrace.

"I'm sorry it's taken so long to contact you." I decide right then not to get into the agreement I made with Lucien or tell her any of what went down between us. It's best if I tell her just enough to give her hope and to satisfy my family's worries. The last thing any of us need is for them to panic and demand that I return home immediately… and that would be the best-case scenario. Worst case, they show up here and make things worse. Megan's life is on the line, and I will do whatever is necessary to find her. "I've been talking to Lucien, trying to come to an agreement. A soul keeper took Megan from the club and Lucien has agreed to help us find her."

"A soul keeper?" Pamela's distress is palpable, and it mirrors my own reaction when I found out. "How the hell will we be able to find her? If he's removed her soul…."

"Lucien has assured me that her soul is intact for the time being. The soul keeper who took her is a bounty hunter and was likely given instructions not to harm her."

"So Lucien found the soul keeper?"

"No, he's disappeared. Lucien and I agree that he's probably not the only person on the payroll of whoever wanted her taken."

"Do you trust him, Scarlett? *Should* we trust him?"

"What other options do we have, Pamela? This is the first and only firm lead we've found regarding what happened to Megan. Others have been disappearing, also."

"What do you mean, others?"

"I mean, there have been humans and Naturals going missing. It's as if they've vanished; there one minute and gone the next."

"Bloody hell. What the fuck is happening?" Pamela asks, her frustration flowing through me. "When will you be coming home?"

I knew I wouldn't be able to avoid that question for long and I know she really isn't going to like my answer.

"I'm not. I've agreed to stay here until we find Megan." I tense, waiting for her response and feel relieved once more that this conversation isn't happening face-to-face. Pamela can be downright terrifying when she's scared and angry.

I start to wonder if we've lost the connection. She's completely silent and I can't feel any emotions coming over the line. Suddenly, I'm hit with her white-hot rage, strong enough to rocket pain through my skull.

"Are. You. Fucking. Kidding. Me!? You will not stay there. You will come home this instant; do you hear me?"

"Pamela. Stop. I'm not a little girl anymore. I've made my decision and I'm staying. I promise that if I sense that I'm in any danger, I will come straight home." I reassure her.

I wait, but all I'm met with is silence. "Pamela," I call across the link. "Pamela, talk to me."

I feel more than hear her sigh. I know she's worried about me, hell, I'm worried about me. But we really don't have any better options at this point.

"I don't like this, but I do see the logic in you staying. If you're adamant about this, then we are going to come and make sure you're not in any danger."

"You don't need to do that," I protest. I don't want them here. I love them and don't want them in any more danger than they're already in. "I'm fine, I promise. And I will contact you every day. Twice a day, even."

"NO," She shouts down the line. "If you insist on staying there, fine. But we will be coming to see you, whether you like it or not. Lucien Sinclair is going to have to put up with a family of witches on his property."

I groan. This is not what I wanted to happen at all, but I know there's no sense arguing the point further. We're all the same when it comes to our stubbornness; nothing can change our minds once we've decided on a course of action. I'm just going to have to resign myself to them coming here and find a way to keep them safe.

"Fine. When will you arrive?"

"I will inform the others about what's going on and plan to arrive late afternoon on Saturday. If something happens before then and you need us, let me know. If you think it's best that you get out of there, don't hesitate. Just come home."

"I will; I promise. And I will let Lucien know to expect you." I tell her with a sigh. "I have to go now. I'll contact you later."

I'm distracted when we say our goodbyes, trying to figure out how to tell Lucien that my family of witches will be descending in just a few days. I don't really blame my sisters for wanting to come check things out. If I were in their position, nothing would stop me from ensuring their safety, either.

Opening my eyes, I look around and find Alex standing in the exact same place, a look of wonder on his slim face. He appears to have been rendered speechless, his mouth hanging open slightly, and I resist the urge to get up and close it for him. I hear him mutter "Wow. This is unbelievable," and I know what he means. Because of my mixed powers, when I make a mental link with someone, my body emits a bright glowing light. The rest of my family is the same. If he's never seen a witch before, I can play it off like it's normal for all witches. I just have to hope he doesn't mention this to anyone who does know about witches and their powers.

I give him a reassuring smile and ask, "Was I glowing?" I let out a light laugh, hoping he doesn't hear how forced it is.

He nods, his eyes lit up with the wonder of a child discovering magic for the first time as his body radiates a slight nervousness. He finally manages to speak in a reverent voice, "You're the first witch I've ever seen." His admission is accompanied by a shy smile. "I can't believe what I just saw. Did you know your entire body was lit up? Your hair looked like the flames of a raging fire."

I continue to smile at him, even as I mentally scramble for an explanation. My omega wakes up and chimes in. *Be truthful.* I know what she means. Tell him as much of the truth as I can without giving anything away. As a shifter, he can smell lies, so that is the safest route.

"I know what it looked like, but I'm not that special. I'm a witch, but I'm also human." I leave out any reference to my omega. "I have a mental link to my family, and what you just saw is what happens when I connect with them." I hope he buys that explanation and that he doesn't go asking around… that could really cause problems for me. More than I'm already dealing with, that is.

I don't want to go back inside. There's something about this garden that has infused my body with a sense of peace, a certain tranquility I don't remember experiencing before. Unfortunately, I know he will likely get in trouble for allowing me to stay out here any longer and he's been nice to me. I don't want him getting into trouble on my account.

Hopefully I'll get to come out here again. This would be the perfect place to relax and write. I make a mental note to memorize the route from here to my room so I can retrace my steps later.

"I suppose you'd better take me back to my cell," I huff, dragging my feet as I walk over to the door leading back into the building. I pull the door open and stand to the side so I can follow Alex back to the room I only left a few hours ago, though it feels like it's been much longer. So much has changed since then. I hope the items I requested are waiting for me in my room. At least then I'll be able check my email.

"Are you hungry?" Alex inquires as we're walking down the hall, stopping and looking at me.

His question seems to wake my appetite because I suddenly smell food and my stomach rumbles loudly. "Sorry," I shrug sheepishly, embarrassment staining my cheeks. "I haven't eaten since breakfast. I could definitely do with something to eat."

His grin lights up his face and he says, "The kitchen is just up here. We usually eat in there during the day. Dora's our cook and her food is fantastic."

I walk slightly behind him as he leads me through a door into a vast kitchen. Three women are working away at a long counter, two younger and one older. Sitting at the largest dining table I've ever seen is another woman and two men, eating what looks to be beef stew.

"Dora," Alex calls out in greeting, "This is Scarlett. She's a guest of Lucien's."

Upon hearing his voice, the older woman turns around with a delighted expression on her plump face. Her build is stocky, and her black hair has streaks of grey running through it. I'm not getting any vibes indicating that she's a Supernatural, so I know she must be human, which is surprising given Lucien's distaste for humans in general.

"So, he let you out at last." Dora states, rather than asks. "Don't hide behind him, girly. Let me get a good look at you." I hear a slight Irish lilt to her voice, and I follow the lead of her hand waving me forward, hoping she doesn't try to touch me.

All eyes turn in my direction, assessing me. Bloody hell, I hate being the center of attention. I'm not here to make friends, but I can't help the twinge of nerves that comes from wanting people to like me. I remind myself that I'm here for one reason and one reason alone; to find my sister. I shouldn't care if people accept me or not, but the human side of me always does. I can feel my witch shrug her shoulders and hear her say, *Tough shit if they don't like us.* Sometimes I wish my human side shared that attitude.

Dora nods her head in what seems like approval as she looks me up and down. She offers me a satisfied smile. "You'll do. Take a seat," she says, nodding towards the table. "I will get you a bowl of the beef casserole I have on the stove. I expect you'll want some, too?" She asks Alex, laughter in her eyes.

"Of course. You know why I come to your kitchen. To see your beautiful face and eat your delicious food." He offers a cheeky grin as he pulls out a chair for me and takes the seat to my left.

She works on spooning up two bowls of food and giggles, waving a wooden spoon at him. "That charm is going to get you in trouble one day." I observe them in silence, listening to their banter. Alex reminds me of my male cousins and their ability to captivate any female audience.

"So... *you're* the witch everyone's been talking about?"

The room goes still and silent as seven pairs of eyes look over at me, watching for my reaction. I turn toward the voice and find it came from one of the women helping Dora in the kitchen. I meet her cold-eyed glare, undisguised hatred radiating from her expression. She's undeniably beautiful with her willowy frame, flowing blonde hair tied back loosely, dark blue eyes, and full pink lips. I roll my eyes at her. That reaction is *really* growing old.

"If that's what you've been told, then I suppose it must be true," I reply with a shrug, turning my attention to Dora as she places a bowl in front of me.

I offer the kind older woman a smile. "Thank you. It looks and smells incredible," I gush, picking up the spoon and taking a bite.

"Well," the angry woman huffs, her animosity searing my flesh, "are you a witch?" She demands. I feel everyone's eyes on me again.

"Julie, stop questioning the poor girl. Just leave it be," Dora tells her, shaking her head with a slight frown on her face.

It's plain as day that word's gotten around about a witch staying here but nobody knows for sure that the witch is me.

"It's fine," I assure Dora with a smile, trying to brush over the awkwardness of the situation. I have nothing to be ashamed of and nothing to fear. None of these people would risk incurring Lucien's wrath by laying a finger on someone he considers a guest. "Yes, I'm a witch and so are my family." I meet Julie's eyes as I say it and wait for her response.

"We do not welcome witches here," she informs me with a curled lip, slamming her mug on the wooden table and causing it to spill out.

What a fucking bitch. Can I hit her? My witch perks up, hoping I'll let her out, but I ignore her. If I let her out, it will only make matters worse.

Antagonism twisting her beautiful face, Julie continues. "We haven't seen witches in years. Where the hell did you even come from? Why are you here?" She demands, her body shaking with anger. "I know there's no way Lucien would invite you here as his guest," her voice sounds like a caress on his name, but the final words are delivered with a hiss. Her teeth are grinding together, her breathing labored from her heated interrogation. I hear a low growl coming from beside me and glance over.

Shit. My eyes widen. The person sitting to my left is no longer the friendly, happy-go-lucky guy I entered the kitchen with. Alex's affable expression has been replaced by that of a raving savage. Shit. This is bad.

I turn my attention back to Julia. I can almost swear that her words are coated in jealousy. I wonder if Lucien has fucked her. That would partially explain her ridiculous behavior. I have a feeling I'm going to face the same animosity from half the women in this building. It's looking more and more like he shares his cock with anyone who's half-willing.

Bloody hell. How did I end up in such a mess?

It feels like the oxygen has been sucked from the room as everyone waits with bated breath to see my reaction. I feel Alex twitching in the chair beside me, his anger rising. I can't tell if it's directed at Julie or at me.

"You have no business knowing anything about me, my family, or where we come from," I tell her as I stir my food, keeping my voice and expression flat and emotionless. "I am here at Lucien's request, and I intend to stay for as long as he wants me here, or until I choose to leave." I turn my attention to the bowl in front of me and take a large bite of the casserole, hoping she drops it. If Lucien considered her important, he would have told her who I was and why I'm here.

"Julie, back the fuck off," Alex growls. "Lucien ordered me to keep her safe and to ensure that she was treated like a guest. Don't make me tell him that you couldn't manage to follow his orders."

From the corner of my eye, I see how close he is to losing his temper. The tension in the room goes up a few notches. "If you wish to remain in one piece, I suggest you keep your mouth shut and your thoughts to yourself," Alex sneers, his eyes flashing an intense yellow. "That goes for anyone else who thinks they have something to say." He looks around the room, making eye contact with each person until they drop their gaze. "Of course… If anyone agrees with Julie here, you are free to seek Lucien out and share your thoughts with him. I'm sure he'd be very interested to hear them."

"Now, now, Alex. We don't want that. I'm sure Julie didn't mean to offend Lucien's guest." Dora forces out a laugh while shooting daggers at Julie with her eyes. It's obvious she's more than a little irritated but wants to diffuse some of the tension in the room.

"She needs to learn to keep her mouth shut. I'm not giving her any more chances," Alex warns Dora before turning his head and glaring at Julia. "If Lucien didn't want Scarlett to be here, she wouldn't be. This is your only warning. Keep your mouth shut and your opinions to yourself. If I hear you aren't doing that, I will make sure you are out of here before you can even blink."

I tune out of the remainder of the conversation, lost in my thoughts. It is going to be really uncomfortable staying here, knowing that Julie likely isn't alone in her prejudice and anger. I wonder if anyone here has ever even met a witch before. I'm not used to experiencing this kind of vitriol, most people I come across have no idea that I'm a witch. We don't exactly go around advertising our powers.

With a start, I realize Alex is talking to me. "If you've finished with your stew, I will walk you back to your room. Hopefully, the things you requested have been delivered." There's a look of apology painted across his youthful features, and I am flooded with gratitude towards him for standing up for me.

I tell everyone good-bye, noticing Julia's lack of response. I can feel her eyes shooting daggers at my back as I follow Alex out of the kitchen. I can only imagine what the conversation will be like now that I've left, and I wish for a moment to be a fly in the wall to hear it. But Julia and the rest of those people are the least of my concerns. I just hope Aria doesn't track me down.

SCARLETT

SEVERAL HOURS LATER

I'M IN BED TRYING TO FALL asleep but haven't been able to due to the tumble of thoughts running through my mind. I need to be sure to always keep my guard up, and with my family coming, I need to make sure to warn them about Aria. I've yet to tell Lucien about my family coming. I could be wrong, but I doubt he'll object to their visit.

I turn my head towards the window and feel my eyes growing heavy as I yawn. I'm exhausted. As my eyes begin to drift shut, I see the lights outside flicker, seeming to bounce off the ground before going black. I fall into a deep slumber.

"I hate you," I spit, my hands curling into fists as I fly at him.

He catches my wrists and pins me to the wall, his thigh wedged between my own. "Did you really think I would let you go?" He mocks

Heat floods my body, my heart pounding in my chest. I can't tell if I'm aroused or furious... probably both. I try to yank myself from his grip but no matter how much I struggle, he's just too strong and seems determined to keep me pinned to the wall.

"Get your hands off of me," I grind out angrily. I struggle harder, causing my clit to rub against his leg and making my core flood with need. A moan slips from my lips as I grind myself against his thigh.

"I can feel how much you want me," he growls. "That's right. Ride me." He shifts his leg to create even more friction as he pushes himself closer to me. I can feel every inch of him pressed against my body. His flesh is so hot, I feel like I'm seconds away from catching fire. Yet I want more. I crave more. I can feel every ridge and contour of his throbbing cock, and I gasp at the size of it. I squeeze my eyes shut, trying to block him from every one of my senses. I cannot let this happen. I will not fall for his lies again.

An angry flush covers my body. I hate him for what he's done, how he has broken me. Even more, I hate how he awakens every part of me, body and soul, the way I feel when I'm with him. I despise the need rushing through my veins, a need only he can fulfill. Even as I struggle to break free from his grip, I can't stop myself from rocking back and forth, pleasuring myself against his thigh. He thrusts into me again and I let out a mewling whine. He groans, his eyes flashing red.

"Stop it. Stop touching me," I beg, tugging my arms to free them from his grip.

"Admit you made a mistake in leaving me," he demands.

"It wasn't a mistake." I spit back, turning my head away from him.

"Tell me you forgive me," he says softly against my ear before taking the lobe into his mouth and gently biting down on it.

"You expect me to forgive you after all the lies you told me!? How could I possibly forgive you after what you've done?" I barely manage to choke out.

"YOU. ARE. MINE!" He roars, thrusting harder against me, panting as he bites down on my shoulder.

"I might have been yours, but you were never mine." I whisper even as a moan slips out when his teeth sink into my skin.

I wake with a jolt, heart hammering.

What in the ever-loving hell did I just dream?

CHAPTER TWELVE

LUCIEN

HALF AN HOUR AFTER LEAVING SCARLETT

I CAN'T STOP MYSELF FROM GOING over the conversation Aria and I had when I escorted her from the room and left Scarlett waiting. She'd completely lost her shit.

"You're going to keep her here?" She asks through clenched teeth, shooting daggers at me with her eyes. Her body is tense as she paces the floor, waiting for my reply.

"Yes," I answer her with a raised brow, eyes meeting hers. I wait for her reaction, knowing it's coming. Her expression changes, darkening with displeasure and annoyance before being replaced with a blank stare.

"How long?" She moves towards me, pressing her slim body against mine and running her long fingers down my chest.

"How long what?" I shoot back. Most never dare to question me. Aria has always been the exception to that rule and it's something I've allowed to some extent. But if she goes too far, I have no problem putting her in her place.

"How long are you going to keep her here?" She practically whines at me.

I can't tell her the truth about my intentions. It would send her into a rage. I knew the moment I laid eyes on Scarlett that I'd wanted her. Hell, I'd known before that from the dreams I was having, even if I hadn't realized it. I tried to avoid her, but as each day passed, my need for her only continued to grow. I want to binge on her body. I need another taste; she's turned into an addiction I cannot stop and cannot deny. My demon is relentless in his demands to seek her out, to claim what belongs to us.

"Are you planning something you haven't told me about?" Aria questions with feigned curiosity, her fury barely hidden beneath the surface. She tips her head to one side, her fingertips running down to my belt and back up, her nails dragging across my chest. I feel them digging into my skin through my shirt. I know what she's trying to do, but it isn't going to work. I used to keep her in the loop, telling her all my plans. Knowing she has an informant in my ranks, that she's been having me watched, has made me more careful than ever.

"What, my love, are you planning to do with her?" She demands, her lips drawing back in a sneer.

I give her a hard look and catch her wrist, tightly closing my fingers around it. She'd been going for my cock, as though she could seduce the information out of me. "I haven't thought that far ahead," I reply, somewhat truthfully. I really don't know what I'm going to do with Scarlett, I just know I feel a desperate need to keep her close to me at all times.

Needing to put Aria in her place, I harshly pull her arm behind her back and pull her close.

I yank myself from the memory as I reach the door I was headed for. Aria has become a significant problem; one I know will need to be dealt with sooner rather than later.

Scarlett has somehow managed to mesmerize me. Even her name tastes like decadence and feels like silk as it rolls around in my mouth. It's fucking with my head, and I need to get my shit together. I wasn't lying when I told her I had an appointment. Eddie Marshall has been causing problems and it is past time I handled him.

It's been brought to my attention that he hasn't paid back the money he borrowed. Though that isn't something I can overlook, it isn't the primary reason he's here. I've given him two warnings about not paying on time, not something I would normally do, but a foolish exception I made with him. A decision I now regret. It is never good to mix business with pleasure and he granted me permission to fuck his twenty-five-year-old twin daughters a few years ago. I'd gone back for more several times. My demon enjoyed the taste of them.

Now I've found out about his disgusting habit and it's something I cannot tolerate. I know I'm an evil fucker, but the things I've learned about him have turned even my ironclad stomach.

"Help! Help me, please, someone help me!"

I tilt my head to the side, cracking my neck and rolling my shoulders to release some of the tension that built up with Aria and Scarlett volleying back and forth in my head. I walk down the long hallway, Damien by my side, until we reach the door on the end. Pushing it open, we walk inside, and I let satisfaction roll through me at the sight of my victim bound to the chair, naked as the day he was born.

Eddie Marshall is a little piece of shit. He likes to molest little girls, the younger the better. How he thought he could keep this disgusting habit a secret from me, I have no fucking clue. Fucking despicable. I hate monsters like him. I've put the word out about his vile addiction and warned everyone in his circle that to do business with him would be to suffer his same fate. I didn't have to threaten, even criminals draw the line somewhere. Marshall is the lowest of the low.

As soon as he sees us enter the room, he crumples, tears streaming down his fat face, and I haven't even touched him yet. Fucking coward. I unbutton my navy blue, tailor-made, double-breasted jacket, sliding it off and hanging it on a hook behind the door. I'm not keen to soil it with this fucker's blood, sweat, and tears. The damn thing cost far too much money. I ignore his begging as I walk over to him, the putrid smell of shit and piss hitting my nose. I'm glad the little bastard is sitting directly over the drain. Once I'm done with him, one of my men will hose him down and all evidence of the fun we're about to have will slide down that very drain.

"I can get you the money, Lucien. I swear," he sobs as he pulls at the binds around his wrists. "I just need a little more time."

"How much time do you think I should give you?" I ask him with a blank expression, meeting his terror-stricken gaze. I can't resist the urge to toy with him, make him think he might get out of this. I unbutton my cuffs and roll up my left sleeve. "Damien. How much more time do you think I should give him?" I ask, not taking my eyes off Eddie.

"I think you've given the dirty little fucker plenty of time," Damien sneers from behind me.

"Please Lucien. Please, just a little more time," Eddie pleads, imploring me with his tear-filled eyes, as though he has a chance of swaying the outcome of this meeting. "Damien, man, please. Please, you know me. We're friends."

Damien laughs cruelly and I glance back as he leans against the wall, arms crossed over his thick chest, his legs crossed at the ankles, looking as though he's settling in for the duration. "You're no friend of mine," He replies with a disgusted look on his face.

I roll up my remaining sleeve and walk over to the tools hanging on the wall.

"You know how this works," I say, taking the hammer down and holding it up the light. Setting it down, I look back at Eddie. "It's quite simple. You do not fuck with me. You play by my rules. If you don't…" I let the rest of the sentence hang as I hold up a set of heavy-duty pliers, examining them.

"Please, Lucien. It's not that simple," he argues, his voice shrill. "I've been trying to get the money together. I've asked everyone I know, but nobody will even consider helping me."

I let out a roar as I approach him, my leather shoes splashing in his piss and shit. I'm so enraged, I don't even notice. I'm sick of his whining, it makes me want to end him right now. But that would be too easy. Dealing with this motherfucker hadn't been on my agenda for the day, and if he weren't such a revolting piece of shit that I had to deal with, I could be balls deep in my little witch this very moment.

"I promised Damien here a souvenir," I offer a feral grin as I turn my head in Damien's direction. "What would you like? A finger? A toe? Maybe his tongue or even his little pencil dick?" Damien smirks at me.

People think I'm the worst there is, but they've never seen Damien in action. He exists on an entirely different plane. Whereas I do what is necessary to maintain order, Damien *loves* this kind of shit.

Eddie trembles, struggling against the ropes holding him to the chair, eyes wide as saucers. I tighten the rope around his wrists and make sure it's secured to his ankles and that they're attached to the legs of the chair. Lifting my leg, I place my soiled shoe on top of his tiny limp dick and press down hard, crushing it against the chair. He howls in pain, and I push further, smashing his balls as well.

"Please. P-p-please. D-d-don't cut off my dick," he begs, snot dripping from his nose onto his chin. Repugnant little fucking bastard. He can beg, plead, cry, and scream. None of it will change his fate. Eddie Marshall is a dead man. How long it takes for him to die is up to me.

I slap his face playfully. "Oh, Eddie. You're not going to talk me out of what I have planned for you. Nobody can save you from me. Besides, you and I both know nobody cares what I do to you."

"Pleeeease?!? Lucien. I'm so sorry. I have the money. It's in a safety deposit box," he cries, his face blotchy from sobbing. "Take everything I have, just please don't hurt me anymore."

Is this motherfucker for real? "You think this is just about the fucking money?" I roar in his face. I remove my foot from his crushed genitals and step away. Pulling a burner cell from my pocket, I bring a picture up on the screen and hold it in front of his face. "This isn't about the fucking money you owe me. You like to fuck little girls, don't you? The younger, the better. How old is this girl? About the age of your youngest daughter, do you think?" I shake my head in disgust and push the phone closer to his sniveling face. "I showed your beautiful wife these pictures. She didn't believe me at first, not until she saw all the evidence with her own eyes."

I press a button on the phone and his eyes widen with horror when he sees the recording of his wife. She went bat-shit crazy when she saw the pictures, the evidence of her husband's heinous proclivities sending her into a rage. She flipped over the table we were sitting at and demanded I inflict as much torture and damage upon her husband as I could, insisting that I make sure he suffers as much as his victims had.

"As you heard, she had some pretty explicit instructions for how I am to deal with you. I'd really hate to disappoint her. Oh, and after I stopped recording, she kindly told me where to find your money. She gave me everything I needed, so now, you have nothing I want. Everything I do to you will be because I want you to suffer excruciating, agonizing pain."

I turn back to the toolbox and pick out the piece I'm going to start with. Turning to face him, I see that his face is purpling as he hyperventilates in terror. I hum, not having a care in the world, as I make my way back to him. Squatting in front of him, I push his tiny dick to the side and grab hold of his hairy balls, yanking them up. He squeals like the dirty fucking pig he is as I wrap the thin wire around them and twist. When will people learn not to fuck with me. I own this fucking city.

I attach the pliers to the ends of the wire and continue to twist, his testicles bulging and turning a dark mottled purple. He screams louder the more I twist, and I grin as I stand up.

"Someone will come by each day to give that another twist or two." Slapping his face, I walk over to the toolbox and toss the pliers down into it. "In case you weren't aware, at some point, your balls will just pop right off."

As I rinse off at the sink, he cries and begs for me to listen. "You've got the wrong guy! I'm not into little girls, I swear!" He screams.

I give him one last look as I stride for the door, grabbing my jacket off the hook. "I can't promise that Damien here won't cut your dick off and feed it to you. He really hates revolting little weasels like you," I tell him before walking out and closing the door behind me. Damien's wild laughter follows me down the hallway. Crazy bastard.

I roll my shoulders. Fuck, I'm on edge. I need to release some tension and there's a little red-haired witch who can help me with that problem. I'm done denying myself the taste and feel of her sweet flesh. There's also the matter of the bomb she dropped on me about her family of witches practically living right on my doorstep. I need to know how long they've been there and how the fuck they managed to remain hidden. I intend to get answers.

LUCIEN

SEVERAL HOURS LATER
—

Fuck. This isn't at all how I envisioned my day going. I'm still vibrating with sexual tension and if I don't find a way to release the pressure soon, I'm going to explode. I can feel my demon trying to claw himself free, and I know my hold on him is slipping.

Just as I'd been going to find Scarlett, I received word that Aria had attacked one of the women who works for me. Alison has been with me for years and is a single mother with two young children.

I ordered my men to take her to my physician immediately. By the time I'd gotten back to my quarters, news of the attack had reached Damien and sent him into an uncontrollable rage. I had to restrain him to keep him from doing further damage to my office. I didn't think his loathing of Aria could have gotten any worse. I was wrong. Once I got him calmed down, we went together to check out the situation.

We arrived at Alison's room to find utter devastation. Her furniture was flipped over, the floors and walls covered in her blood. My men were in the room and filled us in on what they found when they arrived. Her arms and legs at an odd angle, blood matting her hair where her head had been repeatedly bounced off the floor. I'm amazed she survived the attack. It only shows how strong she is. I've since arranged for her children to be looked after by a relative and once she's healthy enough to be released, I will ensure that she and her children are well cared for the rest of their lives.

I had to fight hard against my demon to contain my temper. I've seen a lot of death and destruction in my long life. Hell, I've caused most of it. But to hurt someone like this, for no reason other than a desire to vent rage, it's beyond monstrous. Not to mention, attacking one of my people is the same as attacking me personally. Alison has been loyal to me for years. Thank fuck she wasn't human, or she never could have survived.

Once I felt confident I wouldn't behead Aria immediately upon seeing her, I asked my men to bring her to me. I demanded she tell me what the fuck happened and was enraged by her response. She told me that Alison had looked at her the wrong way before going on to rant and rave about Scarlett. She was angry that I didn't intend to share the witch with her and that I wasn't making plans to wipe Scarlett and her whole family off the face of the earth. If it had been anyone else, they wouldn't have lived long enough to explain, let alone survived *that* explanation.

I was unable to deal with her shit any longer, so I asked my men to take her to a room and lock her in. Hurting a member of my staff, someone under my protection, could not be left unpunished. Until I figure out what the fuck to do about Aria, she will remain locked in her room like a spoiled child, which is exactly what she has become. A dangerous, spoiled-rotten child who acts out when she doesn't get her way. The only reason I stopped myself from ripping her apart was so I could find out who she has spying on me. I do not tolerate moles.

I left Damien to deal with the mess and Alison's room and went to handle arrangements for Alison's children, check on Alison's status, and do damage control with the rest of my staff. Before I walked out of the room, Damien gave me a look, his demon just below the surface. I could make out the shimmering dark purple scales. I know what the look meant. He was telling me that if I didn't handle Aria soon, he would take matters into his own hands.

I must find out who her mole is before that happens.

DAMIEN

I DON'T KNOW WHAT THE hell is going on with Lucien. His fucking head has been all over the fucking place since the witch came on the scene. It was a surprise to everyone that he allowed her to stay, but even more of one to find out that witches have been living so close without any of us knowing about it. How long they've been here remains a mystery.

The witches of old were unstable; I remember them well. They'd been unable to control their powers and were aggressively violent. They would attack anyone in their path for no reason whatsoever. We thought they were extinct, as nobody had seen or heard from them in generations. Apparently, we thought wrong.

Lucien has an unpleasant history with them that few know about, which is why I'm even more shocked than the others that he's keeping her here as his guest. This new witch, Scarlett, does seem different, but only time can tell how different she is. I cannot understand Lucien's attraction to her, though. Sure, she's beautiful, but she doesn't in any way resemble his usual type.

I can tell she's holding something back, can sense something lurking underneath the witch. I plan to find out what the fuck is going on with her. Something doesn't sit right, and until Lucien manages to pull his head from his ass, it looks like I'm the only man for the job.

More than all that, though, is this situation with Aria. I never hid my feelings about that nasty bitch. My loyalty to Lucien is the only thing that has kept me from acting on them. Aria's beauty is skin-deep, and underneath she is hideous, malicious, and unstable. I never understood what he saw in her but at least he used to have some control over her, kept her on a short leash.

She's gone too far this time. She attacked Alison out of sheer spite. She knew there was never anything between her and Lucien, but she also knew that Lucien regarded Alison as a trusted employee. She hoped to leverage this attack as a way to get in closer and I can only hope that her plan fails.

Aria has attacked someone I care about, and I will not stand for it. I would hate to go against Lucien's wishes, but if he doesn't handle her, I will.

Chapter Thirteen

SCARLETT

TWO DAYS LATER

Lucien never came to show me around the other night like he was supposed to. In fact, I haven't seen him at all. As much as I hate to admit that I'm bothered he hasn't sought me out, I'm having trouble pretending otherwise. But the thing that has gotten to me the most is the dream I had the other night. I've been unable to push it out of my mind. Lucien draws me like a moth to a flame, and as much as my saner, human side tries to deny his pull, my witch and omega are fighting back, wanting to tempt him, tease him.

I'm growing increasingly angry at his absence. I want to know what progress has been made with finding Megan. Alex hasn't been much help. All he's offered are platitudes; *Lucien is handling things and when he knows something, he'll let you know.* I haven't even had the chance to inform him my sisters will be coming for a visit. I'm at the end of my rope and my temper is on the brink of explosion.

I've been trying not to touch things, wary of the images or visions that might bombard me. I've already seen a few of him and Aria; sexual visions, and they turned my stomach. I hate thinking about him with other women. The other visions I had were of Lucien talking to his men. In one, he threw a chair across the room in a blind rage while Damien tried to calm him down. That one left me agitated for hours, Lucien's fury becoming as much a part of me as my witch.

Now I'm sitting at the window in my room, watching the day pass. I can sense my family through our connection, trying to get me to link in. I ignored them the whole first day, but when I felt their concern growing, I reached out and let them know I was okay and told them I would contact them tonight. I'm currently waiting for Alex to arrive. I've decided to demand an audience with Lucien and not take no for an answer. If all else fails, I will open a portal and leave. It will be as though I was never here at all.

I hear a tap on the door and glance at the clock. Alex is early.

"Come in," I call out, watching the door open, and Alex steps in, closing it behind him.

"Hey Scarlett, I'm a bit early today," his warm smile fades as he moves closer and gets a look at my expression.

He lowers his large frame in the chair across from me and settles in, his gaze meeting mine with a raised eyebrow. "What's wrong?"

"Wrong?" I laugh in disbelief. "What could possibly be wrong?" I reply sarcastically, pressing my lips together to hold back a torrent of hateful words.

Alex gives me a thoughtful look. "Scarlett, I know things are hard."

"Hard," I mutter. I feel like I'm going around in circles. I grip my hair in both fists but manage to stop myself from pulling the auburn locks. I loosen my grip and drop my head into my hands, letting out a loud groan. I'm sick of being kept out of the loop! I'm going to murder that stupid, bloody man!

I hear Alex laugh and then cough to hide it and realize I must have spoken my thoughts aloud. He laughs again, unable to contain it apparently, and I lift my head and glare at him. Does he think I'm joking? I'm propelled from my seat by rage, my body shaking and face heating up. I feel my control start to snap.

"Alex. I like you. I think of you as my friend. As a friend, I can overlook certain things, but right now, in this moment, I need you to know that I am not amused. I'm not fucking joking. My sister…" My voice breaks and I take a deep breath, clearing my throat and calming myself. I continue as if I'd never faltered. "Not only is my sister missing, but other people, humans and Naturals alike, are going missing. They are being kidnapped and nobody knows who is responsible or where they're being taken. So. You tell your dumb dick of a boss that I want an update, or I am going to completely lose it and he will pay the price." I take another deep breath, attempting to gain control. I know this isn't Alex's fault and I don't want to take it out on him.

Alex stands up and puts his hands in his pockets, a frown on his face. He starts to speak but stops as he takes his hands back out and rubs his eyes before meeting my gaze. He opens his mouth again and snaps it shut immediately.

Standing up straight and pulling my shoulders back, I speak with a firm voice, hoping Alex misses the tremor running through it, "You tell Lucien that Scarlett wants to see him *now*; otherwise, I am leaving."

The witches of old may have been powerful, but they were no match for my own powers or that of my family. I can tell he doesn't think me capable of getting out of here, but I don't care. I know that everyone thinks I'm just a weak little witch, that I have little power to speak of, and I have no intentions of telling them differently. Not yet anyway.

"I'll relay your message, Scarlett. But don't be surprised if he doesn't come running at your whim." Alex warns, his brows drawing together as he gives me a tight-lipped smile. "He's not one to be told what to do. Lucien calls the shots."

"Not now, he doesn't," I shoot back. I look away and sigh before turning back. "Look, what is going on right now is too important. Far more important than whatever power trip Lucien wants to play at. Families are losing their loved ones. Tell me, how many people have been reported missing since I last saw him?" I look away again, this time gazing out the window. "Alex, I will not keep repeating myself. Tell him I need to speak with him immediately or I will be leaving." I sigh heavily I hate making Alex deal with this, but I will not run after Lucien. He assured me that I would be kept in the loop, and he's broken that promise. I walk to the door and open it. "Alex, I am sorry for putting you in this position," I apologize, feeling guilty that he will likely have to deal with his boss' wrath. "He needs to realize that I am not messing around. I don't care if he's busy playing with his girlfriend or all the other women in this place. Either he agrees to meet me today, or I am gone. We will find another way to find out where my sister is and who's responsible for taking her and the others," I tell him with confidence I don't really feel.

He gives me a curt nod and, turning on his heel, strides to the door. Just as he gets there, he turns to face me. Meeting my defiant gaze with an admiring one of his own, he says, "I know Lucien is a difficult man to understand and I know he seems hard. Unforgiving. I don't deny he can be that way, but he's also fair and loyal to those who are loyal to him." He walks out of the room, closing the door behind him with a click.

SCARLETT

THE NEXT MORNING

THE BRILLIANT RAYS OF THE sun streaming through the open curtains wakes me from a deep sleep. Yawning, I stretch and look the other way to shield my eyes from it. I stayed awake last night, waiting, until my eyelids gave up the fight and I passed out. I foolishly thought he would show up or at least send someone to tell me a time he'd be available to meet. He did neither. To say I'm angry would be an understatement. I went to sleep furious and woke up feeling even more so. I punch the pillow in frustration. Bloody. Fucking. Man. It's plain as day he doesn't take me seriously.

I roll over with a sigh and look up at the ceiling. I had another dream last night, this one different than what I'm used to. From what I can remember, it seems to be a warning of some sort, but of what, I have no clue. Something is coming and it has to do with the past. I'll have to mention it to my family. They might be able to help me figure it out, or at the very least, they will be warned to stay on guard. Pushing it to the back of my mind, I go over the conversation I had with my family last night. After about an hour of arguing, we came to an agreement. I would wait until morning and attempt to seek Lucien out first thing.

I was surprised to find Melissa and Evelyn with my sisters on the link. If I decide to leave, Melissa is going to make me a portal that is stable and strong enough that I will get where I need to go, and nobody will be able to stop me from going through. Spells aren't really my specialty; Melissa is the expert. We don't want to do it unless we absolutely have to because it can give away the fact that we aren't normal witches.

It may not be the best idea to seek Lucien out in my current mood, but I know it's necessary and it cannot wait any longer. At the very least, I need to try to get some more information about what's happened since we last spoke. With a sigh, I throw the covers off my body. I can't lay here all day, no matter how tempted I am to do just that. There's no time to waste, far too much is at stake.

If I happen to run into Lucien's she-demon, I'll just have to deal with her. Logan and Adam haven't been stationed at my door the past few days and when I asked Alex about it, he said Lucien wanted to show me that he trusted me. He also said that Aria hasn't been in the building, so I know that if my guards show back up, she's likely the reason why.

After taking a quick shower and dressing in a pair of black jeans, pale blue top, and my black boots, I leave the room with one thing on my mind. Finding out what the fuck is going on.

I walk down one corridor after another, a smile on my face. I stop to say hi or give a slight wave to people I've met the past couple of days. There aren't many, but there have been a few who have shown me kindness and respect. Encountering some of the ones who are hostile towards me, I toss my hair over my shoulder in an act of defiance and ignore their whispers. I feel like stopping and demanding to know what the hell their problem is, but I don't. They aren't worth my time.

I feel a little smug knowing that it's only a matter of time before one of Lucien's little minions tells him I'm wandering the halls. That's if he doesn't see me on the security monitors first. Hopefully the thought of me not being where I'm supposed to be and not having a guard will irritate him enough to seek me out.

CHAPTER FOURTEEN

LUCIEN

"SHE'S GOT SOME BALLS; I'LL give her that." Damien states, sitting his massive frame in the chair next to mine as we watch Scarlett walk around the club as if she hasn't a care in the world. She stops to chat briefly with various members of my staff.

The ones she speaks to display a liking for her, while others show open disdain. I make a note of the ones she didn't bother with, planning to deal with anyone who has shown her disrespect. I want her to feel comfortable staying here.

"She looks pissed off," Damien comments, his head cocked to one side, curiosity shining in his eyes.

I've been waiting for him to comment on me allowing her to stay, but so far, he hasn't said a word about it, which is a surprise. He's never withheld his opinion before, whether I liked it or not. He's one of the few males I allow such liberties from, and if he were anyone else, he'd be six feet under by now.

I scratch at my cheeks, feeling the hair that has grown over the last few days, and watch her on the TV monitors. I haven't slept much lately, and shaving has been the last thing on my mind. I keep trying to figure out my fascination with her. It just doesn't make sense. Fuck. I can't explain it. I hate witches and seeing as though none have been spotted in so long, I really thought they'd been wiped out. Finding out how wrong I was shook me. I've been avoiding her, and my demon is less than happy about it. He's pissed about how much time I've been spending with Aria, too. He keeps urging me to hurt her, but I cannot allow it to happen. Not until I get to the bottom of who has been feeding her information.

I finally let Aria go a few hours ago and she left. For how long, I have no idea. It wouldn't surprise me if she shows up unannounced again, but I have informed my men to let me know the second she sets foot back on my property. I know I can't trust her.

Intel came in late last night and I plan to share it with Scarlett soon. I instructed one of my men, Logan, to investigate the tapes from the night her sister went missing. She was seen entering the club with her friends and spoke to several different people in the time she was here. Other than that, nothing; not one speck of evidence. We don't know if she left on her own or with a male or female. There was no footage of her leaving the club, only of her friends leaving without her. She just disappeared.

I now have him reviewing the video from the private areas of the club and some of my other men have been out questioning people in my territory. Their goal is to find out who else has gone missing and see what connections there might be between them. I was livid with the information that came back; more people have gone missing than we expected. I have feelers out, looking for informants and the lack of response has been infuriating. I've instructed Damien to send men out to other territories for information, to have them stick to the shadows. They should be able to find more out that way.

Something is happening, something bad. I can feel it in my gut. I sent invitations to the leaders of the other territories. Two of my men, Jasper and Rowan, have gone to the Fae's region, and I don't expect them back anytime soon, if at all. The Fae aren't exactly known for their hospitality. They are not at all like the tiny, winged people from human fairy tales. Most are full-sized; six feet or more in height. They're striking to look at, so beautiful it's hard to look away. Long white hair and piercing blue eyes are their calling card. I've only met a few, and it was many generations ago.

The Fae are very private and it's rare for them to leave their territory. They don't like mixing with other Naturals, let alone humans, and getting information from them can be nearly impossible. I'll be surprised to get anything back from them at all, but I must try. They will be needed if my suspicions of what is coming prove correct. I just hope I'm wrong.

I've also sent Duncan and John into Nathan's territory, and Parker and Asher into Jacob's. Now all I can do is wait to hear back.

"How the fuck have they managed to be under our noses this whole time without us knowing?" Damien asks, startling me from my thoughts. He's clearly baffled, his eyes locked on Scarlett. "From what she's told us, there could be fucking hundreds of the bastards. When was the last time either of us ran into a bloody witch? It must have been at least a century, maybe more. There's been no sign of their existence for generations. Surely we should have known?" He turns his head to look at me.

I'm just as perplexed as he is, and it's starting to piss me off. How the fuck had they managed to hide in plain sight? I have every intention of finding out. "I don't know," I reply, taking the last puff of my cigar before stamping it out in the ashtray. "She's been truthful up to a point, but I know she's hiding something. I don't know what, but rest assured, I will find out." I pause, thinking back to the last witch I saw. It was incredibly unpleasant. She had been chased down and gutted, nothing left of her.

"I saw what I thought was the last one about a hundred and fifty years ago. She was from one of the last covens," I tell him, never taking my eyes off the red-haired witch on the monitor. The old witches were evil cunts, every last one of them. Ice ran through their veins. We were all better off with them dead. The witch in front of me though, she's... different. I know she's a witch, she hasn't tried to deny it, but she is nothing like the witches I remember. There's something about her, something she hasn't told me. "She was believed to be from the last coven to exist. The old council wanted to make sure none were left alive. You know they had them hunted down and gutted."

Damien's phone rings, interrupting the conversation. I focus once more on the monitors; on the woman I can't seem to get out of my mind. I notice she's stopped to speak to Dora. Dora's great-great-great grandparents had been the first people to work for me and her family has remained in my employ all these years. They are some of the only humans I've ever trusted. I can still remember how her mother looked when she was pregnant with her.

Dora and her children are part of my... family. I know it would shock most people to know that I have anyone I consider family. I like to keep my ties close to my chest, out of fear that the people I care for could be used against me. I would never allow anything to happen to her or her children. Dora's ancestors knew about us before we stepped out of the darkness many centuries ago and remained by my side through the war between Naturals and humans. They've been with me since.

Damien's phone call grabs my attention away from Scarlett and my thoughts about Dora. His expression has hardened in anger, and his voice has been rising steadily. He's yelling into his phone now, obviously displeased by the results my men are having in their search.

I have a shit feeling about all of this.

"Are you fucking kidding me!?" Damien shouts. Cursing under his breath, he growls as he listens to whatever he's being told by the person on the line. He runs his hand over his bald head, eyes flashing crimson with anger. "Make bloody sure it does not compromise you and get your asses to the pickup point. Ben and Tony will wait for you," he commands just before hanging up, not giving them a chance to respond.

He violently slams his phone down on the desk, and I wait, knowing he will tell me what's going on once he's calmed down a bit.

He groans, scrubbing at his face with his hands, and mutters under his breath before turning to me. "They think they were spotted in Nathan's territory."

"Think?" I reply, frowning. This could turn into a shitshow. Are they really so incompetent they couldn't manage to stay hidden? These assholes are meant to be some of my top trackers. That does not bode well.

"They either were, or they weren't. Fucking hell. Bloody useless assholes." I shake my head in disbelief, my face darkening in anger. My demon lets out a low growl; even he knows how bad this could be.

Nathan is a right bastard. A deadly one. All the rulers have to be in order to survive. Otherwise, we risk being challenged by those who are supposed to follow us, and chaos would ensue. The law states that if one of us must enter or send men into another's territory, we are to send a personal message to the leader of said territory. The laws are old and enforced by the council. It is rare for the leaders to go past their own borders, and rarer still for invitations to be granted. I haven't attempted to meet with another leader since the last conflict.

By sending my men into other territories without seeking permission, I was breaking the laws meant to protect us. But sometimes the situation calls for rules to be bent, and I know I'm not the first leader to have broken this particular law. Hell, some of my men came from Nathan's coven of vampires and Jacob's pack of shifters. I'm torn. The men I'd sent out have shown me their loyalty, and I return my people's loyalty tenfold. However, if my men are caught, then it's the right of the leader of that territory to deal with them as they see fit. All the rulers agreed upon that when the law was first made.

"Something is going down," Damien says. "There are more patrols than usual." He pauses, pouring two glasses of brandy and passing one to me before sipping his own. He begins to pace in front of me. "In every single one of the patrols they saw, at least two of Nathan's top men were among them."

It isn't unusual to send high-ranking soldiers on patrol. I even go out with my own men on occasion. What is unusual is to see so many of them in such a short period of time. I agree with Damien. Something is going on, and I have a sickening feeling that when I find out what it is, it will be bigger than my worst nightmare.

"We need to find out what the fuck is going on," I grind out, my fingers clenched around the arms of the chair as violence rings in my ears.

"They will be telling me every detail of what they saw when they get back," Damien assures me, stopping his pacing long enough to throw the rest of the brandy back. A frown is etched on his face and his eyes are still flashing.

Something is going on with him too, but I don't know what it is. I watch him carefully as he places the glass back on the desk and refills it.

I know him well enough to know when he has something on his mind, and the way he slung the brandy back like water only confirms my suspicions.

I know he's been unhappy about Aria being around, even before she attacked Alison. The way she kept coming by unannounced really bothered him and, truth be told, it didn't sit well with me either.

She's been more demanding than usual, and it started before Scarlett came on the scene and has only gotten worse since. I know she wants me to share Scarlett, my beautiful obsession, with her, but it's not going to happen. I don't ever remember feeling this way, but I have no intention of sharing my little witch with anyone. Fuck. I've always been willing to share, even Aria, who has been the only long-term lover I've ever had. Scarlett's just different. My demon is ecstatic that my feelings align so closely with his. Me, not so much. I keep fighting against myself and my demon, but at some point, I'm going to lose the battle. I am so fucked.

I also know Damien is aware I've been keeping some things from him. I haven't felt ready to tell him everything, so I've been keeping the fact that Aria has become completely unglued close to my chest. For months now, I've had the feeling that she was up to no good and those suspicions have been confirmed.

I continue to watch him pace around the room, waiting for him to speak up and tell me what's wrong. I'm not the type to ask and he knows that if he has something to get off his chest, he needs to come out with it. He's never gotten along with Aria, but I don't think that's all that is bothering him. The hatred he's had for her has been carved in stone since the day they met, but he's always put up with her being around. I know something has crawled up his ass and I want to know what it is.

His phone rings again and it breaks me from my musing. He stops pacing and answers. I hear Ben's voice screaming through the line, panic rising with every word he utters. I can't make out his words, so I gesture for Damien to put him on speaker phone.

"… arrived at the pickup point and we were ambushed. Tony and Duncan are hurt," Ben shouts. "We need backup NOW!"

I grab my own phone and call the one person I know I can trust to handle the current situation while Damien gets more information from Ben. Chamuel is going to be pissed that I'm calling him, but tough shit. He came to me a few months ago and asked for, no demanded, leave. I'm not so much of a bastard to refuse such a request, especially since I know he would have left whether I'd granted him permission or not. Chamuel is much too valuable to me to not have him on my side, so I generally let him come and go as he pleases. I haven't even attempted to get ahold of him in the six months he's been gone, but things have changed. I need him to come back, and I need it now.

Who else can I trust, if not my own flesh and blood?

The attention my little witch wants from me is just going to have to wait. I make a mental note to have a word with Alex. He was given strict instructions that she wasn't to be left alone for even a moment. If he was unable to fulfill those orders, he should have informed me or Damien. Somehow, she managed to walk out of her room and wander the whole damn place, without a care in the world. As though it were her home rather than mine. Alex is lucky Aria left before Scarlett went on her little walkabout. If my witch had gotten hurt, Alex would have taken the full brunt of my rage. Once I find out what the fuck is going on with my men, I intend to have a little talk with Alex and have him tell me what the hell he was thinking not accompanying her the second she stepped over the threshold of her room.

SCARLETT

I COME AWAKE WITH A JOLT. Something must have roused me from my sleep, but I don't know what it could have been. I'm alone in my room and I don't feel afraid. I glance out the window and see the moon, high and bright in the dark sky. I remember coming back to my room after being unable to locate Lucien, planning to try again in the morning. Now I'm awake and something is screaming at me to get up and get my ass downstairs immediately. I climb out of bed and dress, knowing what my sisters would say if they were here. They would tell me to ignore the urge to go, to stay in my room. I wouldn't have listened to them.

I follow my intuition through the hallways, and step outside. I have no idea how exactly I got here; I merely walked the way my instincts told me to go. Looking around, I'm surrounded by carnage and mayhem. Men are all around me, some I recognize, some I don't, but most of them bloodied and broken.

Several of the men are lying on the ground, being tended to. I hear orders ring out left and right, and scan the vast area, looking for Lucien. Finally, I spot him to my left, having a heated discussion with some of his men. I thought I'd seen him angry before, but this is something else. Now isn't the time to approach him and ask what's going on, so I turn my eyes to the scene before me.

I look around at the injured, and spotting a trolley filled with bags of medical supplies, I grab one and go over to the man lying closest to me. I can see as I approach him that he's wary of letting me near him, his brown eyes flashing a warning, but I ignore his reaction and examine him anyway. I spot two deep gashes, one on his left forearm and the other on his right thigh, blood pouring from both. The one on his thigh is of higher concern, so I focus on that one first. The bone is showing through the gaping flesh, and I fight against the bile rising in my throat.

He growls, low in his throat, and I place my hand on his arm, holding up the bag of medical supplies. "Please, I only want to help you," I assure him. "Just let me clean and stitch your wounds." It feels like several minutes, but is likely only a few seconds, before he nods his head for me to continue. I give a sigh of relief and pull on a pair of disposable gloves.

Using a pair of scissors from the bag, I cut his pants up to his thigh, revealing the full severity of the injury. It's worse than I'd thought. I don't know if I can help heal him without giving myself away. My thoughts race as I begin cleaning the wound. Would I be able to live with myself if I didn't use my powers to help him? Dozens of Lucien's men may die without my help. Healing this one will sap my energy and might give me away, but I don't think I can handle watching him die when I have the ability to save him.

Making up my mind, I pour antiseptic into the wound and a flash of pain flickers briefly across his dark face. I see the flare in his eyes and a slight lengthening of his teeth and know he's a vampire. A shiver runs down my spine. Vampires are some of the deadliest creatures alive. I know to avoid them at all costs, but I push away my fear and force myself to pretend he's human.

I need to stop the blood loss as quickly as I can. If he loses too much, he'll need more, and I have no desire to be his next meal. Vampires, like most other Naturals, typically heal on their own, without intervention. Looking down at the wound again, I realize that his healing process has been slowed by something, perhaps the severity of his injuries. I'm going to have to work quickly. I grab a needle and thread with one hand and lay my fingertips of the other at the edge of the open wound. I shortly pray in my head that nobody will hear me chanting above the chaos surrounding us and begin.

I call forth my omega, immediately aware of her essence coming through. She knows she can't use the full strength of her healing powers, so I don't have to remind her. Heat begins radiating from my head, down through my shoulders, to the tips of my fingers. We are two entities in one body and, together, we start whispering the healing spell, making sure our voice never rises above a whisper. We both know what we are doing is dangerous, possibly reckless. I am putting my family and friends in danger, but I couldn't just sit by and allow these people to suffer on my watch. My omega is careful not to fully close the wound, merely healing it just enough so the vampire's natural healing will kick in.

I watch as his injuries start knitting together from the inside out. I can't go any further. If I do, I won't have the energy to help any of the others. Besides, I've done as much as I can without bringing attention to myself. As I come out of the healing process, I notice the vampire looking at me and that the expression on his face has changed. He no longer looks suspicious, in fact, there seems to be a certain recognition in his eyes, as though he understands what I just did.

His words confirm my suspicion. "Your secret is safe with me, girl," he says in a low, gravelly voice, as he makes eye contact with me. "Not all of us means your kind harm," he assures, laying his big hand over my smaller one. "I'm Jaden. I thank you sincerely for your help," Jaden lowers his head in a sign of respect before continuing. "If you ever need anything, ask Alex to bring you to me. I owe you a life debt. Now please, go help the others as much as you're able."

"You need blood, and soon," I tell him, looking down at the hand he placed over my own. I don't know what else to say; I'm in shock. How does this man, this vampire, know about us? What exactly *does* he know? Shit, how many know we're here, existing among them? Question after question races through my mind. I don't know if this is good or bad. How will my sisters react when I tell them? I know I won't be able to bluff my way out, not with a vampire, and I can't allow myself to panic.

"I will be fine, as will you be. Accept your fate, embrace it." I feel his fingers tighten around mine as he speaks, and then he lets go, letting his hand fall to the ground. "Hard times are coming for us all. Now go. Your work here is done, and the others need you." He nods to the injured men around him and shoos me away with a flick of his hand. Part of me wants to stay, even knowing I'm needed elsewhere. I want answers to the questions bombarding my brain. Pushing away the impulse to stay and question him, I stand up and go to attend to the rest of the injured.

CHAPTER FIFTEEN

LUCIEN

Even surrounded by chaos, I sense her the minute she steps outside. I resist the urge to turn and look at her. I want to grab her by the shoulders and shake her until her teeth rattle, demanding to know what the hell she thinks she's doing. Doesn't she realize how dangerous this is? Anything could happen to her, and I wouldn't be able to get to her in time if my men decided to cause her harm. Most of my men are Naturals; they could easily tear her apart in seconds. What made her think to come out here, anyway?

I want to walk over and demand answers, but I force myself to remain where I am and order my men to fetch the doctors.

The injured are coming in thick and fast and if I don't get things under control, I will lose more of my men than I already have. The doctors finally arrive and rush off to work on the men who are most severely injured. There aren't enough uninjured to help all my men, but at least the ones in peril are being treated.

The voices around me drop to a murmur and I notice a look of admiration spreading across Damien's face. He nods to whatever's happening behind me, and I turn to look. There, on the ground, Scarlett is sitting and tending to one of my men.

Aside from Nathan, Jaden is the oldest vampire I know. He's been with me for two hundred years. He's also one of the deadliest and for him to be injured in such a way tells me all I need to know about how bad the ambush was. It looks like he's losing blood rapidly, and that alone is a danger to not only the witch tending to him, but to any who may cross his path. I step forward, getting ready to drag her away from him but stop when he places his hand over hers. In that moment, I know she is safe. I can't hear what he says to her, but whatever it is, she's clearly shocked by it. I watch as she stands and moves to another of my injured men.

LUCIEN

NEXT DAY : LUCIEN'S OFFICE

FUCK, I'M SHATTERED. BEING UP all night will do that to a man, Natural or human. Chamuel still hasn't responded to my phone call or to my message. Usually, even if he doesn't pick up when I call, he will still respond within a few hours. I have no other way of contacting him and I'm frustrated at having to wait for him to get back to me. I can only guess at how long it will take. My brother is a remarkably private person. He works beside me at my request. Few know of our relationship, it's nobody's business. If people were to find out, it could raise a lot of questions for the both of us.

Last night had been a clusterfuck, totally catastrophic. I lost a lot of good men, and many others are injured, though some more severely than others.

One of my most loyal men, Duncan, hadn't survived the attack. As a human, he stood little chance against the siege. He left behind a young wife and son, and I intend to make sure they're well taken care of. According to Ben, they were on their way to the rendezvous point when they were struck by unknown attackers. The description Ben gave made little sense. We destroyed those fuckers a long time ago! What the hell is going on!?

Tony also survived the attack but is still unconscious. I will have to wait for him to come to so I can get his account of what happened, but the other men's reports closely matched Ben's. Once Jaden got his bloodlust under control, he was able to fill in some of the gaps.

Then there's Scarlett. I don't even know what to think about her. How had she known to show up outside? At first, Damien and the rest of my men were displeased by her presence, their distrust had been more than evident. It hadn't stopped her from helping, though. She followed any orders thrown her way, even to the point of helping get the injured into the on-site hospital.

Blood had been everywhere, limbs missing, skin torn. The sight would have turned even the hardest of stomachs. I know it turned mine. I would have thought she would run from such a sight and was utterly shocked when she did the opposite. Without batting an eye, she tended to every injured man my doctors had been unable to get to. By the time the sun rose, Scarlett had gained the hard-earned respect of my men.

According to the latest report, fifteen are dead and thirty wounded; eight of them critically injured. They know as well as I do that they're lucky to be alive. I've already sent the order out for all patrols to be doubled. I won't put my men in more danger than necessary. What worries me most about the attack is my men's descriptions of their attackers. I've been trying to convince myself they were mistaken, but the feeling in my gut is telling me otherwise. It just doesn't make sense. No one has seen or heard from them in years. Fuck, as far as we knew, they were all dead.

I'm struggling to come to terms with the events of the last few days. Witches we believed to be wiped out turned out to be living on my fucking doorstep. Aria has a spy in my ranks, and she attacked and nearly killed Allison. Nathan has doubled his patrols and clearly knows something is happening. The list of shit hanging over my head is endless.

The only positive thing to happen were the responses from Jacob, Reid, and Archer, the other territory leaders I'd reached out to. All three accepted my invitation, though they requested to bring more of their men than usual. I agreed. There's definitely something going on, and even if they don't know exactly what it is, they sense something coming. I sent messages to the leaders of some of the smaller territories as well, and three of them let me know they would be here.

I've yet to receive a response from Nathan or Gil-Galad, though I expect to hear from Nathan today. I'd be surprised if Gil-Galad acknowledges my summons at all. Jasper and Rowan haven't checked back in, though they radioed in the previous evening just before entering the Fae's territory. For the time being, I'm considering them MIA and I don't feel confident that situation will change.

It isn't unheard of to gather so many territory leaders together for a meeting, though it is rare. Both councils have gotten wind of our little gathering and requested an invitation, making it clear they weren't really asking. They acted like I had no choice but to agree, clearly forgetting I once sat in one of those seats. I reluctantly agreed, knowing I didn't need to add a pissed off council to my growing list of concerns.

The meeting is in five days, which means I have enough time to get extra security in place before everyone arrives. All weapons will need to be turned in and everyone will go through digital image screening prior to being permitted into the meeting. One can never be too careful as you never know who may try to double-cross you.

A rapid banging sound brings me out of my thoughts. It sounds like whoever is at the door is trying to break the bloody thing down. I know it can't be Damien, he's off making sure everything will be in place for the meeting. Besides, he doesn't usually knock. I call out for them to come in and take a sip of the scotch I've been savoring.

"Boss?" Alex questions in a tentative tone as the door swings open. "Sorry," he apologizes, stepping inside the office. "She wanted to talk to you," he indicates Scarlett, who's standing directly behind him.

She moves around to stand beside him, lifting her chin boldly. Her gaze locks onto my own, her face unflinching. She's more confident than she ever has been in my presence. This isn't the human standing before me. It's the witch. I take in her dark auburn hair that's piled atop her head, making her look taller than she is. There are a few curls hanging down from where they escaped the bun. Tight black jeans hug her curves and low-heeled black boots make her look like she's ready to go to battle. The jade-colored top brings out the green in her eyes and contrasts perfectly against the red of her hair. The fierce expression she's wearing makes her more compelling to me than ever.

"What can I do for you, Scarlett?" I keep my tone even as I lean back in my chair and cross my feet at the ankles. I have a feeling she heard about the meeting and that she will likely want to attend with her sisters, but I can't allow it. If the other leaders got even a whiff of the witches I have living freely in my territory, all hell will break lose. I have way too many things to deal with to add pandemonium amongst the Naturals to my plate.

"What the hell happened last night? Your men were fucking attacked, some of them killed, way too many injured. What are you hiding from me? How can I trust that you can keep me safe or protect my family when they arrive?" She fires the words at me, hands on her hips and a frown marring her face. She waits a few seconds for my reply and when none is forthcoming, she huffs softly before walking closer. My eyes are drawn to her swaying hips, and I have to force myself to focus on her next words.

"Have you found the soul keeper yet?" Her eyes narrow on my face, and she leans forward, planting her hands on my desk.

I take a sip of my scotch and watch her. I know the longer it takes for me to respond to her questions, the more enraged she will become. Her green eyes flash at me and I can see her trying to rein in her anger. I wonder what it would be like to see her explode. No doubt it would make those incredible eyes glow like green embers. Sometimes she seems to be able to peer down into my soul with them, almost as if she can see my demon.

If she thinks I will allow her to demand things from me, she has another thing coming. I got information about the soul keeper last night, but with everything that happened, I hadn't had a chance to share it with her yet.

Standing from my chair, I place my hands on the desk next to hers and lean forward. "Don't think you can come in here, throwing out demands." I'm positive my eyes flash red as I grind the words out between clenched teeth. I pull back and relax a little. "Seeing as you helped my men with their injuries, I'm going to overlook your insolence. This time."

"I'm not throwing out any so-called demands. I want answers and you promised to keep me in the loop. What the hell happened to your men? Hell, do you even know what attacked them?" She spits the words at me, standing her ground and not showing even an ounce of fear. Even though I have no intention of telling her, I feel my respect for her grow.

"My sisters will be arriving soon," she says, as though I, Lucien Sinclair, need to be reminded that I'm not only allowing fucking witches to live safely in my territory, but that I invited them into my club. I know it will eventually get out that I have a witch living under my protection, in my home, and I know it will cause me innumerable headaches when it does.

She continues, "There had better be some extra protections in place to keep them safe. And they will want to be updated. If we get even a whiff that you aren't being completely honest, our agreement will be null and void."

"You might want to watch that mouth of yours, Scarlett," I warn in a deadly quiet tone. I feel my demon stir inside of me, his excitement rising, fighting to come out and play. I feel my eyes flash again as my skin flickers, the texture changing.

Her beautiful eyes widen, and her mouth drops open as she stumbles back in shock. From the corner of my eye, I see Alex take a step towards us, and my demon growls a warning to stay back. My beast will not harm her; nor will I. While I haven't completely come to terms with the feelings that have been growing inside of me for her, my demon has, and neither of us wishes any harm to come to her.

"Don't overstep, Scarlett. I can only allow you to go so far before I have to teach you a lesson." I rake my eyes over her menacingly, showing her I mean business. "Your sisters will be safe while they are in my care, but anything that happens to them outside my compound is outside of my control." I shrug and ease back down into the seat behind me. My demon is still right near the surface, and I shove him back, taking full control.

I turn my attention to Alex, who has stood silently throughout the entire exchange, watching and listening. "Alex. Jacob will be coming to the meeting. As you know him best, I want you to handle the meet and greet. Make sure they leave any weapons they're carrying in the storeroom designated for that purpose. You can let them know their weapons will be returned to them when the meeting has concluded." He nods, his expression neutral.

"Jaden will deal with Nathan, and Ben will be assigned to the Fae, if they accept the invitation. Also, both councils requested an invitation and six members from each will be attending, as well as a few of my regional leaders." I run one of the larger territories and I've appointed leaders to some of the regions within my territory to help me keep a handle on things. Aria is one of them. All of them answer to me, and they all know that I can take their regions back from them with a snap of my fingers. Most of the territories are run in a similar manner.

I turn my attention back to Scarlett, who is now sitting in one of the chairs in front of my desk, watching me give Alex the orders. Her expression betrays no sign of surprise at hearing of the meeting.

I decide, then and there, to allow her and her sisters to attend the meeting. I know it is going to cause issues and that I will have to handle the questions that arise, but I have a strong feeling in my gut that they need to be in attendance.

Scarlett is still visibly angry, but news of the meeting seems to have shut her up for the time being. Hopefully, she can push it all to the side while I share the information I gathered about the soul keeper. I now know where he's staying and have gathered a group of my men to collect him and bring him back here. I warned them of the danger they were facing by going after a soul keeper and given them the option to back out. Every last one of them assured me they would be on guard at all times and that they were up to the task. If the soul keeper manages to get his hands on any of them, it will be nearly impossible to reacquire their souls and put them back in their bodies. I hate sending my men on such a dangerous mission. I don't want any of them injured or dead, especially when the loss of my men from the night before is still with me.

"Alex," I call over to him, not taking my eyes off Scarlett. "Go to Damien and let him know I've assigned you the task of rearranging the storage room for our visitor's weapons. Tell him I want to use the room next door for the meeting. I need you to make sure the storeroom is ready and that everything is in place for their arrival. Choose a few men you trust to help you. Damien will brief you on how to handle collecting weapons and how to work the digital scanning system. If you have any questions, Damien is in charge."

He looks at me, then at Scarlett. I can tell he's hesitant to leave her alone with me, that he takes his role of protecting her seriously, even against me. He doesn't know that I have no intentions of harming her, and I admire his commitment to the task, although he should know he's completely outmatched against me. Normally I would simply order him to leave, but I'm willing to give him a little bit of leeway. It's clear he's grown some attachment to her and it's likely that attachment goes both ways. I'll let it slide for now, so long as it doesn't go any further than a friendship. There are questions in his eyes, and I can see him trying to gather the courage to speak them. I decide to answer without him needing to ask.

"Alex, you have my word she will be safe." I meet his eyes and watch as a muscle twitches in his jaw. I know he wants to say more but is aware that questioning me would have dire consequences. He swallows roughly and nods.

"Scarlett," he calls out, breaking eye contact with me to look at her. "I'll see you later, okay?" He says with a smile, before nodding at me once more and leaving the room. The door shuts behind him and I relax in my chair, taking a sip from my glass.

I turn my full attention to Scarlett. I know she has questions she wants answered and I plan to answer them as honestly as I can. She's still hiding information from me, and I'm going to expect some answers of my own.

CHAPTER SIXTEEN

SCARLETT

I CAME IN HERE DEMANDING answers. I got far more than I bargained for.

I can see Lucien fighting with his demon, can see it close to the surface. His eyes flash red when his demon starts to push forward, but it's subtle enough that I'd miss it if I weren't watching for it. Earlier I saw his skin shift and was surprised when Lucien was able to push the demon back. His demon doesn't scare me, though I know he probably should.

I could tell from the expression on Alex's face, he hadn't wanted to leave me here alone with Lucien. He didn't need to worry; I know Lucien wasn't going to hurt me. But if he tried, I would fight back, and I'm far more powerful than either of them realizes.

After Alex leaves, Lucien and I sit in silence for a few moments, just staring at one another. Time seems to stand still until he grabs the decanter on his desk and pours some amber liquid into his glass. "Scotch?" He offers, nodding to the glass in front of me.

Without a word, I shake my head. Part of me thinks a drink could be useful right about now, but I'm not much of a drinker and the liquor would go straight to my head and leave me unable to defend myself, should the need arise.

He sighs before standing and removing his suit jacket. He drapes it across the back of the chair and settles back into it, taking a sip of his drink, his muscles rippling under his shirt. I long to run my hands over them, to press my body against his. I want to feel those powerful arms around me as his breath caresses across my skin. Trying to shake the lustful images from my brain, I cough nervously as he stares at me with predatory eyes, making me feel like his next meal and sending delicious shivers down my spine.

He continues to watch me in silence as my heart hammers in my chest. Where the hell my witch has gone, I haven't a clue. I can't seem to find her inside of me, as though she's all but disappeared in the recesses of my mind. I know this is her way of telling me I can deal with him on my own, but shit! I'm not entirely sure I can. I force myself to focus on why I'm here. I can't allow myself to fall for this man, this demon, who so easily makes me forget about everything but him.

I tune back in and register what he's saying. "… our disagreement is getting us nowhere. We need to work together to figure out what's going on. You have questions," he states rather than asks. Biting down on my lower lip and releasing it, I take a deep breath as I stare into Lucien's coal-black eyes. I nod lightly and he raises an eyebrow at me as he takes another sip from his glass. "So do I," he informs me.

He looks down at the swirling liquid and continues. "News has come in about the soul keeper. He's been staying in a hotel not far from here, and I've sent my men to pick him up and bring him to me. I will be questioning him when he arrives." He stops talking and lifts his dark head, his eyes searching mine for a reaction.

I'm sure he can see my surprise. I hadn't expected him to find the soul keeper so quickly. I'm pleased at the news and by the fact that Lucien finally seems willing to work together, but also a little afraid. If the soul keeper manages to get his hands on the men sent to retrieve him, their souls will be ripped from their bodies. It's almost impossible to put a soul back once it's been removed. Fuck.

"Your men are in grave danger," I whisper, letting my concern show on my face.

With a deep sigh, he inclines his head in agreement. "Yes. Yes, they are." His eyes continue to watch me intently. There is so much power inside of him, it lingers in the air around his body. He's menacing, hard, complex, utterly forbidden and so damn sexy. His presence makes my heart beat faster and my skin tingle as I meet his unwavering gaze. "If it makes you feel any better, they knew what the job entailed before they agreed to it. They know exactly what they're walking into."

Shaking my head, I reply. "That doesn't make it any better."

I appreciate him trying to ease my concern, but I know too much not to be afraid for his men. I may not know all, or even any, of them, but I don't want anyone getting their souls ripped out of their bodies on my account.

"I don't relish the idea of sending my men into such a dangerous situation, but it was necessary. I made sure they were as prepared as they could be, and I'm confident in their abilities. I wouldn't have sent them otherwise." He reassures me, placing his empty glass on the desk in front of him.

"How did you know to come outside last night? How did you know what was happening?" He asks, changing the subject so swiftly, I feel like I have whiplash.

His question doesn't surprise me, though. I knew he would demand answers, but there really isn't much I can tell him but the truth, which doesn't really explain anything.

I shrug. "I woke up, but I don't know what woke me. Something told me I needed to go downstairs, so I followed my intuition and ran into, well, chaos."

"Why did you help my men? You didn't have to." He looks at me suspiciously, his dark eyes not once leaving my face or even blinking as he scrutinizes every expression, looking for lies.

Oh, shit! I start praying to anyone or anything that may be listening. Please don't tell me he realized I was helping speed up his men's healing. I knew I was taking a chance, and I would do it again. But I hoped Lucien would only be aware of me bandaging and stitching, not of the powers I used. When the vampire, Jaden, acknowledged what I'd done, I was shocked. I couldn't get away from him fast enough and I kept looking over my shoulder, waiting for heavy hands to drag me away and demand answers. I was actually shocked when it didn't happen. Without anyone stopping me or impeding me, I healed as many men as

I could without anyone watching. At the end of it, exhausted, I dragged myself to bed.

I try to keep my face free of any and all emotion that could show him the rising panic inside of me. If he were to figure out what I am, it could spell disaster for me and my family. Knowing better than to lie to a demon, I consider my next words carefully.

"They needed help and I had the skills to give it. I cannot in good conscience leave anyone, human or Natural, to suffer untreated as they bleed out. I knew I could help, so I did." My body is tense as I wait with bated breath for his reaction. I didn't lie about why I helped; I just didn't mention my Omega and how she helped me heal his men.

Lucien merely continues to watch me in silence for several minutes. Not knowing what he's thinking sends a small fissure of anxiety down my spine. I resist the urge to shudder. His expression finally changes, a small smile appearing on his lips. "They appreciate it," he says, "as do I. I likely would have lost even more of my men had you not stepped in to help."

"I hope the need doesn't arise, but I would do it again." I inform him, returning his smile with one of my own as my muscles relax in relief.

"So, the soul keeper," he backtracks, running his inked hand through his tousled hair. "From the intel that's come in so far, it appears he wasn't working alone, which is what I've suspected all along. I will know more once I get the chance to interrogate him" He stops, his dark eyes locked on my face, his expression suddenly morphing into one that speaks to his formidable rage.

"You'll be updated as soon as possible. You can go ahead and let your sisters know everything we've found out so far. As you know, though I'm curious to know how you found out, the meeting is taking place in a few days. I've decided to extend an invitation to you and your sisters. As you heard me telling Alex, the leaders of the other territories will be in attendance, along with representatives from both councils. I'm warning you now, it will not be pleasant, particularly if they get even a whiff of the fact that you're all witches."

I feel my face go pale with his warning. If we go to the meeting, we'll be surrounded by Naturals. Everyone knows who the leaders of the territories are, it isn't kept secret. It's bad enough being in Lucien's company, trying to keep my omega a secret. I can't even imagine what it will be like with Naturals all around me. Lucien isn't wrong. Having the entire Supernatural world find out there are still witches among them could spell disaster, but it's the least of my worries at the moment. While unlikely, it's possible they could see the benefit of having witches as allies. But if they were to find out we are also omegas… this meeting could spell our demise.

I lean back in my chair, allowing myself time to formulate a response. "We've stayed hidden for so long, I can't see my sisters accepting the invitation," I finally reply, my mouth so dry I have trouble getting the words out.

They are already displeased about the fact I refused to come home and that they're being forced to come here to see me. They have no desire to reveal themselves to Lucien, I can't imagine how they would feel being asked to attend a meeting among nearly every leader of the Natural world. Just the idea of it has me nearly trembling in fear.

"Make them see sense," Lucien states simply, leaning back in his chair.

"The very idea…" My words trail off, a sigh leaving me as I shake my head. "I will speak with them, but I see only one way they will agree to be there. You would have to agree to allow us to use a concealment spell which would hopefully keep anyone from sensing our true nature." Part of me really hopes he refuses, saving me and my sisters from having to worry over the concealment spell failing us and dooming us in the same breath.

He steeples his hands over his mouth, thinking over my proposal. I can see he isn't happy with the idea. I know he's still grappling with the fact that he's had witches in his territory for so long without being aware of it and it doesn't sit well with him.

A small, thin smile appears on his face as something occurs to him. "The spell didn't work on me, and I doubt very much it will work on the other Naturals. How have you stayed hidden for so long? I sensed you were a witch the moment I saw you."

I've known I wouldn't be able to avoid the question forever. I wonder how much I should tell him. We need his trust, and he already thinks he knows exactly what we are; half-witch and half-human. Giving him the information on how we control the witch part of us won't make much of a difference at this point. I don't need to tell him just how powerful we are.

"You forget we are part human. The human part controls the witch," I explain a calm voice.

Fixing me with a stern look he demands, "How the fuck can you control that thing inside of you?"

I try not to fidget in my chair as I think of how to explain it to him without freaking him the fuck out. I feel my nerves bubbling up inside of me; I hate being nervous. How is he going to react, knowing the humans stepped up and helped the witches? I definitely don't intend to tell him about the Naturals who helped us, no matter that it was centuries ago. Some of those Naturals are still alive, and the ones who aren't, have descendants who could be in danger if the truth came out. Thinking about it now, I wonder if perhaps Jaden was one of those who supported my ancestors.

"It wasn't easy. It's taken a long time, generations, to get where we are now. I can control my witch, so can the rest of my family. When I need her, I call her forth, but my human is always in control," I tell him, hoping he understands that he isn't in danger of rogue witches attacking him in a fit of anger. "No matter how close she is to the surface, I have full control." I can see the battle being waged inside of him as he tries to accept what I'm saying. I can imagine how difficult it must be, considering the destruction caused by witches in the past.

"You have a demon inside of you; you're not human, though you look the part. How do you control him? Is it possible for him to gain control and take over?" I ask.

"No. He's part of me. I am the Beast and the Demon; we are one," he explains thoughtfully, his eyes never wavering from me.

"So basically, we are the same," I shrug and point between us. "The difference being that my family and I are part human, and you're not. Our witch, when necessary, protects us. You're powerful enough on your own not to need your demon to protect you."

Tilting his head to one side, Lucien narrows his eyes as his they travel over my face and upper body, a glint appearing in them as he asks, "How powerful are you?"

I shift uneasily in my chair, not realizing I'm biting down on my bottom lip until it starts to throb. My knee starts to bounce as we stare at one another across the large wooden desk. I fight the urge to get up and flee, to get as far away from him and his questions as possible. What can I tell the man sitting before me? Not the complete truth, but I already warned him and Aria that I was capable of protecting myself when threatened. Speaking of Aria, I've since learned she is his partner, confirming what she told me when we met. One of Lucien's employees told me they've been together for years.

I take a deep breath before answering. "I've already told you. I am capable of protecting myself when necessary, against just about any threat. I know Aria is your partner, but you need to know that if she attempts to harm me or any of my family members, I will not hold my witch back and neither will they.

"I see someone's been talking out of turn," Lucien grinds out with clenched teeth, his dark eyes glaring at me.

After what I just told him, that's all he has to say? Bloody hell. I shrug. "What can I say? You're a hot topic of conversation and there are more than a few people here who just love to gossip. You and your little plaything are a favored topic, whether I wish to hear about it or not." My lips twist as I allow my gaze to travel over his face, shoulders, and chest before locking eyes with him once more.

What does he see when he stares at me with such intensity? Is he trying to see inside of me? To see my soul? I know it's impossible to see inside of someone in such a way, but I can't help the shudder that runs through me at the thought.

"Don't believe everything you hear or see, little witch," he tells me, raising a hand and stroking it over his jaw, a hint of annoyance glimmering in his eyes.

"I don't believe everything I hear, but I can't help but believe what I've seen with my own two eyes. I've seen plenty," I retort, rolling my eyes as I cross one leg over the other. "I know what I saw that day from my window and what I witnessed in the security room."

He stiffens at my words. "As I said. You cannot believe everything you hear or see. Looks can deceive." An expression of intense frustration comes over his face, a muscle twitching in his jaw.

Is he trying to tell me in a roundabout way that she isn't his partner? I might believe him if I hadn't witnessed not only with my eyes, but in my visions.

"Are you saying that Aria isn't your partner, your wife?" I ask incredulously, lifting my eyebrow as my head cocks to the side. Does he think I'm an idiot?

As he pours himself another drink, he replies, "It's complicated." His stare is bold as his eyes slide down to my breasts before returning to meet my gaze. A shiver of lust runs down my spine at his heated look. Bringing the glass to his lips and taking a long sip, he hesitates before saying, "What Aria is to me has nothing to do with the undesired feelings I have for you."

His words catch me off guard, shocking me. I know he can read the astonishment on my face. He watches me as I try to take control of my emotions and still my hammering pulse. I know I can't avoid what he just said, it needs to be addressed, if for no other reason than my sanity. I track his movements as he places the unfinished drink on his desk before standing and making his way around to where I'm sitting. I swallow hard, my mouth dry, as he moves closer. I can feel a burning need growing inside my body. I fight to keep my eyes anywhere but on him. I don't want him to see the longing in them, don't want him to know that he has me right where he wants me.

His large body looming over me, he gently grabs my chin and tilts my face up to his. "Why can't I get you out of my mind? You're always there, no matter who I take to my bed or how often." His voice is cloaked in wonder, a smoldering flame growing in his eyes.

I'm speechless, both from his words and the way he's looking at me. I feel my entire body start to shake as his scent fills my senses. His touch is melting all the walls I thought were firmly in place and it takes every ounce of control I possess to stop myself from pouncing on him.

Finding my voice, I tell him, "I will not be your plaything or some trophy you show off to the men who bow down to you." His eyes flash red and I remove his fingers from my face, even as an unwelcome surge of heat flows through me. My breath catches, my heart racing inside my chest.

A low growl emanates from his chest, and I close my eyes.

His deep voice is thick with emotion when he speaks. "Open your eyes." He gives me a gentle shake, and at his command, my eyelids lift to meet his black gaze. "Is that what you think?" He asks with a frown, observing and assessing my expression. "You think I want to use you? You couldn't be more wrong."

"Your feelings are unwanted; you just said that," I reply, my voice catching as I fight back the tears I feel gathering. I lower my gaze, not wanting him to see my despair.

"Look at me," he demands, his voice rough but gentle.

Even as my eyes meet his, I curse myself for giving in. His gaze is heated, his expression one that speaks of dark desires. I know if I were standing, I would try to flee. He usually keeps his emotions so guarded, to see his face full of such… yearning… it feels as though my soul has been bared to him.

He shakes his head, his ebony eyes holding me in their thrall. "Unwanted, yes. I've never wanted another female the way I want you. Not even Aria. I cannot stop this craving I have for you. It's all-consuming. I've done everything in my power to stop myself from seeking you out. I've been at war with myself and my demon for days now. He wants you like he's never wanted another; he wants to lay claim to you. I've never had to fight him so hard for control. When I'm near you, he wants out. He keeps pushing me, trying to force me to take you as our mate."

I blink, convinced I'm imagining this entire exchange. There is no way he just said the words I think I heard. This is madness. I hold my breath, my eyes frozen on his lips. I force my gaze to his and the look I see in them tells me that this is really happening.

"Am I meant to believe you?" I ask, surprised when my voice comes out steady. "You want me to believe you have no feelings left for the woman you've been with for so many years?"

His dark eyes rove over my face, drinking me in. "Do you remember the first night we met, when I made you give me a promise? You stood before me, scared out of your mind, but still worked up the nerve to stand up to me. You looked like an angel passing through the depths of hell, refusing to back down. I knew then that you were the one for me, no matter how many times I've tried to deny it. The circumstances that have brought you here are irrelevant. I cannot deny what you are to me any longer. Fuck, I don't have it in me to fight with my demon any longer. I know he's right. This goes beyond any business agreement; I know you see that. I know you feel it too, whatever this is between us. I can see it in your eyes every time you look at me."

His words hit home, making it difficult to breathe. Can I believe him? Can I trust him with my heart? What he's saying is an echo of what I've seen in my dreams. My dreams have been trying to tell me that this man, this demon standing before me, he is my destiny. Do I have the courage to embrace it, embrace him? He has the power to hurt me, not only physically, but emotionally. He has the power to obliterate my soul.

Distracting me from my worries, he takes my hand and kisses it, as though I'm the most precious thing on earth. Who is this person in front of me? No longer the brutal, dangerous, deadly demon of lore, but somehow even more powerful. He is everything I've ever wanted. Lucien is, literally, the man in my dreams.

I know I need to decide to walk away from him, from my destiny, or to place my trust in him, in my dreams, and give myself to him. What happens if I do the latter? What happens with Aria. I refuse to be his dirty little secret. How would I handle my family and their reaction to our union? With a start, I realize I've spoken my thoughts aloud.

"There is no way I can keep you a secret. My feelings for you can no longer be hidden. I will deal with Aria," he assures me, pulling me out of the chair and into his arms. "We will deal with any problems as they arise. For this moment, and every moment hereafter, you are mine. No one will dare take you away from me."

His smell engulfs me, making my thighs clench with desire. The only thought running through my fog-filled mind is having his lips and hands on my body. All the promises I made to myself to resist him have vanished.

I watch his lips descend towards my own and I meet them willingly, eagerly. This kiss is so much more than all the ones before. It threatens to swallow me whole. A protest forms in my mind, that I have no guarantee he will end things with Aria, but it is washed away by the sensation of his body against mine. I am his for the taking and I'm powerless to stop it. I tangle my fists in his raven hair, allowing my body to mold to his hardness.

Even with lust battering me from every angle, there is one thought that hasn't left my mind. Though I am his, is he truly mine?

CHAPTER SEVENTEEN

SCARLETT

I STAND IN HIS ARMS AND breathe in his scent, a heady mixture of his cologne and his natural essence. It surrounds me, engulfs me, causing my thighs to clench. All I can think about in my fog-filled mind is having his lips and hands on my body. His lips meet mine and my mouth opens for him willingly. There's nobody nearby who can stop what is going to happen. I am his for the taking. A part of me tries to protest, but deep down, I really don't want to.

Gripping his hair with both fists, I arch against him, as if doing so will connect us on a deeper level. I feel his rock-hard cock pressing against my stomach, twitching with impatience. He stifles the moan rising in my throat when he wraps his large hand around my neck. All the while, he's directing me towards the wall behind me, pushing me against it before grabbing my thighs and wrapping them around his waist. I whimper as I feel his hardness rub against my heated core.

As I writhe against him, he skims a hand over my breast, and I never want the sensation of his touch to end. I'm not a small woman, but his large frame towers over me, completely surrounding me. I've never felt more alive. I feel protected…wanted. As though I'm the only woman he will ever desire from this moment forward. Gripping him tightly between my thighs, I whimper as an intense longing overwhelms me, and though it excites me, the fervent emotions he pulls from the depths of my soul terrify me.

I want him deep inside of me, need to feel his hardness plunging deep and taking me to places I've never experienced. The tempo of the kiss changes, becoming even more demanding as his lips ravish my mouth in an explosion of passion and desire. I moan, pushing my body against his, writhing in anguish to get closer. I've never felt this burning need before and it's consuming me in a way I never thought possible. A shiver of pleasure races down my spine as he nips at my throat. I dig my nails into his back and hold on tight as he sucks roughly on the soft spot where my neck meets my shoulder, his tongue and teeth making me cry out with longing. The husky sounds escaping me are raw, animalistic. I need him to fuck me, to take me with abandon.

He lifts his head, placing his lips against my ear. "I want to fuck you. I *need* to be inside of you." His voice comes out in a low growl before he slams his lips against mine once more, stealing my breath.

The need to claim him, to have him claim me, chases any trace of coherent thought from my mind. As his hard body pins me to the wall, I grab his shirt in both hands and pull, buttons flying everywhere as I rip his shirt off. With a hungry moan, I run greedy hands down his firm back, the muscles flexing under my fingertips. Trailing my hands down his chest and abdomen, I feel a light dusting of hair, his abs rigid as I graze them with my palms.

Pulling his chest away from mine, he grabs my top and strips it off in one swipe, baring my breasts to his ravenous gaze. He leans down, nuzzling and biting them, causing me to arch my back in bliss as he tastes the sensitive skin before moving down to take a stiff nipple into his mouth. Closing my eyes, I brace myself against the wall, allowing him to lick and kiss his way down my torso. He untangles my legs from around his waist and rips my pants down my body, taking my panties with them.

He teases me open with his fingers and my hips thrust forward to meet them. Lucien growls and I feel the vibrations travel the length of my body, every nerve ending alert. Now that I've been laid bare for him, there's no turning back. I will never crave another as I do him. No matter who I may try to give my body to in the future, none will compare.

Abruptly, the door slams open, hitting the wall with a loud thud and causing me to shriek and stiffen in Lucien's arms.

"Fuck! "Shit, sorry boss, but we've got trouble," an obnoxious voice calls from the doorway.

I'm frozen in shock and feel my cheeks flush with mortification as all the passion fades quickly from the room.

"GET. THE. FUCK. OUT!" Lucien roars, his expression full of rage as he detangles himself from me and turns around to face the man who barged in without knocking. Thank heavens his body is large enough to hide me.

"Sorry, Lucien," is muttered before the door clicks shut.

Lucien turns back around to face me, placing his large hand on my waist. He pulls me towards him, and passion engulfs me once more. I have no desire to break from his embrace, the mere touch sending a shiver through my entire body. Knowing what's coming, disappointment washes over me as I feel the brush of his lips against my cheek before settling at my ear.

"I have to go," he whispers, his breath hot against my flesh, hand flexing at my waist. "Stay here until either Alex, Adam, or Logan arrives to take you back to your room. Don't leave without one of them," he orders, his voice husky.

I feel my skin tingle under his hand and nod my head at his request. I feel a strange sense of loss as he releases me and hands me my clothing, which I hurriedly pull on as he grabs a spare shirt from the other side of the room.

Eyes tracking him hungrily, taking in every inch of his incredible body, I watch with disappointment as he opens the door and closes it behind him.

I'm left once more with my thoughts and emotions swirling in overdrive. The emptiness of the room is magnified tenfold without his presence, the silence allowing room for doubts to surface. Could I trust the things he told me? My warring emotions make me want to believe him, but I can't help wondering if I *should*. How is it possible to feel such a strong connection to someone I hardly know? I know it won't be long before he seeks me out again, the chemistry between us is too strong for him not to. Excitement and fear threaten to overpower me, and I know I need to gain control of my emotions before I spiral out of control.

Making an effort to push Lucien from my mind, I think about the man who walked in. I'm certain I recognized his voice. I'm almost positive he's the snake shifter who was watching the monitors a few days ago. He gave me the creeps then and I felt the same this time around. Those beady eyes of his give me the willies, and even though he's gone, it's like I can still feel them on me. If Lucien hadn't stood in front of me, blocking me from view, he would have seen all of me, and I don't know if I would have ever been able to scrub the sensation of his eyes on my bare flesh.

Yuck. Fingers of unease trail down my spine. I hope I never have to see him again.

My witch and omega are bouncing with excitement, elated about what happened between me and Lucien. Although I can feel the pleasure radiating from my omega, it is nothing compared to the unbridled desire pouring out of my witch.

Behave yourselves, dammit. Don't get so fucking excited. It might have meant nothing! I scold and feel them deflate at my reprimand.

I need to focus and in order to do so, my feelings for Lucien must be pushed to the side. I cannot believe I stupidly agreed to attend the meeting without discussing it with my sisters. They have a right to decide whether or not to attend a meeting with other Naturals, humans, and the two councils. I need to talk to Pamela as soon as possible, but I'm dreading it. I know they're all going to flip the hell out when I tell them.

My mind wanders back to our last conversation, when Pamela told me that they were going to try to find the woman who broke through our defensive spells. I'd forgotten about her with the stress of finding Lucien and everything that has happened since, but now that I think back, something about her niggles in the recesses of my brain. At the time, we'd all agreed that she felt familiar, but couldn't remember having seen her before.

Whoever she is, she knows who we are and knew how to find and bypass our spells. She was clearly sent to warn us, but by whom? Can we trust her? Should we take her warning seriously or could it be a trap?

Pamela told me she was going to get in touch with an old friend who could trace certain waves which, according to Pamela, are sort of like radio waves. Apparently, the mystery woman would have left them behind even after disappearing. I don't really understand all of it, complex science tends to go over my head.

Ava was the one to contact me with an update after the wave science guy left. She had a hard time getting the words out around her laughter over the way he acted. According to Ava, he was rude, hadn't even bothered to say hello. He merely grunted at them, muttered a few spells, and waved his bloody arms up and down like he was trying to take flight. After doing that for about five minutes, he stopped, walked over to the bag he brought with him, and took out two thin silver metal sticks which he waved around his head while running in circles and screaming in a high-pitched tone. Ava said Pamela was pissed at how the rest of our sisters couldn't seem to hold back their hysterics during his visit, and I wish I'd been there to witness the whole thing.

In the meantime, we're still waiting for the results of whatever test he performed. I don't want to say anything to Pamela, but it sounds like it may have been a waste of everybody's time.

Pulling myself back to the problems at hand, I know I must tell them about all the different factions attending the meeting. I can't avoid it forever and I need to give them a chance to prepare themselves beforehand.

Hearing footsteps, I notice someone walking down the hallway. There's a short pause as they reach the door to the room I'm in before continuing on. That's strange. I shake my head. It can't be Alex, Logan, or Adam because they would have come in. One of them should have been here by now.

Looking down, I notice I've been rubbing at my arm and that there's a slight tingling under my skin. Breathing in deeply, I can still smell Lucien, almost as if he were still in the room, standing next to me even. It's distracting and it's everywhere. Shit. I need to take a shower. I have important things to think about and I can't focus with his intoxicating essence surrounding me.

I know Lucien told me to wait for one of his men, but my nerves can't hold out any longer. I move over to the door and start down the hallway, leaving behind the perplexing emotions he caused.

I make it about halfway down the dim corridor to my room when an uneasy feeling comes over me. The hairs on the back of my neck stand on end, and I could swear I'm being watched as goosebumps break out over my body. I glance over my shoulder with a frown. Nothing. After a quick look around, I shake my head and tell myself to stop being silly, but it doesn't stop me from moving faster towards my room.

Without warning, I feel a sharp pain on my shoulder. Heart racing and eyes wide, I glance down to see long skeletal fingers curled around it. Dark red nails like eagle talons are digging deeply into my flesh, drawing blood and causing me to cry out. I don't need to turn around to know who's behind me. I smell her heavy perfume.

I can't say I'm all that surprised. I'm actually shocked it's taken her this long to approach me. Only a fool would underestimate a creature such as Aria. I'm no fool. As dangerous as the situation is, I decide to give her one chance to walk away, mostly intact, although I know the chance is pretty much nil that this confrontation will end nicely. I allow her to spin me around, letting her believe she has the upper hand.

"Look what I found wandering around all alone. It seems there's nobody around to save you, witch," she says menacingly.

I lift my chin and stare directly into her eyes. "Hello, Aria."

I've never looked into eyes so full of madness that the only thing left is death and destruction. Until now. Looking at her, it's clear to see how much hatred she holds for me; it's written all over her face. A twisted, venomous expression slashes across her features and causes me to take an involuntary step back. Fuck. Fuckity fuck fuck fuck. That was a mistake. With that one step, the desire to hunt me like prey and kill me lights up her eyes.

I freeze, my gaze wary and watchful as I take in her every move, waiting for her body language or facial expressions to indicate an attack. I've known since I met her that given the chance, Aria would do everything in her power to destroy me. Trying to talk her down is a waste of time and oxygen; I have no choice but to fight her. This is what I've trained for my whole life.

Her eyes burn a deep blood-red, and before I can react, her arm raises, fingers curled into her palm, her fist brought back towards her chest. Invisible bands close around my throat, like an icy hand gripping me, tightening until I can't breathe. My eyes widen, bulging from their sockets, as her magical grip attempts to crush my airway. Grasping at the imaginary hand with both of mine, I frantically try to pull away. As my feet start sliding across the floor towards her, my witch rages to the surface. Fuck this! Calling my witch forward, I allow her past the barriers I have in place to keep her under control. Surging up from deep down inside of me, I feel her well of power boiling under my skin.

Giving her room to ascend, I step aside and allow her to take over my body, only staying in control enough to reestablish my hold on her once the job is done. I wait, taking a front row seat for the carnage about to go down.

Within milliseconds, my skin tone changes to the chalky white of my witch, my red hair turning a silver grey. My eyes, now deeply set and shadowed, are silver with a black line rimming the edges and there's a line across my forehead, connecting them. My witch is giddy with excitement.

She wants to play? Well then. Let's give her a taste of just who she's fucking with. I hear my witch clearly, her voice just this side of sane, maniacal laughter ringing in my ears.

I feel my entire body go limp as my witch fully reaches the surface, head and hair draped forward. None of these changes draw attention. My body still hangs listlessly as Aria drags it forward, stopping my witch inches from her face. With a vicious strike, quick as an adder, my witch jabs forward with extended fingers, straight into Aria's trachea. I hear her gasp for breath as she clutches her throat, bending at the waist to catch her breath, causing her to lose the invisible hold she has on my body.

I watch as Aria staggers back from the impact and the electrical blast that follows comes lightning fast, catching her unaware. The pulse my witch sent out travels the room and hits the bitch square on the chest. Aria's body hits the wall with an impact that cracks the stone behind her and causes the floor to tremble slightly. Grinning madly, my witch's eyes narrow as she charges towards her, not giving Aria a chance to retaliate.

"You stupid, silly bitch. How many warnings does my human have to give you?" She spits in a low deep voice, grabbing Aria by the throat and lifting her until her feet dangle several inches above the floor. Bouncing Aria's head off the wall with each word, she continues. "I'm not going to kill you. At least not today." She offers an evil grin. "My human would be quite displeased with me if I did. But heed my warning, for I will only give it once. Go near her again, look at her the wrong way even once, and I will not hold back. I will kill you." She releases the hand wrapped around Aria's neck and lets her crumple to the floor. "Now fucking go. Before I change my mind." I can see the imprint of my witch's hand on Aria's neck as she crawls along the floor before scrambling to her feet and running down the hallway. As she reaches the corner, she pauses, turning head back towards us. A smug look crosses her face before she scurries around the corner.

That was way too easy, my omega says, finally making an appearance. *Aria's up to something. She's supposed to be an extremely powerful demon, but she didn't even put up a fight. And what was that last look? It seemed as though we gave her something she wanted. It just doesn't feel right.*

I agree with my omega and so does my witch. Something is off and I need to figure out what it is. I pull my witch back and feel my appearance revert to normal as I finish walking to my room. I already know Aria will run to Lucien and try telling him her side of things. I somehow doubt she'll tell him the truth of what really happened, but I guess I'll find out sooner or later.

LUCIEN

ONCE AGAIN, I HAD TO LEAVE her. It's really starting to piss me off.

I can still taste her on my tongue and all I want is to get back to her and finish what we started. I just have to take care of this nuisance first.

The shifter will be lucky if I don't kick the shit out of him. I noticed how he stood there with a glint in his eye, his tongue practically hanging out, staring at Scarlett, hoping to get a glimpse of her body, even as I tried to block her from his sight. I felt Scarlett's reaction to him, and I plan to question her about it later. Though he's a shifter, he isn't a powerful one. He is a slimy little fucker, though.

"Damien, what the fuck is going on?" I demand as I stride towards him, the weaselly fuck of a shifter not far behind. Damien is standing with two more of my men, both of whom seem to be covered in blood. With relief, I notice it isn't theirs. As I approach, they both nod in my direction before walking away, leaving me with Damien.

"They found the soul keeper. Dead," Damien informs me as I reach him.

"FUCK!" I roar, hitting the wall with my fist, causing the brick to crumble. This isn't good. There will be no way to get answers about where Scarlett's sister was taken or who he was working for. I wanted him alive and in one piece.

"I'm not finished," Damien states, not showing any reaction to my fist hitting the stone wall, "they found a soul eater in the house with him."

Bloody hell. Soul eaters are far more dangerous than soul keepers. Once one of them gets ahold of you, there's no returning your soul to your body. At least with a soul keeper, there's a chance, albeit an unlikely one. "Shit! Did it touch anyone?" The words are spoken between clenched teeth.

"We got lucky; he didn't get anyone. I put him in the holding room. Lucien, he will not last long," he tells me as we start walking down the long hallway. "We don't think he's the one who killed the soul keeper. It appears someone else gutted him from stem to sternum."

"How long do you think he has?" The soul eater must be questioned. I highly doubt it's a coincidence they were found together.

"A day, maybe two at the most. He's muttered a few incoherent words, but otherwise has been quiet. If you want to question him and find out what the hell he was doing with the soul keeper, you need to do it now."

It's important I get any information I can from him. It's unheard of to find a soul keeper and a soul eater in the same vicinity. It's a well-known fact that they tend to kill each other on sight.

"Why is he in the holding room?"

"We still have that fucker Eddie Marshall in the darkroom," Damien reminds me. Fuck. I'd completely forgotten about that sack of shit.

"Dispose of him," I order. I've gotten what I needed out of him. "Make sure the fucking dirty pedo suffers, but first, line up the cleaning crew and make arrangements to have the soul eater transported to the darkroom. I want it done in the next hour."

Damien immediately pulls out his phone, dials, and starts barking orders.

"Alf," he says into the phone, "get rid of the vermin and get the clean-up team in there." He pauses, listening to what Alf is saying. "Are you fucking kidding me? Yes, now. Alf, you better stop bitching and get the fucking job done because you don't want me to come down there. It needs to be done within the hour. Make sure the fucker suffers," he growls before hanging up and shoving the phone back in his pocket. "Fuck that asshole. I swear, one day I'm going to end up killing the fucker," Damien says with a shake of his bald head, a frown on his face.

"He is a little shit," I agree with a shrug, "but he's a loyal one."

Damien scoffs. "He might be loyal, but he's a fucking asshole."

Catching sight of the shifter still standing behind me, Damien narrows his eyes and curls his top lip as he snarls, "I told you to go back to the compound once you followed out your orders. Why the fuck are you still here?" he demands, taking a step towards him. I turn, glaring at the shifter behind me.

Taking a step backwards, his eyes widen as he stutters, "I-I-I o-overh-heard about the soul keeper and soul eater. I was just making sure everyone was okay," he entire body trembles as he raises his hands in surrender. I doubt he's telling the full truth; he's known for his lies. Sneaky fucker.

Baring his teeth, Damien gets in the shifter's face as his eyes flash red. "Do as you are bloody fucking told before I cut your goddamn head off your shoulders."

I hear him whimper in fright as he shakily nods his head before turning and practically running down the hall away from us.

"I don't trust that shit bag," Damien tells me, narrowing his eyes as he watches the shifter disappear around the corner. "There's something off about him and it pisses me off that I can't put my finger on it."

"He's being watched. Two of my female employees have complained about him and I noticed he makes Scarlett uneasy."

"Good. He's up to no good. I've noticed that most of the females avoid him as much as possible and was planning to question him, but with everything going on I haven't gotten around to it. You could just send him back to Jacob, let him deal with the weirdo," he says, turning to look at me.

"No. If our suspicions are correct, I want to catch him in the act and deal with him. Then you and I can deal with his creepy ass."

Damien nods before a sly smirk creeps over his face. "So… you and the little witch Scarlett," his eyebrows wiggle, "you a thing now?"

"What? Are you a child?" I ask with a sigh, shaking my head at him.

"Maybe," he barks a laugh. "Are you claiming her as yours?" He asks with a raised brow, expression suddenly serious.

"Fuck yeah. She is mine." I admit, hesitantly. I'm not the type to expose my feelings to anyone, particularly not my men. It can be used against me and be viewed as a sign of weakness. But this is Damien and I trust him more than just about anyone else.

"Good, it's about damn time. You've been moping around for fucking days. I was starting to get sick of it," Damien replies, leaning back against the wall behind him, staring at me. "What are you going to do about Aria? To say she's going to be unhappy is one hell of an understatement. You know she will do everything in her power to keep you away from Scarlett."

A ball of frustration fills my stomach. She's becoming more and more unstable. Aria has become a problem, even before Scarlett. I will have to find some way to deal with her soon. If I don't, there's no telling what kind of damage she will inflict.

"It doesn't matter if I claim Scarlett as mine or not. Everyone better fucking know she's off-limits, even if my mark isn't on her. I am still working on a solution to keep Aria away from her. She has shown far too much interest in the witch. And I don't know why she started showing up unexpectedly. How the hell did she even find out I had a witch staying here? She must have an informant placed among my men.

Someone I believe to be loyal is passing her intel. It's the only explanation. She's up to something and it's making me uneasy not knowing what her endgame is," I confess.

"Shit, Lucien. How long have you known she was up to something?" Damien mutters, a disconcerted expression on his face. "Why didn't you bloody tell me? While I don't know Scarlett well, I can tell she's not the type of woman who would be okay with you seeing Aria at the same time as her. What woman in her right mind would be?"

"I've suspected something was going on with Aria for a while, but I didn't have any solid proof. Plus, I didn't want to believe the woman I've kept close all these years could be a traitor, didn't want to admit that someone I trusted would betray me."

"And now?" He asks.

"Like I just told you, Scarlett is mine. I will do everything in my power to protect her. I might have to do things that will leave a bitter taste in my mouth to make it happen, but I won't hesitate to do them. I will not let anyone harm her. Aria isn't mine anymore, she hasn't been for years." I tell him. "She's more than just a little twisted. Something is wrong with her, and she has become volatile, to the point she may need to be eliminated." I couldn't fucking lie to myself or to him any longer. It's past time I tell him the truth; I will likely need his help before all is said and done. "If Scarlett sees me with Aria, she's going to have to accept that I'm doing it for her. I need to make sure Scarlett isn't in danger of Aria coming after her while I figure out what the hell she's up to."

"Thank fuck. I've kept my mouth shut for the most part about Aria, just like everyone else has, but you've always known how I felt about her. It's not like it was a secret. But do you know why I never spoke up more about it? I'm going to be real with you. We may be right bastards and be downright unscrupulous at times, she has been everything to you for a really long time. Lucien, you've done everything she demanded. But can you say the same about her? The thing is, she's a sick twisted cunt and she's always been batshit crazy. You just had your head too far up your ass to see it. It wouldn't have done me a bit of good to speak up, because you weren't ready to see it. You've finally woken up and can see her for the monster she is, what everyone else has always seen." This is the first time he's been totally honest about his feelings on the subject. I'm not surprised to hear it, nor am I surprised to find out the rest of my people share his views.

He continues, "But Lucien? Don't be shocked if Scarlett doesn't accept your reasoning." He gives me a knowing look and I turn away. I really don't like what he's saying, and the worst part is… I know he's right. Shit. I really hate that.

The sound of his phone ringing breaks the silence hanging over us after his last revelation. He pulls it out and answers. "Yeah?"

"Okay, we're on our way. Make sure the fucker is secure. We don't need any bloody surprises," he tells them before hanging up.

He turns to me and says, "The soul eater has been transferred to the dark room."

"Let's go question the fucker then," I growl, making my way to the door with him right behind me.

In the next forty-eight hours, I'm going to be overrun by witches, Naturals, and humans. What could possibly go wrong? Fuck me. Shit is about to hit the fan.

CHAPTER EIGHTEEN

LUCIEN

DARK ROOM

THE SOUL EATER SITS IN THE chair placed in the center of the room, arms and legs bound. His pale face shows no sign of emotion, his eyes empty and soulless. I've been up close and personal with many a soul eater, but this one appears different. I'm standing with my men, taking in his appearance. He's completely bald except for the small brown horns on either side of his head. His pale pink eyes stand out against his pasty flesh, and his face is reminiscent of a Billy goat.

I feel my demon rise until he's close enough to the surface that my appearance starts to shift. The bones of his skeleton push up against my skin and two large blood-red horns curl out of the sides of my head; they look like spirals breaking out from my skull. My nose sharpens, becoming more pointed, my face elongating. Spikes sprout from my shoulders, the edges sharp enough to slice through skin like butter. My teeth become jagged and my skin changes to a reddish-brown hue, completing the shift. This is the demon who lives inside of me, and he is the reason most think twice before crossing Lucien Sinclair. Because of the pain he's capable of inflicting, not to mention his hair trigger temper, I tend to keep him on a short leash. With everything that's happening, I need answers and I need them now. I have no choice but to cut the leash.

Confronting a soul keeper is one thing but confronting a soul eater is another thing entirely. I need the extra strength my demon affords me.

If I stood before the soul eater without him, I would be putting myself at risk.

The men standing closest to me need to be on guard. My demon only trusts people who have shown unwavering loyalty to me.

"Damien, question him." My voice is a combination of my own and my demon's, making it lower in tone and rougher. It practically echoes through the room.

The soul eater doesn't react, sitting still as a statue as Damien walks forward until he's only a few feet in front of the chair. He snaps his fingers in the soul eater's face, trying to get his attention.

"Did you kill the soul keeper?" He growls, his expression dark. The soul eater remains expressionless and doesn't respond.

Damien snarls. "Listen, you bloody bastard. Either you answer, or we're all going to take turns taking you apart bit by bit," he threatens. "Answer the fucking questions. There was a woman who disappeared from The Fallen Angel. Did you take her?"

If I hadn't been watching closely, I might have missed it when the soul eater's jaw twitched slightly with recognition. He can hear everything Damien is saying, and he knows exactly what Damien is talking about. He's fucking with us.

I let out a vicious roar. "MOVE!"

My men part like the Red Sea for Moses and I walk between then as they try not to touch me, their backs against the walls. I taste the soul eater's fear when he whimpers, shock radiating through his body as he recognizes the demon standing before him. Muttering under his breath, he shakes his head from side to side, struggling against the restraints.

"Get away from me," he says under his breath as my eyes lock onto his and I see them fill with horror.

A mere touch of my hand would cause him total agony and I would relish the sound of his screams echoing throughout the building. But I need to probe deeper. My demon is practically bouncing with glee at the torment we're about to inflict.

As a joint entity, my demon and I enter the mind of the soul eater. A feeling of bliss courses through my veins as we enter his mind, the soul eater splintering from within. We crave his misery, his pain, and as the screams fill the air around us, we relish them. I sense the hunger emanating from my men as I twist and dig my way deeper. I need to find out who he's been in contact with, need the information he's trying to withhold from me. But no matter how hard I try to push; I can't seem to get past a barrier keeping me from going deeper. I give more control over to my demon, letting him explore. He obliterates the barrier and pushes forward, flicking away one blockade after another. Finally, I see a glimmer of what I'm looking for, just out of reach.

Just as my demon reaches for it, blood begins trickling from the soul eater's eyes and nose, his skin turning blotchy and red. I watch in morbid fascination as his hands clench the arms of the chair, his nails digging deep into the wood and his mouth opening in a silent scream. It feels too easy, like his mind is just giving up and letting us in.

My thoughts stutter as what I sensed earlier flickers and shimmers, growing into a solid black mass with no physical features. Though its form appears human, looks can be deceiving. It wants me to know it's there. Just before I feel the soul eater's mind begin to disintegrate, I hear a hint of echoing laughter, as though the mass is mocking me. I stay where I am, unable to stop what's happening. I feel his brain rupture as I watch the light fade from the soul eater's eyes, just before his head expands, exploding with a loud pop. Brain matter flies everywhere, saturating everything and everyone in the room. I hear my men's ravenous growls from behind me and don't have to turn around to know what's happening. They're feeding.

I continue to study the soul eater's body. It looks like a bomb went off inside of him, the whole left side of his skull is gone. Whatever was in his head sensed my demon's probing and had, without a doubt, killed the soul eater. I have a much bigger problem on my hands than I could have imagined.

We are in deep shit.

Everyone is in danger, Naturals and humans alike. I must inform the leaders of the other territories of this outcome.

A rage-filled roar bursts out of my chest as I feel my anger meld with my demon's. My body is sharking with rage, my hands clenched, as I try to beat back the desire to destroy everything and everyone around me.

I vaguely hear the words coming from my men.

"Fucking hell."

"Bloody hell, move back."

"What the fuck just happened?"

Damien's words clear some of the fog. "You should probably all get out of here."

I hear muttered voices and shuffling feet before the door opens and shuts with a click.

My eyes are glazed over and I'm barely managing to keep a hold on my demon. I need to stop him before he hurts my men. If I don't, he will leave their dead bodies scattered throughout the building.

I let my thoughts drift to the woman I made promises to such a short time ago and the rage begins to recede. I will have to reveal my demon to her at some point, but I don't think she could handle me like this. I hope she never sees this side of me, the beast that would gleefully eviscerate the men and women who have come to rely on him, the people who have proven their loyalty.

I feel my demon settling down, my skin and features slowly going back to normal. I turn to Damien and find him on his phone, ordering the cleaning crew to get their asses down here and clean up the mess. He meets my gaze and gives me a nod, watching as I finish changing from the monster rooted inside of me to the man I allow the world to see. No emotion registers on his face. Why would it? His own demon doesn't differ much from mine.

I look around the dark room to find that most of my men have left. I can't say I blame them. Seeing my demon in full force would scare the shit out of just about anyone, even other demons. Hell, especially other demons. The demons amongst my men would know who my demon is and are smart enough to get as far the fuck away from me as possible when I lose control like that. Only a few of my men remain, and they are fools. I do not intend for them to witness what will happen next. I desperately need more intel on the soul eater and who he was in contact with.

As I take note of who stayed behind, one catches my eye. Tall, and so skinny he looks emaciated, with greasy black hair reaching his shoulders, I see a gleam in his pale blue eyes. His expression is one of sick delight and I know he's getting his rocks off on the carnage. Fucking Jack. I've had trouble with him before. He is one twisted fucker and Damien has had to warn him more than once, beating the shit out of him the last time. So far, he seems to be toeing the line, but the look on his face sickens me. Even a twisted bastard like myself has some standards.

"Jack. You will wait for the cleaning crew to arrive. Make sure this shit is gone by the time I get back. I don't want a single fucking trace left behind."

"Okay, boss," Jack replies, a delighted grin on his face as he rocks back and forth on the balls of his feet.

Before I walk out of the room, I turn to the others, dismissing some of them. Once they're gone, I address the rest. "I want intel on the fucker whose head just exploded. Get it for me. Now!" I feel my demon roar inside of me as they scurry from the room, desperate to do my bidding.

A deep growl leaves my mouth. I need to rip something apart. I didn't get the satisfaction or the answers I so desperately needed, and as Damien and I walk down the hallway, I pause. Letting out an almighty roar, I punch the stone wall beside me. I hit it repeatedly, watching as my hands leaves a dent; the more I hit, the larger it gets.

Damien just stands there, eyebrow raised and a smirk on his lips, as he watches me obliterate the wall. Chunks of stone crumble and fall off, leaving a pile of rubble at our feet. Whatever I felt inside the soul keeper's mind wanted me to see them. I can't catch a break. Things keep flying at me from every direction.

I still need to find out who is snitching for Aria. I have an idea of who it is, but I won't act until I have proof. I want them to hang themselves and given enough rope, they will. I put a certain level of trust in all my people, and they know if they ever betray me, I will handle it, and the likelihood of them walking away in one piece is slim.

"Fuck, Lucien. If you don't get control of yourself, the fucking wall is going to come down around us," Damien warns. Fuck me, he's right. I hit the wall one more time, causing it to splinter. "What did you see inside that fucker's head?"

Taking a deep breath, I close my eyes and take a few moments to calm myself before opening them. I look down and frown. Blood is trickling from wounds on my hands I hadn't even felt. I wait as the open wounds knit back together.

I pull my jacket sleeves down and brush the dust from my suit. "There was something or someone on the edge of his mind. Not only could I sense it, I saw it." I meet his gaze, running both hands through my hair. "Whatever it was, it had some kind of power over the soul eater. The worst part, it was just a fucking shadow."

"Shit," Damien mutters under his breath, scrubbing a hand over his face. I can almost hear the wheels turning in his head.

"Shit is fucking right," I agree as we walk down the hallway. "We need more fucking intel. Like yesterday. We're in the dark here, and if we aren't careful, we're going to end up being blindsided by something we can't possibly prepare for."

Damien turns to me. "When I was on the phone, they told me the men you sent into Fae territory are back and that the Fae accepted the invitation. Apparently, the men were unharmed." He gives me a knowing look. To hear that the Fae not only accepted the invitation but allowed my men to leave without injury is a surprise, to say the least. "Nathan said he will be sending his second-in-command to the meeting in his place."

In all the years I've known him, Nathan has never declined an invitation to meet with a leader. Something is going on and I want answers. His second had better be prepared for my questions. Nathan and I have a fragile alliance, and though we have called on one another for help in the past and we each have people from the other's territory living among us, the treaty is tenuous still.

With a frown, Damien asks, "Have you heard from Chamuel?"

"No, I haven't," I reply, wondering where he's going with the change of subject.

"Don't you think that's…"

Interrupting him, I say, "So unlike him?" I knew exactly what he was going to say, and I don't want to hear it. The same thought has gone through my head a million times, and I don't want to hear Damien confirm my suspicions. "I can't fucking get ahold of him. He hasn't answered a single one of my calls or texts. And no, I don't have a bloody clue where the hell he is. I've already considered the possibility of him being taken. Does that answer your bloody question?"

From the expression on Damien's face, my words appear to have shocked him. "Fuck, Lucien! When was the last time you spoke to him?"

"About a week after he left," I answer, thinking back to what my brother said during our last phone conversation. "He told me he was going dark and if I needed to get a hold of him for any reason, to call or text as usual."

"And you've called and texted and he hasn't responded?" He asks, a look of disbelief on his face. "Nothing at all?"

"For fuck's sake, Damien. That's what I just said, isn't it? You think if I'd gotten a response, I'd be so fucking worried?" I shout. "Chamuel can look after himself, though. Him not answering didn't worry me at first, but the more time that passes and the more I try to reach out without receiving a response…"

"Shit, Lucien! Why the hell didn't you tell me it was this serious? You have to start telling me shit," he exclaims, his voice rising in anger. "We have enough shit going on around us without you keeping things from me. How the hell am I supposed to help you, how am I going to be an effective second if you don't bloody tell me anything?!" He takes a deep breath, trying to calm down. "Look, I have this contact. He's high in the heavens and owes me big time. I'll reach out and see if they've heard anything."

I nod and show my appreciation by squeezing his shoulder. I don't give a fuck who his contact is if they can find out where Chamuel is. If I could get some idea of where he is or where he's been, I can trace my brother from there.

There is one place Chamuel might have gone, but I hope I'm wrong because there would only be one reason for him to go there. Damien's right, though. I should have told him; I have to stop withholding information from him.

The world as we know it is changing. I need all the help I can get.

CHAPTER NINETEEN

ARIA

I'VE KNOWN THERE WAS SOMETHING off about her since the moment I laid eyes on her. Yes, she admitted to being a witch, but to have the ability to change like that, right in front of my very eyes... That speaks to powers the likes of which our world hasn't seen for generations, and I hadn't been prepared for it at all.

Letting me see her power was sheer stupidity on her part. Now I know what I'm facing. She isn't a mere half-witch; she is something more. I wonder if she has another being inside of her, something besides her witch and her human. It could even be a demon, not unlike my own. I cannot attack her again, I know that. Not yet anyway. I will have to be more cunning than I was today. I will need to come up with a plan and make sure everything is in place before going after her again.

I remember she mentioned her family. Are they all like her? What else is this bitch hiding from Lucien, from me? Question after question whirl inside my head. I must have my little pet do some snooping for me. I will find the answers, of that I have no doubt.

I can't believe how stupid she was. She fell right into my hands. How delightful! I'm unable to stop the laughter that bursts from my mouth as tears of joy stream down my cheeks. It may have been unwise to attack her as I had, but when I saw her wandering alone, it had been far too tempting to resist. At first my intention had been only to scare her, to warn the witch away from Lucien, but that had gone out the window the second the scent lingering on her skin hit my nose. I recognized it right away; the smell of Lucien's cologne is unique and smelling it on her sent me into a blind rage.

I shouldn't have been caught off guard, shouldn't have been so surprised. I'd known from the way I've caught him looking at her that he's taken an unhealthy interest in the bitch. I can tell from the way he's been putting me off that he doesn't want to share her. He wants to keep all that yumminess to himself.

Well, if he thinks he can get rid of me so easily, he has another thing coming. I will not allow him to replace me with that stupid witch. I will make him watch as I kill the little cunt right in front of him. Does he think I will just step aside while he has his fun without me? That bastard! How can he do this to me? I am his everything, not her!

Lucien has *always* belonged to me, and it is past time I reminded him of that!

I turn on my stool and face the mirror, raising my chin and turning my head, first one way, then the other. I can clearly see the bruises marking the skin all over my neck. I don't bother to hold in a satisfied laugh. Oh goodie! This is even better than I could have hoped.

I feel something drop from my hand and look down. I realize I must have grabbed my knife in my fit of rage and sliced the palm of my hand wide open, causing blood to drip from the wound. I watch, fascinated, as the blood spills onto my pale blue dress. As the blood continues to gush, I lift my hand to my mouth and lick it away with my tongue. I look at myself in the mirror as the blood drips from my mouth and runs down my chin. Running my tongue around my mouth, I lick it away. I look down and see the edges of the cut knit together.

I look into the mirror once more and examine the injuries the witch inflicted on me. To my dismay, they don't look as severe as they had only moments before.

I run my fingertips over my bruised neck. Hmmm. I will have to do something about this. The marks she left behind won't be enough, not for what I have planned. She cannot get away with trying to take Lucien away from me and he needs to be punished for wanting her, for crossing me this way.

LUCIEN

"Lucien?" The voice speaking my name is laden with emotion, a tremor in the tone. Bloody fucking hell. What is Aria doing back here?

I don't have time for her melodrama right now. With a frown, I turn my head. She's standing in front of the door, her chin quivering. When she sees me looking, her face crumbles and a lone tear slips from the corner of one eye. I take in her appearance. It looks like someone beat the shit out of her; her face is covered in bruises.

I close the distance between us until I'm only a few inches away from her. With clenched teeth, I demand, "What the hell happened to you?"

"I'm sorry, Lucien," Aria sobs, her entire body trembling as she throws herself against my chest. "I-I-I don't understand why she attacked me. I know we got off on the on the wrong foot, but I th-thought I could make amends by going to s-see her."

I cup her chin in my hand and tilt her face up so I can examine it. I see an outline from where someone's fingers have pressed into her slender neck, a bruise is forming around one of her eyes where someone hit her, and her lip is split and bleeding.

"Shhhh. Everything is going to be alright, Aria." I soothe, running my hand down her slim back. "You need to tell me who hurt you." Shit. Whoever hit her gave her a real beating. There is no way I can just let this go.

"It was that witch. Scarlett. I'm sorry, Lucien," she sobs against my chest. Fuck, fuck, fuck. What the hell was Scarlett thinking? It doesn't make any sense, not after she warned me to keep Aria away from her and her family.

I nudge Aria away gently and trail my fingertip down her temple, moving a few stray tendrils of her hair away from her cheek as I meet her gaze. "One minute…" She stops and gulps, closing her eyes before continuing. "One minute she looked as she always does. The next… Lucien, her whole appearance changed. From her hair to her face, everything. It was like a completely different person stood in front of me!" She turns her face away as tears fill her eyes and spill down her cheeks.

I dip my head down and whisper into her ear. "What happened after she changed?"

Her body trembles. "She grabbed me by the neck and punched me repeatedly. She wouldn't stop. I tried to fight back but she was too strong. Lucien, I didn't think she was ever going to stop."

I try to keep my voice calm. "What happened then?" My knuckle caresses her cheek.

Aria's hand grips my forearm as she speaks. "After she stopped punching me, she grabbed me around the neck again. She must be more powerful than we thought, Lucien. She chucked me across the hallway as though I were light as a feather. I flew through the air and only came to a stop when I smashed into the wall behind me. Then she grabbed me by the hair and started slamming my head against the wall, screaming at me the whole time." Her voice breaks at the end, and she starts sobbing.

She presses her head into my shoulder, and I stroke her hair. "What did she say?" I ask.

She lifts her head and looks into my eyes. "She told me I needed to leave you alone. She said you belong to her and if I don't stay away from you, she will end me."

My demon doesn't believe a word coming from her mouth. I push him down and he growls at me, "You're not falling for this crap, are you?" I ignore him, knowing what I say next is going to piss him off all the more.

"Promise me, my love, that you won't go near her again," I coax with a frown. "I will deal with her."

Aria tilts her head back and looks at me with a tremulous smile. Whatever she reads on my face must convince her because she says, "I promise. But you must promise me that you'll be careful. You can't be alone with her. She's dangerous." Her last words are barely a whisper. She lays her head on my shoulder, wrapping her arms around my back.

To find out the truth of what really happened, I would promise anything.

"I promise," I assure her, taking her face in my hand and gently brushing my thumb across the soft skin of her cheek. I take her lips with mine, kissing her tenderly.

I don't notice the figure standing in the doorway, shock and horror written across her face. I don't see the tears running down her face as she witnesses me kissing Aria. Nor do I see as she turns and runs back the way she came, long red hair flowing behind her.

CHAPTER TWENTY

SCARLETT

MY MIND IS WHIRLING WITH CONFUSION and hurt. All the promises Lucien made were nothing but lies. Tears surge up unexpectedly and spill down my cheeks. With the back of my hand, I swipe them away.

If I close my eyes, I know I will see Lucien holding Aria in his arms as he kisses her passionately. I feel an overwhelming urge to hurt him the same way he's hurt me, but I will not let him break me.

I grab my laptop and sit on the bed, forcing myself to focus on work. Between the confrontation with Aria and what I saw between her and Lucien, I'm on edge. Letting my witch come to the surface was impulsive and foolish. In doing so, I revealed just how powerful I am, but the moment I saw the look in her eyes, I knew she was there to hurt me, to kill me if she could.

As if that situation weren't bad enough, the memory of Aria in Lucien's arms is haunting me. I feel hurt, sick to my stomach; confused. How could Lucien tell me he cares about me, that I matter to him, and then turn around and be with her like that? I wonder if he knows I saw them together. I doubt it. He looked quite engrossed in what he was doing. If he thinks I'm willing to just be one of many, he has a surprise coming. I do not share. And if he thinks I'm going to gullibly swallow his lies… I'm nobody's fool! He told me he was going to deal with Aria. I guess we just had different ideas of what that would look like.

After seeing them together, it was apparent they are still very much intimate with one another. The images rushing through my mind are giving me a headache. I feel like such an idiot for believing he cared about me.

I feel a presence in the room and look up to see Lucien standing in front of the bedroom door, leaning against the wall. I hadn't heard him knock; I must have been too distracted. Either that or he just walked in as though he had every right to do so. His muscular arms are crossed over his thick chest, his eyes locked on my face. Our eyes meet and time seems to stop for a moment.

He's so beautiful it makes me ache inside. I try to keep my face blank, devoid of any emotion. I remain still and stare at him, waiting for him to say something.

A muscle in his jaw flexes. Oh shit. I swallow a lump in my throat and attempt to appear confident. I don't want him to see the effect he has on me. Darkness rolls off him in waves; he is the dark to my light. His intense stare feels like an inferno scorching across my skin, setting my body on fire. I know that if I don't get out of this room, get as far away from him as possible, he will be inside of me before I can even think to protest.

I watch with wide eyes as he pushes himself away from the wall, his long legs eating up the distance between us. He wraps his hand around my upper arm, his grip firm but gentle, and pulls me up until I'm standing in front of him. My hand flies to his chest, stopping him from pulling me closer.

"Don't," I whisper, my eyes closing briefly as I try to ward off the pleasurable sensation of standing so near to him. I open my eyes and find his attention locked on my lips. For just a second, I forget what I witnessed, forget how hurt and angry I am.

He starts to close the distance between our lips and my fury rushes in, more potent than ever. I yank myself out of his arms. "How many women have you been with since you told me I was yours? Other than Aria, of course!" I grind the words out between clenched teeth.

Curses fall from his mouth as his eyes flash red, blazing a fiery red. He growls. "Who told you?"

My own eyes burning, I glare at him, my temper rising further. "No.

One. Told. Me." My words are quiet but deadly. I step further away from him. I need to not be so close to him or I may lose touch with why I'm so angry and let him take me anyway. "I saw you."

"You saw me?" He replies sharply, his expression clouded. "When?"

Rage threatens to choke me. "Does it matter!? You're nothing but a liar. I saw you kissing her. Now answer my question!" I shout, and his jaw flexes at my demand.

"You think you can question me?" His curt voice lashes out at me, his body vibrating as he takes a threatening step in my direction. "You think you can demand answers when you keep your own secrets?"

"Secrets!? What secrets are you talking about?" I ask, spreading my arms wide. I may not have been totally honest with him, but it's only been to protect myself, to protect the people I care about. I haven't lied to him; not like he's lied to me. And it isn't like he's proven that he can be trusted. Every time I turn around, it seems like he's saying one thing and doing another. Why would I give someone information that could spell the end of me, the end of my family, when I can't trust them?

"Tell me, Scarlett, why Aria is black and blue, why she looks like someone beat the shit out of her. She said you attacked her, that she was trying to smooth things over with you and you lashed out for no reason." His tone his cold, his teeth clenched so tightly together, I'm certain they will crack.

A peal of manic laughter escapes me, the sound echoing around the room. Oh, Aria is good. She's really pulled the blinder over his eyes, hasn't she?

Black eyes flash red and I watch Lucien try to rein in his temper, his hands clenched in fists. Losing the battle, he shouts, "You think this is fucking funny? You changed in front of her and assaulted her!"

Color rushes to my cheeks. "Funny? Of course, I don't think this is funny!" I shout back, marching towards him and only stopping when we are toe to toe. Our eyes lock, his blazing into my own, his dark eyebrows merging into a savage line. "You should get your facts straight, Demon." I growl.

Can't he see what she's doing? She thought she could best me, could scare me, and ended up losing the fight. When she realized I wouldn't be taken down so easily, she decided to run to him, try to make him get rid of me.

Stabbing him in the chest with my finger, I shout, "I warned you to keep her away from me. She came after me, attacked me, and I defended myself, exactly as I said I would!"

"Stop. Fucking. Poking. Me." he says menacingly, grabbing my hand and forcing it down to my side.

"Oh, am I hurting you? The big, bad, dangerous demon." I scoff, yanking my hands from his. I step back. I don't want his hands on me.

Scowling, he looks me up and down. "You don't have a single mark on you."

I yank down the neck of my jumper, revealing the deeply embedded scratches around my throat. "What the fuck are these then? You think I did this to myself?" I demand.

My body tenses when he lifts his hand, extending it towards my neck as though to touch me. "You're telling me Aria did this? That she attacked you first?" He asks with a frown, examining the marks. I back away further. I don't want him touching me, not if he doesn't believe me. I can tell by his expression he doesn't like it when I move away from him.

Letting go of the neck of my sweater, I sigh. "I did not seek her out. She came at me. I told you I would defend myself, and I did."

"She said you changed…" he begins, trailing off as his eyes search my face for a reaction.

I take a deep steadying breath. I'm not surprised she told him about my witch. How can I get him to understand? I can already picture his reaction and I know he isn't going to like what I'm about to say.

Rubbing my forehead, I try to come up with the easiest way to explain. "You know I'm part human and part witch. The witch is inside of me. I told you that when my witch senses I'm in danger, she comes forward. When that happens, when she comes out, she reveals herself fully. I can either call her forward or, if she senses I'm too injured to call her, she can come forward of her own accord."

Lifting my chin, I lock eyes with him. I watch his as they flash red and back to black. I study him intently, his face seeming to flicker, as though it's changing in appearance, and I know I'm witnessing his demon. I stand my ground, trying my hardest not to panic. I know there's no point in trying to run; there's no way I could outrun him.

"So, you didn't attack her?" He asks through clenched teeth.

Hasn't he been listening?! Bloody hell. "I didn't say that. How many times do I need to repeat myself? She approached me, she attacked me. I defended myself. My witch had no choice but to come out and protect me. If I'm in danger or if we see someone worth saving in danger, she comes out and deals with the situation."

I feel my witch bristling at his questions. She wants me to release her so she can answer for herself, but that would only make things worse. I push back against her, telling her to stay put.

Feeling miserable, I close my eyes. I can't bear to look at him. "If you believe Aria, that is your choice, but I'm telling you the true account of what happened. I won't keep repeating myself," I tell him, defeat ringing in my voice.

"I believe you." My eyes fly open in shock. Lucien is standing in front of me, an expression of satisfaction painted across his face. "It is in my nature to question everyone around me. Even those I trust. It's how I've managed to successfully rule my territory for so long. But I believe you. I was skeptical when she came to me, and I only kissed her to make her think I believed her so she wouldn't come after you again. It was to buy me time to figure out how to handle things."

I don't believe my ears. Can I trust what he's saying, that he believes me over Aria? She's been in his life for so long. I want to believe what he's saying is true, but I've seen them together. I've witnessed the affection he has for her with my own two eyes, and if that was all a ruse, how can I trust that the emotion he's showing me now is genuine?

My doubts must show because he steps closer to me and gently cradles my face in his rough hands. His touch is tender, yet still commanding. His fingertips run softly down my skin, sliding down to the top of my jumper. He slowly pulls it down, revealing the marks on my neck. I feel the tips of his fingers caress over the deep red scratches.

I hadn't realized how badly she marked me until I got back to my room and examined the area. Her hand hadn't actually touched me, so I didn't expect to find anything. I was wrong though, and the scratches are still sore. They're deep and raw, and while my omega is trying her best to heal them from within, she's having trouble doing so, for reasons unknown to both of us.

"I'm sorry," Lucien whispers. I can feel the rage flowing out of him, even as he trails his knuckles over my cheek with care. The look on his face is unlike any I've seen on him before, almost as though he thinks I'm the most precious thing he's ever seen. His lips touch my neck and shivers of desire race through me as he places soft butterfly kisses there. With a sigh, my eyes flutter shut. "Lucien." His name is a plea on my lips.

"I will deal with this. Aria will not touch you again. I promise." His voice is quiet, and I can tell most of his rage is directed at himself, that he's taking responsibility for her actions.

"I can protect myself," I protest, opening my eyes and meeting his gaze. "I can take care of myself. But that isn't the problem, Lucien. What I witnessed, between the two of you… I can't get it out of my head. It's embedded deeply in my mind, and I keep seeing it over and over again."

I hear the sigh that falls from his mouth. His lips brush against my brow. "Whatever you think you saw…"

I scoff! Does he really take me for a fool?! "Really!?" I interrupt him. "So, you putting your tongue down her throat meant nothing? There was no other way to handle the situation? Don't take me for a bloody idiot, Lucien." I tear myself from his arms and walk away, wanting to be alone with my thoughts.

"I don't think you're a fool, Scarlett," he says, walking towards me with fire burning in his eyes. "I will do everything in my power to protect you. Even if that means hurting you in order to keep you safe."

I shake my head. "You being with her doesn't just hurt me, Lucien. It is killing the feelings I have for you. If you keep things up with her, no matter the reason why, those feelings will die a slow death. If you give yourself to another, there cannot be an us," I explain, moving away from him again. I need to get my head on straight and standing so close to him is messing with my ability to reason. I sit on the edge of the bed and look at the floor. Does he really think I can accept him being with Aria, or anyone else, and still be with him? "Tell me Lucien, what the hell did I witness exactly?"

"I handled her the only way I know how. I'm sorry, Scarlett. I will make it up to you somehow." His apology surprises me. Lucien Sinclair is not the type of man to apologize.

His intense stare burns into me, lighting my body on fire. Even though he's apologized, I feel I should be fighting the lust building inside of me. He has a lover, for heaven's sake. I hate how weak he makes me.

I watch with bated breath as he stalks towards me. With powerful strides, he reaches me quickly and before I know it, he's pulling me to my feet and lifting me into his arms. My traitorous body leaves me no choice but to wrap my legs tightly around his waist as his hands firmly grip my ass.

His lips crash down on mine in a punishing kiss before he tosses me onto the bed, my hair fanning across the mattress like a flame. His body presses down on mine, his heat engulfing me. Using his knee, he spreads my thighs apart, his fingertips skimming the flesh on my stomach. Goosebumps erupt all over my body. I know I should be fighting him, shouldn't be letting him touch me, but logic has left me. All I have left is the pleasure he makes me feel, pleasure unlike anything I've known before.

A jolt of excitement hits me as he looks down at me. Hunger, matching my own, burns in his eyes. They flash from black to red and back again; I know what that flash means. His demon is right under the surface. I bite down on my bottom lip, loving the intensity in his gaze.

My breathing becomes labored as he continues to watch me, more so when he leans in and presses his lips down on mine. His mouth is rough and my lips tingle, electricity popping through the air like a lightning storm as his tongue enters my mouth. His hips roll against me, his hardness pressing against my pussy. I gasp into his mouth and his lips leave mine, allowing me to suck in some much-needed air as his mouth assaults my neck. His teeth are gentle, nipping along the tender skin before he sucks hard, using enough force to leave a mark. I grip his hair, wanting more. Needing more.

Pulling my hands away from his head, Lucien stands, grabbing my hips and pulling me down the bed until my legs are dangling off the edge. He grabs my top and yanks it up over my head.

"Don't hide from me," he growls, as I start to cover my breasts with my hands. He grabs my wrists and pins them down on the bed, his hungry gaze roving over my body. Letting go of my arms, he places his hands on my knees, sliding them up the inside of my thighs. My breathing quickens with his slow progress. His fingers reach the top of my jeans, and he unbuttons them before slowly pulling down the zipper. He roughly grabs the waistband and yanks them down my legs, getting them off in one pull and leaving me completely bare.

Lucien stands back and stares at me for several minutes, my body spread over the bed. "You're fucking gorgeous," his voice deepens sending a shiver down my spine. "I'm going to have so much fun with you." He gives me a wicked grin before his teeth clamp down on my earlobe, pulling it into his mouth and sucking hard. My eyes close in sheer delight and I let out a small whimper. My insides flutter with excitement when he backs off the bed and turns around, looking for something.

A devious expression appears on his face as he grabs my robe from a nearby chair and pulls out the belt.

What the hell does he think he's going to do with that? My omega asks. I'm asking myself the same question.

"What is that for?" I ask in a whisper.

"I'm not going to hurt you, I promise. If you ask me to stop, I will." Lucien assures me. "Now slide up the bed," he demands with a deep growl.

I swallow, watching as his eyes turn red. I sense that the person standing before me is no longer Lucien Sinclair, but the demon hidden inside of him. He has something in mind, and I think I know what he's planning. The question I keep asking myself is, should I be worried? My body, unable to resist the promise of pleasure in Lucien's eyes, acts of its own accord, moving up the bed as he commanded.

He smiles in satisfaction. "Put your hands together above your head, near the headboard."

I glance behind me at the headboard then at the belt in his hands and swallow hard.

"Now, Scarlett," he orders in his deep voice.

I take a deep breath. Oh, shit. I can't believe what I'm about to do, but want what he can give me, even if it scares me. It might be crazy to trust the man in front of me, but I somehow know he won't hurt me. Not like that.

Biting my lip, I place my hands above my head and lock my fingers together. He kneels on the bed, sliding his body over mine, and I gasp as his massive form caresses my bare flesh and he looks down at me with hunger. The smell of his aftershave fills my senses as his hands slide up my arms and fix the belt around my wrists, tying them to the headboard.

He moves back down my body, and I swallow hard at the look in his eyes as he gazes hungrily at the sight of my body spread out before him, his for the taking. I long to touch him.

"Don't move unless I tell you to." He stands at the edge of the bed, staring at me with red eyes. He grabs my legs, spreading them wide, and looks down at my pussy like a man starved for a meal. My body tenses. I'm not shy about being naked, but I am feeling nervous. It is an uncomfortable yet pleasant sensation to be laid bare for him, helpless with my hands bound above me.

"So fucking perfect," he growls, licking his bottom lip as he kneels and lowers his head between my legs. He wastes no time, sticking his tongue out and sliding it over my flesh. It flicks against my clit, and I jolt, my hands banging against the headboard. I clench my eyes shut at the sudden pleasure racing through my pussy and up over my entire body. Waves of intense desire crash over me and I moan, thrashing my head from side to side.

"Oh, God," I shout, and he chuckles against my core before pulling away, leaving me wanting and hungry for his touch.

He looks down at me as he gets to his feet. "You're so responsive," he marvels, softly stroking over my wetness with his fingertips.

I gasp as he moves closer and shifts his body so he's once again between my thighs. He brings his hand up and I see he's gripping something. It looks like a can of whipped cream. Where the hell did that come from!?

He licks his lips as I watch him and chuckles at my confused expression. The can comes up and I gasp as he squirts a long line of the whipped cream along my inner thigh. The sting of cold renders my senses useless for a moment, before the contrast of his hot mouth sends me into overdrive. My clit tingles from the pleasurable sensations coursing through my body.

He sprays another blast of whipped cream at the top of my pussy, and my body trembles as he licks from one side to the other. His mouth is so close to my clit. My breathing picks up, his warm tongue melting the cream on my skin. My hands wiggle against their restraints as I try to contain the energy building inside me. I'm desperate for more but he seems content to keep licking me slowly, torturing me. I had no idea this could be so erotic. My heart races when I hear him shaking the can again.

Oh my God. Where will he spray next? I close my eyes and wait, my body strung tight as a bow. My body arches in shock, a moan escaping my mouth, when I feel the cold hit my clit. His mouth lowers, his tongue circling and lapping away. Heat radiates from my skin as he continues to work me over. The noises coming from my throat are like nothing I've heard before, but I barely even hear them over the sound of blood rushing in my ears.

He moves a hand up to cup my breast, his fingers tweaking my nipple, just hard enough to be painful as I get closer and closer to the edge. His tongue is relentless; the more he builds me up, the hotter my body gets. I don't know how much more I can take. I pull against my restraints. The thrill of being tied up only adds to the pleasure I'm feeling.

He wraps his mouth around my clit and sucks hard and lights flash behind my eyes. My entire body quivers as everything around me shatters into pieces. Fire explodes in my core, the orgasm more intense than I ever could have imagined. My body is overwhelmed with ecstasy. I scream out his name and then I'm coming down, gasping for air.

"It feels like I've been waiting forever for a taste of you. That was so worth the fucking wait," he growls, nipping at my clit. "You taste like the sweetest, most delicious honey." He sucks my clit one more time, making me moan as my body continues to climb down from the intense high, before pulling back and swiping his hand across his mouth, taking the last of the whipped cream and my juices from his face.

"What are you doing to me?" I whisper, hating that he can see how much he affects me.

"Giving you pleasure like you've never known," he whispers in my ear. I jolt. I didn't realize he had moved up my body so quickly.

Letting my head flop to the side, I try to avoid his gaze. I feel embarrassed. Not just because I've never done anything like this before, but because it's Lucien Sinclair. A demon. And I'm about to let him claim me with his body.

His weight pins me to the bed, and he growls. "I'm not even close to finished with you yet. I need to be inside of you." A shudder runs through my body at his words.

He stands, kicking off his shoes and yanking off his socks before unbuttoning his pants. He pulls them down his lean thighs and throws them across the room. All I can do is stare at his enormous cock with astonishment. I've felt his hardness against my body and knew he wouldn't be small... but I was in no way prepared for the sight before me.

I hear my witch giggle. *Shit. How the hell is that monster going to fit inside of you?*

Shut up! I snap back at her.

I'm nervous enough without her input.

He doesn't give me much time to gaze at his perfection and I whimper when his body is on top of mine and I'm no longer able to look at his body. That dark hooded look I've grown accustomed to is back on his face. Looking deep into my eyes, he runs his hands over my arms.

His eyes flash red as his demon growls, "MINE," before his hands are fisting in my hair. I gasp, my pussy tingling.

"I am not yours," I shoot back, even as my body rebels against me, arching closer to him.

"You are mine, witch. Ours," He insists gruffly, sniffing my hair. "You belong to us." His other hand moves down my body, reaching the juncture of my thighs. His fingers dance along the edge of my folds and my legs spread further, almost without my permission, granting him entrance. His touch is dominant, possessive, as he takes control of my pleasure once more. Fingers slide slowly inside of me, and I moan as his thumb presses hard against my clit.

I feel myself open for him, walls stretching, and my hips buck up against him, wanting more. I feel beads of sweat forming at my temples. He knows exactly how and where to touch me. I'm already close to the edge again. I moan loudly as he massages my clit with his thumb. When he stops, pulling his hand away, the orgasm fades, making me whine in protest.

He trails his fingertips up and down my thigh, his touch so soft it almost feels like he's using a feather. He grips the outside of my thigh and brings it up around his waist. I move with him as his cock shifts in line with my pussy. I'm so engrossed in the sensation of him pressed against me, I don't even care that he left me hanging just a moment ago. All I care about is having more of him.

"This pussy is mine," he murmurs as he thrusts inside of me, and I moan and gasp, his length stretching me. He stills, allowing my body to adjust to his size, and I feel him pulsing. He looks into my eyes, resting his forehead against mine. We stay like that for a long moment, basking in one another's closeness, before he lifts his head and begins moving in and out of me. Now that my body has gotten used to him, his cock feels so fucking good as he thrusts deep. His fingers dig into my thigh and I'm sure I will have marks there later, but I don't care.

He lifts himself up, wrapping both my legs around my waist, and fists my hair in his hands. His thrusts are hard, deep. Calculated. They hit the perfect spot as he gets me closer to the place only he has ever been able to take me to. Shudders wrack my body as I move my hips faster, in time with his. He thrusts again and again, causing me to scream with delight. Intense pleasure continues to build inside of me, my back arching off the bed as the heat intensifies, my body so freaking hot I feel I might explode into pieces.

He hits my pleasure spot over and over. Spots dance in my vision, my muscles clenching around him. It feels like I have lightning inside of me. Every part of my body shakes, the orgasm even more intense than the last. My pussy squeezes his cock as it pulses around him, and he growls, the vibration sending a jolt of pleasure through me.

"Fuck me harder," I plead into his ear, thrusting my hips towards him as he pounds me into the bed.

At my words, a loud groan escapes his mouth and his thrusts become harder. Faster. I try to hold on, but my body is spent as I ride out the last waves of my orgasm. I know he's right on the edge, so I tighten my pussy, wanting to send him over. He growls and his head drops next to mine, his teeth latching onto my neck hard. I know there's going to be a mark there, and I'm surprised at how that thought makes me happy. He explodes inside of me, letting out a deep sexual moan. For several moments, he lays on top of me, both of us trying to catch our breath. Finally, with a light groan, he pulls out of me, dropping a kiss to my temple. My legs lower to the bed as he reaches up, freeing my hands.

My breathing is still labored when he lays down beside me and I struggle with what to say or do next. We've both been fighting against this moment since we set eyes on each other, both of us wrestling this insane chemistry between us. It was dangerous to let him touch me, and it can't happen again. I don't want to be involved with someone who has another woman.

I try to forget the look in his eyes when he said I was mine. How can I be? It makes no sense. I reach up and touch my neck, where he bit me. It tingles and burns, and I can feel the indentations from his teeth. When I pull my hand away, there are dots of blood on my fingertips. What the hell!?

CHAPTER TWENTY-ONE

SCARLETT

"YOU BIT ME!" I LOOK AT HIM accusingly, taking in his smug, satisfied smile.

He turns to me and takes me hand gently in his own. He looks at my fingers and notices the blood. "So I did," he replies with no remorse. His eyes flash red as he once again growls, "MINE."

"What the fuck does that even mean?" I demand, pulling my hand away.

He sighs. "My demon has taken a liking to you. He decided a while ago to keep you, and I'm just now getting on board."

"Keep me!?" I screech. What the hell is that supposed to mean? I do not like the way this conversation is going. "You can tell your demon that I am not his pet." I huff, pulling the sheets over my naked body. "He doesn't just get to *decide* to keep me." I point to the mark on my neck. "What's with the biting? I can't believe you actually broke the skin."

"He sees you as his. He feels protective over you. So, he marked you to let everyone know you are not to be touched."

I lay there, shocked, as the words 'mine' and 'his' reverberate in my head. "No, no. NO." My words are emphatic and I'm shaking my head as his words penetrate my mind. "It will never work. You hate witches. I'm shocked you even allowed yourself to touch me."

He studies me closely with those black eyes, his face devoid of emotion. He turns his body towards me before speaking. "Have you quite finished?" He asks, an eyebrow arched. Irritation flickers in his eyes, the sign of emotion so surprising, I find myself nodding at him. "I will not deny my previous disdain for all witches. I had no way to foresee how my feelings for you would develop. I fucking want you and I have from the moment I laid eyes on you, and I will not deny the need I have for you any longer." There's an edge to his voice that wasn't there before, and it causes my heart to turn over in my chest. A tingle starts in the pit of my stomach and courses through my body. I can't let this go any further.

I shake my head at him. "What just happened will not happen again. It can't." Whatever is between us can't go any further, no matter what my dreams have told me. No matter what my heart is trying to tell me now.

I feel a sudden need to get away from him, so I sit up, trying to move to the edge of the bed. I don't get far.

He sits up and places his large hand between my breasts, pushing until my back hits the mattress. His body rolls on top of my smaller one, trapping me beneath him. "What is between us will continue, and this is definitely going to happen again. You can try lying to yourself, but you can't lie to me. No matter how many times you deny what you're feeling, those feelings are still going to be there." His eyes bore into mine, daring me to object. He smirks, and I know he has me right where he wants me.

I gasp in delight as his hand slips between my thighs, his thumb pressing against my clit, strumming the tiny bundle of nerves and waking my arousal. My nipples harden and pebble, and he bends his head, taking one into his hot, wet mouth, sucking gently before biting down. My breath hitches.

I try to fight the hunger clouding my mind. I don't want to be the other woman, don't want to be his dirty little secret.

I jump when he speaks, "You won't be." The voice comes from deep in his throat and is rough like sandpaper. I realize I must have spoken my worries aloud.

Our eyes meet. Should I trust him. My heart is saying one thing, my mind is saying another. I want to believe what he's telling me, but I'm scared. If I give him my heart, will he break it? Is he only using me to get closer to me, to my family?

I tilt my head and ask him, "What do you mean?" I want to be sure I'm not misunderstanding him.

A small smile tugs at the corner of his mouth, a tender look flickering briefly in his eyes. "I have no intention of you being my dirty little secret. I intend for everyone to know exactly who you belong to," Lucien promises darkly, taking both my hands in his and placing them above my head. The look on his face turns to one of hunger, and heat instantly pools between my thighs.

"Are you wet? Does your pussy want my cock?" He whispers, the smoldering flame in his eyes making me squirm.

I can't help my response. I hate being so weak, I'm not this person, but he turns me into a quivering ball of need with little to no effort on his part. Whimpering, I nod my head, arching my hips into him. He doesn't mess around with any foreplay; he simply pushes his hips between my thighs and drives his cock home. There's no warning, no build-up, just his cock thrusting in and out of me, hard and deep. I gasp, clutching at his hands, as my head tips back in ecstasy from his movements. His mouth nips and sucks at my neck as he continues fucking me.

"Oh. God." I cry. I'm so wet for him.

"Your voice goes straight to my fucking cock. All I can think about is touching you. Fucking you until you scream my name." He growls, continuing to thrust, his hips smacking against mine. "I've tried to stay away from you. I couldn't. I can't. You're fucking mine, Scarlett. Your body is mine. All. Fucking. Mine." His last three words are punctuated with his thrusts, harder than ever.

"Lucien," I moan out. "Oh, God."

"There's no God here, baby. Just me." He stops for a second, staring down at me, before pushing into me leisurely. Sliding his cock in and out, painfully slow, intensifying the pleasure I'm receiving from him.

I moan, looking up at him desperately as he gives me a feral grin. Letting go of my hands, he grabs my hips, tilts them up, and drives his cock even deeper inside of me. He knows exactly what he's doing, how good he's making me feel. He is the devil in disguise.

I open my mouth, but no sounds come out. Oh God. It feels so incredible, so fucking good. Fuck. I'm going to come again. I bite down on his shoulder, hard, and he hisses in pain at the force of my teeth sinking into his flesh and squeezes my ass forcefully, making me bite down even harder as my orgasm rips through my body.

"Fuck!" He shouts, his cock pulsing inside of me, and I feel his release. He slows down, dragging his cock in and out of me slowly, my pussy milking every last drop from his length.

"I want you walking around with my scent all over you, my cum dripping down your thighs. I want everyone to know exactly who you belong to," he states, pulling out of me. He rolls off me with a kiss to my forehead before pulling me back into his arms.

His hard chest cushions my head, and I'm somehow comfortable, perfectly content like this. "Aria will not like it," I lift my head to look at him. "She's dangerous…"

"Shhhhh…" He cuts me off. "Let me deal with Aria. My demon and I have marked you. The bite on your neck shows that you belong to me. No one will dare try to harm you. They know if even a single hair on your head is out of place that they will have to answer to me." He tries to reassure me, his fingers caressing the mark on my neck.

"If this is going to work between us, you have to explain exactly what Aria is to you. Even if she isn't your wife, she's obviously someone close to you. Is she your mate?"

"I've never had a wife, partner, or mate." Lucien replies and I hear the truth in his words. "It is hard to explain exactly what Aria is to me," he sighs, rubbing his face. It's apparent he isn't used to people questioning him, nearly everyone is too afraid to do so.

"We've been together a long time. It started after I lost everything. Aria was there. She stood by my side when I had nobody else. I won't deny that I once cared deeply for her, but those feelings pale in comparison to those I have for you." His voice trails off and it's easy for me to see that whatever happened in his past is still causing him pain, the memories still affecting him even to this day. He shakes his head, as though trying to rid himself of his thoughts, and continues. "I won't let anyone hurt you, Scarlett. Not even Aria. I can no longer deny how I feel about you. I don't normally let my feelings rule my head, but I can't seem to help it where you're concerned. I might sometimes appear cold and heartless, especially in front of others, but if that happens, trust me when I say that there is a reason for it. If you let me, I will protect you with every fiber of my being," he promises, running his fingers softly up and down my arm before placing a kiss on my shoulder.

I close my eyes when his lips touch mine. I know he's not going to say anything else; he's said all he's willing to, and even though I believe him, I still feel uneasy. Aria isn't about to let him go easily, and regardless of his belief that his feelings for her are gone, I think he's in denial. I don't share and I have no intentions of being in an open relationship. Will the day come that he realizes he's made a mistake? Will he set me aside?

I know that the moment Aria finds out we're together, she will go ballistic. Then there's my family... I know they won't be happy with me being with a demon! If I give into him, give into my feelings, my whole world will be turned upside down. He still doesn't know about my omega. I can't even imagine how he will react to that news. But if I don't tell him, how can trust possibly form between us? Why is this all so difficult?

As though sensing the conflict raging inside of me, Lucien's hands move up and cradle the sides of my face before pressing kisses all over my cheeks and eyelids, like he wants to soothe me, convince me everything will be alright.

The sensation of his hands and lips on me cause chills to break out over my body. I want his hands everywhere, need more of his gifted mouth. I let him pull me into his embrace and allow the rest of the world to disappear.

CHAPTER TWENTY-TWO

SCARLETT

SEVERAL DAYS LATER

I STAND LOOKING AT MYSELF IN the mirror in front of me and my mind drifts to the other morning. Lucien told me not to worry, but that he would be busy for the next few days, and that I might not hear from him or see him for a while. Before leaving, he gave me a panty melting kiss and told me he would miss me, and before I'd recovered enough to ask what he would be busy doing, he was gone. I was so pissed off. I still don't know how I truly feel, no matter what he's told me or how much I want to believe his feelings are true. I still find myself struggling to trust him.

Alex has become my lifeline. Lucien gave him permission to keep me in the loop, so he's been giving me constant updates. Alex is really sweet, and we've grown quite close. I was right about him being a wolf shifter. He shifted in front of me after I begged him to. His wolf is beautiful with luscious white fur. I was surprised to see that his coat is a different color than his hair. He's basically a giant puppy in wolf form. It was quite the sight to see.

He told me quite a bit about his life and his family. His parents are still alive, and he has three older brothers and two younger sisters. They live with the shifter Alpha, Jacob. Jacob is the principal leader of all shifters and rules over his territory, and like Lucien, he has region leaders who report to him. Jacob is practically famous; nearly everyone in the Natural world has heard of him.

At the moment, Alex is out on a mission for Lucien. He told me he planned to visit his family before returning and that he would see me in a few days. I'm not sure what exactly Lucien has him doing.

For now, I have Logan watching over me. He isn't quite as friendly as Alex, but he is much older. He's polite, in a gruff way, and after a brief conversation between the two of us, he assured me he has my back, which is a relief. Though we don't have the same level of comradery I've developed with Alex, I still feel like I can trust him.

I'm excited about Pamela, Ava, Emma, Mia, and Abigail's impending visit. They'll be arriving tomorrow, and I cannot wait to see them. I wonder if Lucien will be here to greet them when they arrive. When I asked Logan where he was, he wasn't all that forthcoming with the details. All he said was that Lucien is busy with business and is doing all he can to find Megan.

I feel like he's avoiding me, but I'm unsure as to why. I wonder if I'm as much his weakness as he is mine, and if so, whether he's as unhappy about it as I am. The way I react to him throws me at every turn. A mere look from him leaves me reeling. My body yearns to see him, and so does my mind, even if it is out of some misguided hope that the feelings I have for him are merely a figment of my imagination and that if I see him, I won't experience the same intensity I remember feeling around him.

My dreams are getting stronger, more vivid, but I can rarely remember any details upon waking. The only thing I remember from the last one was that Aria was in it. The very thought of her causes me to shudder in revulsion.

I've heard whispers that she's back, and I wonder if she's the reason Lucien hasn't been to see me. When I had gathered enough courage to ask Logan about it, his reply was vague. Even as I asked, I knew he wouldn't tell me if Lucien was with her. He knows that to tell me that would be to put his position with Lucien in danger. My gut tells me Lucien is spending time with her, and if it turns out to be true, I will be gutted. I've been intimate with him and that means something to me. All

I can hope is that so long as my family is here, Aria keeps her distance. I hate to imagine what kind of secrets could come out otherwise. After our confrontation last week, I know there's much more to her than meets the eye. If she comes at me again, I will retaliate, and I don't know if I will let her walk away from another such encounter; I don't know if my witch will allow it.

My thoughts turn to Megan and what she must be going through. Just the idea of her suffering at the hands of her captors wipes all consideration of Aria from my mind. I want my sister found, safe and in one piece, and finding out who is responsible for taking Naturals and humans would be a bonus. The idea of what Megan might be enduring makes me sick to my stomach. I know she's still alive, I would have felt our bond sever. Although the mere thought of her being dead brings me so much pain, I wonder if my witch and omega would block the break in our connection.

No. I will not entertain such thoughts. I can't. Megan is out there somewhere, she's alive, and we will find her. No other outcome is acceptable.

The sound of someone banging on my door brings me out of my musings.

"Come in!" I yell and watch in the mirror as the door pushes open.

"Hi, Scarlett," Logan greets me as he steps inside the room. "There's a group of women demanding to see you. I asked them to wait for you in the meeting room," he informs me with a raised eyebrow.

"My sisters?" I question, turning around to face him with a thoughtful look. That's strange; they're a day early.

"Well, there are seven women down there demanding to see you. I just assumed they were your sisters," he shrugs, rubbing at his beard.

"Seven women?" I know I just keep repeating his words, but the news has thrown me for a loop. The other two women must be Melissa and Evelyn. They're the only two people I know who would dare come here with my sisters.

Though Melissa hardly ever leaves her house, I know she would come if she felt her help was needed. She lives in a vast woodland, preferring to live in the wilderness. The privacy it offers is important to her. If an outsider wishes to see her, they have to make an appointment. Evelyn, being part phoenix, also prefers seclusion. She lives on the outskirts of a small village and mostly keeps to herself.

"What do they look like?" I ask Logan, listening as he describes my sisters, along with Evelyn and Melissa. I'd be lying if I said I'm not surprised they came. Something more must be going on, because for them to leave the privacy of their homes is rare indeed.

Without another word to Logan, I rush out the door as though the hounds of hell are hot on my heels. Logan chases after me.

"Shit, Scarlett. Wait! Everything is fine." I don't heed his words, knowing he can catch up quickly.

I need to figure out what the hell is going on. I hope to God nothing terrible has happened. Pamela didn't mention anything serious the last time we spoke.

I shove open the double doors, causing them to bang against the stone walls, and standing in front of me are my sisters and cousins, with ten of Lucien's men surrounding them; that doesn't include the other men in the room. I watch the women of my family take stock of the people in the room as I feel Logan come to a standstill behind me.

"I told you everything was fine," he whisper-yells over my shoulder.

Taking in the scene before me, my jaw drops. Is he fucking kidding? At least thirty men are standing around the large room, all watching my family as though they're about to explode. I'm relieved to know that my family will only attack to defend themselves.

"It doesn't look fine to me," I retort, worry creasing my forehead.

Melissa is dressed in head-to-toe black leather and standing like a warrior waiting for battle. Her silver hair hangs down her back in waves, her odd-colored eyes standing out against her tawny skin. The tattoos covering both her arms seem to come alive if you stare at them long enough. I feel guilty at how relieved I am that her brothers didn't come. They could have caused a much bigger problem than even a coven of witches showing up at Lucien's door. Male omegas are known to be troublesome and are much rarer than female omegas. I have a fleeting thought to ask her who is taking care of her children, but I push it back.

I'll make sure to find out later.

Towering over Melissa, on her right, is Evelyn. My middle sister is the tallest out of all of us, well over six feet. Her multi-colored hair hangs down her back, setting off her golden honey skin. Her lean, firm legs are clad in black leather and she's wearing a deep cherry red tank top. The rest of my sisters stand to either side of them.

Pamela, the oldest, is dressed in her typical gypsy garb, her long flowing skirt brushing the floor and her top hugging her body, all of it paired with multiple bangles jingling on her wrists. Her jet-black hair is cropped close to her head, her skin the color of fresh cream. Not once has she taken her eyes off the men surrounding them.

Ava is nearly a carbon copy of Pamela, except with long hair reaching her waist. Emma is also quite tall, with skin so pale, it is close to the color of bleached parchment. Her startling blue eyes are a shock against her olive skin.

Mia and Abigail are identical twins. They're watching the scene around them with a look of innocence in their grey eyes, which couldn't be further from their true nature. They always dress identically, as they enjoy the confusion on people's faces when they see them together. One day they'll be the strongest of us all due to their combined powers.

Eight of the most powerful witches and omegas are standing in this room. That realization makes me gulp loudly. If any one of these men knew what we were capable of, none of us would make it out of here alive.

I notice the moment my sisters realize I've entered the room. They rush over to me, trailed by Evelyn and Melissa, relief written on all their faces.

Pulling me into a tight hug first, Melissa bends her head and whispers in my ear, "How long did they last?"

I know what my cousin is referring to. She means the spells and herbs she'd given me to help infiltrate Lucien's club. "They lasted about six hours," I tell her with a small smile. "But they didn't work on Lucien." She gasps and I cut her off before she can say anything else. "What are you and Evelyn doing here?"

"They should have lasted longer than that," Melissa exclaims with an expression of alarm on her face before quickly replacing it with a fake cheerful smile.

I know what she's thinking because I'm thinking the same. Lucien is far stronger than we could have imagined, and if that's true, it means he's older and above a level fifteen. We will have to share our thoughts through the link so my family will know what we know. I'm worried they will have the same fears as me. Are we in danger? Do we need to go back into hiding?

I can't help but think that Lucien is using me for his own gain, but I push those thoughts to the back of my mind. Problems for a different day; I need to focus on my family right now.

Melissa pulls me from my thoughts. "Ava let slip what was happening, so Evelyn and I insisted on coming. We figured at the very least, it would throw Lucien off, surprise him. We didn't know what we would be running into." Her forehead puckers in thought as her eyes widen. "So, he knew?" she asks.

My head is spinning so much, I have trouble thinking straight. "Yes," I reply, keeping my answer short. I don't want Lucien's men to overhear our conversation.

"Fuck," Melissa mutters under her breath, finally stepping away to let my sisters greet me. I know by the look in her eyes that our conversation isn't over. After getting through all the hugs and kisses, we sit around a large round wooden table in the center of the room. Logan stands directly behind my chair, like a guard dog, and I see the confusion on my family's faces, wondering what the fuck is going on and why a complete stranger is acting as my bodyguard. I give them a shrug and a small smile. We have far more important things to discuss at the moment.

I still as I feel someone's mind touch my own. It feels familiar but different than what I'm used to feeling from my sisters. Before he even enters my line of vision, I feel Lucien's presence and realize he's been observing us, taking everything in. Damien walks in beside him.

Lucien doesn't say a word as his dark eyes meet mine. I devour him with my gaze, feeling starved for his touch; I hate myself for it. A flash of hunger comes and goes as his eyes slide down my body. He gives a small smirk and I know the bastard is aware of how he's affecting me.

I feel the surrounding atmosphere shift as Lucien's men become aware of his presence. I look around at my family and can tell they've felt it too. I wonder if they have any idea that Lucien is standing directly behind them. They keep their eyes locked on the men surrounding them and I watch with bated breath as he makes his way towards us, his face devoid of emotion, Damien trailing behind him. I know neither of them trusts the women sitting around this table, and briefly wonder if that sentiment extends to me as well. I know for a fact it does for Damien, but what about Lucien?

Shaking those thoughts, I see the moment my family becomes aware of the presence behind them, and one after another, their expressions change. I know they must want to turn around and look, but they fight the urge to do so.

LUCIEN

I WALK INTO VIEW OF THE WOMEN sitting around the table, Damien by my side, and meet the gaze of each one. I already know all their names. I never enter a situation without all the relevant data. They're all still, as if frozen in place, almost like they're waiting for me to strike out at them.

When I marked Scarlett the other night, it created a mental link between the two of us, so I know she felt me enter the room. When our minds touched, my demon pushed against my hold, reminding me that she belongs to us. Our bond is only a fraction of what it will become and the pull I already feel towards her is a little bit frightening. It's instinctual, primal. I will do anything to protect her, even if it means helping to find her sister and putting up with her family of witches.

"Ladies," I nod in greeting. "You have me at a slight disadvantage. I didn't expect to see you until tomorrow. You all know who I am, I'm sure. I don't know any of you, but I'm hopeful that will change." I pause, observing each of them for a reaction. As they nod, I continue, "I've agreed to assist Scarlett in finding Megan. I'm sure she has made you aware that I know you're all witches?" I raise an eyebrow in question.

They remain quiet, looking as though they're in a trance. I notice the one with short black hair looking pointedly at Scarlett and wonder what she's thinking. Getting no reaction from her sister, she turns her attention to me.

"What exactly has Scarlett told you about us, Mr. Sinclair?" she inquires with a raised eyebrow.

"Scarlett hasn't told me a thing," I answer. "She simply asked me for my help, and I agreed." I give a casual shrug and look down at my nails, a bored expression on my face.

The dark-haired gypsy gives me a disbelieving look. "Lucien. May I call you Lucien?" I nod, smirking. "You just told us you know what we are. I would like to know what you mean by that statement."

"Don't play dumb… Pamela." She gasps, shocked that I know her name. "You're wasting my time and my patience. Tell me, are you willing to take my offer of help?" I ask her. Does she think me an idiot, that I wouldn't have found out everything I could about Scarlett's family and her past when she showed up in my club?

The woman with silver hair pipes in. "I can't see you doing something for nothing." Her odd-colored eyes glance pointedly around the room at my men, carefully gauging their reactions.

"You're right," I concede, turning my head to look at the woman who interrupted Pamela. I never agree to anything without some sort of payment in return, but I don't feel guilty about that. "I'm not a charity. I don't agree to help anyone without some kind of agreement in place."

"What do you want from Scarlett? From us?" asks one of the most beautiful women I've ever seen. Her hair is so light, it looks almost translucent; her eyes a striking blue that contrasts sharply against her deep olive skin. This must be Emma. I watch as she looks over at Scarlett and a silent message passes between them.

"The agreement is between myself and your sister," I reply, showing no reaction to her questions. Catching Scarlett looking at me, I let a mocking smile appear on my lips, daring her to share the details of our little arrangement. "If she wishes to tell you, that is up to her."

I watch as all the women turn and look at Scarlett, the same question written on each of their faces. It's obvious they want to know what the agreement is, that they're worried she has sealed all their fates to the devil himself.

Scarlett shakes her head, making it clear she has no desire to share with them. I hear Pamela mutter a curse under her breath. She must be the de facto leader of this little group.

Pamela looks over at me once again. "Do you have any information on our sister yet?" she demands with a scowl.

I feel my face tighten in irritation before I answer her. "I'm sure Scarlett has kept you up to date on what's been happening and that you're aware I found the soul keeper who took Megan."

Upon hearing this, the women start a round of rapid-fire questioning. Looks like Scarlett hasn't been keeping them in the loop as much as I would have expected. The volume in the room steadily increases and she can't get a word in edgewise. I almost smile at her defensive posture. She's hiding it well, but I can see how pissed off she is.

I hadn't yet informed Scarlett about finding the soul keeper dead or about the soul eater my men found with the body. I'd been on the way to do precisely that when I received word about her family arriving. Aria had unexpectedly arrived this morning, preventing me from reaching out to Scarlett any sooner. She's really becoming a problem and I'm going to have to deal with her soon. My demon and I aren't the least bit pleased with how Aria has managed to keep us away from our witch.

I cut off their arguing by speaking over them, "We do not know where Megan is being kept or who has her at the moment."

The woman dressed in tight leather pants and a blood-red top is the first to recover from my announcement. "We want to be there when you question him."

I chuckle lightly at her request. Based on her appearance, this must be Melissa. Running my index finger over my lower lip, I reply. "Not going to happen. The found the soul keeper dead. A soul eater was standing over the body."

I watch their reaction, their shocked expressions giving them away. It doesn't take long for the shouted questions to start back up. I let them carry on as my thoughts wander.

Melissa must be the witch I've heard rumors about, the one who runs with a pack of wolves. Based on the tattoos running up her slim arms to her shoulders, I figure there must be more to her than meets the eye. I've questioned several of my men about her and they all claim to not know who I'm talking about. It's like she doesn't exist. There's a strong likelihood it's an attempt to protect her. Nobody would have believed that I, Lucien Sinclair, would not only allow a coven of witches into my home, but would also protect them from outside harm.

The volume of their protests and questions continues to rise and I wait for them to calm down. What will their reaction be when I tell them the soul eater is dead as well, that I watched his head blow up right in front of me?

"Stop. Just bloody stop! You all seem to have forgotten how dangerous a soul eater can be. They're at least ten times worse than a bloody soul keeper. If one gets close enough, it will eat your soul. It wouldn't even need to get ahold of you to do it. They can steal your soul with the mere touch of a finger, and you'll be completely fucked. That is why we need to let Lucien deal with this," Scarlett shouts, her face red from frustration.

"Scarlett is right. It won't take much for a soul eater to get a finger on one of us and snatch away our souls. They're crafty little buggers who will do anything to get what they want. If it were just a soul keeper, you would have a chance at recovering your soul, but this isn't worth the risk," one of the lookalikes calmly states.

I see the rest of them take in her words, absorbing them. I wonder if they will manage to come to some kind of agreement. Honestly, so long as Scarlett is safe, I don't give a fuck what they decide. It's up to them if they want my help or not.

"Aren't you worried about your soul?" The other twin asks me.

"My soul?" I can't help but laugh. "You hear that, Damien?" I call out, turning my head and looking at my friend who gives me a wide grin. "How sweet. She's under the impression that demons have souls. That I have a soul," I laugh loudly once more before turning back to face them. "Ladies, I assure you; if I ever had a soul, it is long gone by now," I state, hearing Damien chuckle from behind me.

"Fine, Lucien. We will let you question the soul eater without us," Pamela agrees with a huff. "But the minute you know anything about our sister, we expect to hear about it right away."

"There's already an agreement in place, Pamela," I raise a brow condescendingly. "You all may stay here until I get back. The club will open in a few hours, and you're welcome to enjoy yourselves. I should know more by morning."

I turn to Damien. "Give each of them their own VIP pass. Make sure all my people are aware that they are here as my guests, and I expect them to be treated as such." He nods, and I turn to the men stationed in the room, telling half of them to stay with Scarlett and her family and the other half to come with me.

Damien lifts an eyebrow at me, surprised at my instructions. I know what that look means. He's wanting to know what the hell I'm doing. Having a coven of witches in my club is dangerous; insane, really. I know he thinks I've lost my mind, but he would never think to question me where the witches or my men could overhear him.

"I'll get right on that, boss," he assures me, as he removes his phone from his jacket pocket.

"Tell Alf to handle it," I order. "I need you with me." Damien is my second in command and I have things to discuss with him. My men know to take Damien's orders as though they're coming straight from my mouth, so I'm confident it will be done right.

I turn back to the women and nod at each one of them. "Ladies. I shall see you all later. Scarlett," I nod my head in her direction, but don't say anything else. I let my mind brush against hers, opening my thoughts for her to see. By the look in her eyes, I know she felt me through our link. I give her a slight smirk and look up at the man assigned to protect her.

"Logan. Don't let her out of your sight." He acknowledges me with a slight nod. Logan is one of my most loyal men. There are maybe a handful of people I trust in this world, and he is one of them.

As I turn to leave the room with Damien by my side, I feel a sense of satisfaction at how well things went. Now I just need to go make sure everything is going as planned for the meeting taking place tomorrow.

CHAPTER TWENTY-THREE

SCARLETT

I watch as Lucien leaves with half his men and Damien following. The questions from my sisters and cousins come instantly.

Walking over to where I'm standing, jaw tensed, Pamela demands, "Scarlett, what the hell was that?!"

Thank heavens the bite mark from Lucien is hidden; otherwise, I'd have a lot more explaining to do. It might be a stupid plan, but I've decided to play dumb. "What the hell was what?"

Eyes narrowed, hands on her hips, Pamela scowls at me. "Don't you 'what' me. Did you think I would miss the looks you were throwing back and forth with that demon? What the hell is going on between you and Lucien Sinclair?" Her voice is edged with anger. "Please tell me I was imagining things. He just admitted to all of us that he lacks a soul, for fuck's sake!"

I'm tempted to tell Pamela to mind her own business, but I know she isn't going to leave this alone. She's always been like a dog with a bone until she gets what she wants. I know it will shock them when they find out I slept with him, but I don't believe Lucien's claim that he has no soul. The man just loves to fuck with people. But soul or not, shit is going to hit the fan when they find out about us. All of them forget that I'm an adult capable of running my own life. No matter how good their intentions are, I have no desire to listen to them lecture me on my choices. I'm going to have to tell a few white lies to get them to move on.

We have far more important issues at hand. I haven't even had a chance to tell them about the meeting yet, and I know they're going to have a strong reaction to that particular bit of news.

"We had a moment," I finally respond with a shrug.

Hearing someone scoff behind me, I roll my eyes and ignore it. I hear Lucien's remaining men snicker and notice Logan glaring in their direction, causing them to stop abruptly. I'm unsure if Lucien's men know about what happened between us. If so, none of them have acknowledged it with me.

"You had a moment?" Pamela demands incredulously. "You expect me… us, to believe that's all that happened? Do you think we were born yesterday, Scarlett?" Her voice shaking an anger, her lips pressed into an angry line, she continues, "With all the sexual tension between you two, I'm surprised you didn't just start going at it right in front of us!"

I feel my cheeks grow hot with temper. Why the hell can't she just leave it alone? I feel like pulling my hair out in frustration as I speak in a low tone. "Whatever did or did not happen between Lucien and myself is absolutely none of your business."

Her jaw drops open in surprise and her shock is reflected on the rest of their faces. A wave of guilt rushes over me as Pamela's eyes fill with tears.

Melissa steps forward and pulls me into her arms, kissing me atop my head. I feel calm rush through me from her touch and take a deep breath.

"Forgive Pamela for intruding. You know how she is. Plus, with Megan missing, we're all on edge," Melissa whispers in my ear.

I sigh. I know she's right, but it doesn't give any of them an excuse to try to control my life. "I know she means well, but she's just so infuriating sometimes," I reply in a whisper.

"I know more than anyone how you must feel. Those brothers of mine drive me up the wall, even on their best behavior," she reminds me, her arms tightening around my shoulders.

Melissa has three older, overbearing brothers. They've always kept a close eye on her, even though she's never really needed them to. She's a born fighter, and even if she weren't, she has her wolves if she needs protection. They go wherever she goes and if they feel that Melissa or her family is being threatened, they won't think twice about defending them. Melissa found them as cubs on the brink of death several years ago, after the rest of their pack had been slaughtered. If she hadn't taken them in, they would have starved to death.

"How is everything at home?" I whisper, changing the subject. "Who's watching your little ones?"

"Everyone's good. The kids are up to their usual mischief. Sophia volunteered to watch them for me since my brothers are away. You're going to have to find time to come visit soon."

Shit. "Sophia? Is she in her right mind to take care of them?" I ask, our eyes meeting. We both know Sophia isn't really the problem, Fate is.

"I know Fate can be unpredictable, but I know she would never hurt them. She loves them just as much as Sophia does. I did place a warning spell though, just in case she does drop in."

Melissa's right. Fate wouldn't hurt them, but I'm glad she set up an alert because she can be unpredictable and make bad choices. Changing the subject again, I say, "Your wolves must need to run. There's a huge garden here you can take them to."

A shadow of alarm touches her face. "That would be amazing for them, but if it isn't safe, I would rather wait." I'm not surprised by her caution. The safety of her wolves is always one of her top priorities.

"You can at least let them out for ten minutes or so. I'm sure they'll be fine," I assure her before turning to Logan.

"Logan, do you think Lucien would mind if Melissa went to the garden…" Damn. What the hell am I going to call them? Not wolves, though that is what they are. But nobody outside the family knows about them and she likes to keep it that way. "She just needs a bit of fresh air."

Logan turns at my request and stares intently at Melissa, his head tilted in puzzlement. With narrowed eyes, he studies her tattoos. There are five total on each arm, each one a picture of a wolf. They reach up over her shoulders and down her lower back.

I can tell he's trying to figure out if his eyes are playing tricks on him or if the tattoos really are moving over her skin. Very few people know about the magic involved in the special kind of tattoos she has. I have a feeling he's trying to figure out if she's a wolf shifter based on the adornments, and I can't blame him. I'm not entirely sure what kind of shifter Logan is but based on the way he's reacting to my cousin, I'm starting to suspect he's a wolf.

After what feels like eternity, he finally gives a slight nod of consent.

LOGAN

I CAN'T STOP MYSELF FROM staring at the woman with the mesmerizing tattoos. There's just something about her that I can't quite place my finger on. At first, I thought it was just the tattoos, but now I realize there's more to it than that. I shake my head. I'm sure I know her from somewhere, but I can't seem to remember where. I'm sure it will come to me.

I can see no issues with allowing her to go to the garden. It's considered an open space for any who live or stay here as guests.

"Will half an hour be enough time?" I ask the woman Scarlett referred to as Melissa. She gives a swift nod and I call one of the other men over.

"Luke. Take Melissa to the garden," I tell him. "You don't have to enter with her but give her half an hour and then bring her straight back here. Don't let anyone in the garden with her, and make sure she comes back unharmed. Do. Not. Forget. She is Lucien's guest."

I stare at him until he nods. He gestures for Melissa to follow him, and they head towards the door.

Turning my attention back to Scarlett, I assure her, "She'll be fine with Luke. He's one of the good guys."

I watch as they leave the room together and wonder, *is she the mystery woman I've heard so much about?*

SCARLETT

"SHE'LL BE FINE WITH LUKE. He's one of the good guys," Logan tells me. I can't help but stare at the man in question. He has to be at least six-four, with insanely broad shoulders and jet-black hair tipped with blue. With his light piercing grey eyes, he manages to draw the eye, even if he isn't the most handsome man I've ever seen.

As they're leaving the room, I hear Luke ask Melissa, "Is it true you run with a pack of wolves?" I strain to hear her reply, but they're out the door before she answers.

I'm not surprised to learn that the shifters here have heard of my cousin. I'm actually more surprised none of them tried to approach her before now.

I turn my head and meet Luke's stare. With a slight smile, I tell him, "If the need arises, Melissa is more than capable of looking after herself."

He leans down, whispering, "So she's the one we've heard about?"

I keep my face blank. "I don't know. What is it you've heard?"

He studies me, not answering right away. Finally, he seems to realize I'm not going to say anything more. "Is she the woman we've heard rumors about? The one who runs with a pack of wild wolves? I've heard people go to her for spells and healing, but nobody has ever admitted to actually going to see her."

I manage to keep my emotions hidden even though his words surprise me. Shit. How long have these rumors been going around? This is the first time I've heard anything about it. I wonder if Melissa knows. I decide not to answer him. If he really wants to know and has the balls to ask her himself, he can go for it.

Turning my attention to my sisters and Evelyn, I try to decide how to handle things. I don't want to argue with any of them, particularly Pamela. Melissa was right. Finding Megan is our top priority.

I stare at the women whom I love most in this world and feel my heart fill. Yes, they drive me crazy sometimes, enough to make me want to scream, but I really wouldn't have them any other way. We've been through so much together. Losing our parents so young was heartbreaking, but Pamela and Megan were our backbone from day one when they took over for our parents. I don't want there to be this tension between us.

I promise myself to tell them about Lucien later, but for now, I need to tell them about Aria. I still haven't told them about her attack or about how my witch was forced to make an appearance. While Lucien hadn't seen anything firsthand, no doubt Aria told him everything, probably even embellishing things for her benefit. I must assume he suspects how strong I am.

    I reach out through our link, embracing my sisters in my love and warmth, and assure them I hold no ill thoughts towards them. A feeling of happiness and contentment rushes through all of us, only to be replaced with panic when I tell them about Aria. We agree that we will protect ourselves if she or anyone else attacks us. We will have no other choice.

CHAPTER TWENTY-FOUR

SCARLETT

A FEW HOURS LATER

LUCIEN HAS JUST COME BACK into the room and dropped a bomb, leaving all of us in a state of shock.

The words echo inside my head.

The soul eater is dead.

This is really bad. We are so screwed!

Someone managed to place a trap inside his brain that caused his head to explode when Lucien went digging through memories. By the matching expressions on my family's faces, they don't believe a word he's saying, and who could blame them? Am I an idiot for thinking he's telling the truth? Lucien has no reason to lie to us.

If what he described really happened, we have to figure out what it means. How did someone get into a soul eater's mind that way? What would the person responsible be capable of doing to the rest of us?

Even as I'm asking it, I know how stupid my question is. "What are we going to do?" I look at Lucien who is staring at us as though waiting. For what, I have no clue.

Nobody says anything, we just take turns looking at one another. My family doesn't seem to have any answers, and judging by Lucien's lack of reaction, neither does he.

After an interminable silence, he finally speaks up. "Nothing. There is nothing for any of you to do. I have a few contacts who might be able to help, and they owe me favors."

My family huffs, practically in unison. It's clear they're unconvinced. They do not trust Lucien; despite everything he's done to try to make them see that he's on our side. It's going to take a lot of time for them to get over their preconceived notions of him.

"You're forgetting something, Lucien. We are not human; nor are we your regular, run-of-the-mill witches." Melissa states as she strides back into the room and takes a seat, Luke standing behind her. She was gone longer than thirty minutes, but I hadn't worried. I know her wolves would need more than thirty minutes to run around.

My sisters and Evelyn are whispering back and forth, shocked by Melissa's words. She turns to us and rolls her eyes. "Come on guys, he isn't stupid. He suspects how powerful we are, if he didn't already know, that is." Turning to me, she smiles mischievously. "Am I right?"

Lucien's voice turns our attention his way. "You've got balls, I'll give you that." His eyes roam over her tattoos, a smirk on his face. "I wasn't completely sure, but yes, I suspected you all were more than just the normal witches I've been exposed to."

Shocked, I ask him, "Why didn't you say something sooner?" I can't believe he kept quiet about his suspicions. I thought he wanted me to trust him. Why would he keep something so important from me?

Turning his black eyes on me, he shrugs. "There was no reason to. But now there is," he states simply.

I know it shouldn't matter. It isn't like I've told Lucien everything, but I'm still irked. Of course, I should have known he was too smart to miss the fact that I survived an attack by Aria, too smart not to realize that I must be more powerful than I'd let on.

Bloody Demon, I think, pushing the words at him. *You aren't supposed to hide things from me, Lucien.*

He raises his eyebrow at me, and I know he heard my thoughts. I feel his mind brush against mine, an attempt at comfort, a lover's caress. I know it's his way of apologizing. I understand why he kept it from me, but I'm not happy about it. A small part of me feels guilty, though. I still haven't told Lucien that we are all part omega or that we have a phoenix among us. I'm too frightened to tell him everything.

Frightened that his feelings for me will change. I'm sure he knows I've been holding back, without knowing exactly what it was. I wonder if he suspects the truth now.

I also can't help but wonder if he's still having sex with Aria. I can sense her when she's here and I noticed that I haven't seen him any of the times she's been in the building. I've considered using an orb to follow him and find out exactly what's going on.

Lucien's voice breaks me out of my thoughts. "My men are going to patrol the streets more frequently and in larger groups," he announces.

"Great. And seeing as you now know what we are, you must see there's no reason we can't help," Evelyn states and the rest of my family voices their agreement. "We can patrol the streets alongside your men."

"And how will you be able to protect yourselves?" Sneers Damien. "I know Lucien seems to think you're more powerful than you're letting on, and you all seem to think you're some kind of powerhouses, but we haven't exactly seen any evidence to speak for that. You are, after all, part human."

"You're right, we are part human. But I can assure you, we are far from helpless," says a voice from the back of the room as Mia steps forward and raises her hand, a small discharge of lightning shooting from her fingertips in Damien's direction.

We all watch in fascinated horror as it flies towards his head with a humming sound, just barely whizzing by his ear and hitting the wall behind him with an almighty bang, a charcoal smudge staining the wall in its wake.

Eyes wild and lips curled in aggression, Damien checks his ear to make sure he wasn't hit. "You're fucking crazy! You could have scalped me," he shouts.

"Please. If I wanted to hurt you, you wouldn't be standing," Mia laughs wickedly, her eyes shining with mirth. She flicks her fingers at him again, and this time the lightning grazes his other ear.

"Mia!" I shout, running my hands through my hair in frustration. Bloody hell. Is this really happening?

All hell breaks loose, and I groan.

Lucien and Damien come charging towards us, their faces painted in determination, as the rest of Lucien's men attempt to surround us. I know my sister was only trying to show them that we aren't the helpless little humans they think we are. But they don't know that, and if they get their hands on her, I'm worried they'll hurt her.

Before they can reach us, a clear shield rises up, surrounding me and my family. I don't need to look around to know who constructed it. Abigail's instinct to protect her twin has certainly come in handy. I know she won't lower it until she's certain we're no longer in danger. Any of us can step outside the bubble, but nobody will be able to come inside.

Lucien places one of his large hands against the shield and I watch as it bounces off. "Scarlett! Lower the shield!" he demands through gritted teeth, his intense black eyes meeting mine.

"I can't," I tell him, shaking my head. "I didn't put it up, so I can't take it down."

"Then who the fuck *can* take it down?" Damien asks, stepping closer to the shield and putting his hand against it. He pushes in and watches as his hand bounces back out.

"Me," Abigail replies, stepping forward.

"Lower. The. Fucking. Force. Field." Damien growls, pacing the barrier like a wild animal. If looks could kill, I'm certain we'd all be dead.

"No. Not until I'm assured nobody is going to try to hurt Mia or any of the rest of us," Abigail's voice trembles slightly, but her back is ramrod straight. I'm proud of her for standing up for her family, but this could go terribly wrong very quickly. We all need to learn to trust one another, and I'm not sure this is the way to go about building that kind of relationship. I watch warily as the rest of Lucien's men gather around the shield, standing directly in front of it.

I reach out to Lucien's mind. I need to convince him she means no harm. *Lucien. Please. I promise she was only trying to show you both that we are capable of taking care of ourselves. That we aren't helpless.*

She should have done it some other way. Shooting fucking lightning bolts at us with no warning isn't the best way to build rapport. Lucien snaps back. *And why the fuck did she direct them at his fucking head?!* His voice echoes through my mind, causing me to grip my head with both hands.

I glare at him. *She wanted to get her point across.*

Well, I'd say she fucking succeeded. He replies through the link.

"Lower the fucking forcefield," Damien shouts again, punching it repeatedly. I've only ever seen him calm and collected, and his anger is quite the sight to see.

"Screw you," Abigail shoots back, laughing nervously. "I already told you. I'm not taking it down until I have both your word that nothing will happen to Mia or any of the rest of us."

"Oh, I intend to screw you, witch. By the time I'm done with you, you'll be begging me for more," Damien fires back, a look of lust clouding his face.

"In your dreams, demon," Abigail scoffs, even as her eyes travel his body appreciatively.

What the fuck is happening right now?

"Oh, it will be happening there too," he growls.

Abigail walks closer to the shield until she's nearly touching it and runs her tongue along her bottom lip. "Look all you want, demon, because that's as close as you'll ever get to touching me." She winks at him, and he snarls.

"Don't delude yourself, witch. You'll be begging me to fuck you before I ever lay a finger on you," he replies, licking his bottom lip seductively.

Is this really fucking happening? I seriously cannot believe what I'm hearing.

Pamela finally speaks up, causing everyone to look at her. "Stop. Both of you. Just. Stop. Abigail, you need to release the shield," she says sternly before turning her attention to Lucien and Damien. "What Mia did was stupid, but she didn't mean anything by it. She's young and still in training. They both are." Pamela holds up her hand when she hears Mia's words of protest.

"Get her to lower the forcefield," Lucien orders Pamela. He's clearly ignoring the sexual tension that's building between my sister and his second-in-command.

Abigail turns and looks at Lucien. "I'm not lowering anything until I know none of you are going to harm us," she says stubbornly. "Both of you swear you won't do anything and that you won't order your men to do anything either," she says, pointing her finger at Lucien's men surrounding us.

"Fuck! Fine! I promise, nobody will touch any of you," Lucien shouts, looking at his men to make sure they understand his orders.

"What about him? Is he making the same promise?" Abigail asks with her eyebrow raised, nodding her head in Damien's direction.

I can tell she's trying to goad him; the look in her eyes is one of teasing mischief. What the fuck?! I don't like this at all. Whatever is going on between the two of them is not going to end well. Abigail is normally the sweetheart; the quiet one.

I know Damien is disdainful of humans; he and Lucien are cut from the same cloth. Damien seems even colder than Lucien, though. While Lucien was originally cold towards me, I can now see that much of it was a façade.

I touch Lucien's mind, communicating my gratitude through our mated bond, and telling him how sorry I am for what just happened. I can tell through the link that he's fighting the instincts of his demon to attack Mia. His demon isn't pleased, but I can sense the moment he decides to step back.

Tensions are still high on both sides. Things got out of hand rather quickly. Mia was stupid to shoot lightning at Damien's head that way, no matter what her intentions had been. I know none of them trust Lucien yet, they haven't really been given a reason to. They think he has his own agenda, and I have to admit, I'm still not entirely sure how much we can trust him to act in our best interests, either. But standing here, looking at him and being able to see into his mind, I know he has no intention of hurting me or my family.

"Abigail. Drop the shield," I say softly, laying my hand on her shoulder and reaching my mind out for hers so I can give her a glimpse at Lucien's thoughts. "You can see he means us no harm."

She looks at me and her eyes narrow as she tries to understand what she's seeing in her mind. I can see the moment she realizes that he would protect me with his own life if need be, that the bond we share is for life; her eyes widen in shock. She knows he intends to protect those I love because of how deeply he cares for me.

He might not retaliate; she communicates through our link. *But what about the demon standing beside him? And the others?*

Lucien won't allow Damien or any of his other men to act. They know better than to disobey his orders, I promise.

Her chanted words flow through my mind seconds before I feel the power dissipate around us, indicating the shield is down. Immediately after it drops, Damien takes a step in Mia's direction, his eyes full of contempt, but Abigail steps in his path.

ABIGAIL

I PUT MY HAND ON THE DEMON'S hard chest. "Don't," I whisper, stopping him dead in his tracks. My eyes widen in shock as an energizing blast travels from the tips of my fingers to the warm skin under his shirt. It feels like a thunderbolt, shooting deep inside his blackened soul before slamming back into my fingers, down my arm, and throughout my entire body. He had to have felt it, but he doesn't react. My witch and omega are both shocked; they've never felt anything like that before. My omega finally speaks up, telling me that she thinks I just linked myself to Damien.

My light grey eyes meet his dark blue gaze, and I see excitement and recognition shining inside them. A simple innocent touch has changed us both irrevocably, though I'm not really sure what that means. Not yet anyway.

"Do you really think you can protect her from me?" His tone is soft and low as he steps closer to me. His white shirt is open at the collar, exposing his well-muscled chest and a black swirl of tattoos he appears to be covered in. The sight of his naked flesh causes my mouth to water.

"Maybe," I whisper, my voice hardly audible over the sound of blood rushing in my ears. This cannot be happening. I won't allow it. I clear my throat before speaking. "I don't want us to be on opposite sides, Damien. We're going to need each other if what's been happening is any indication of what is still to come. Mia didn't mean anything by it, she had no intention to harm you. She only wanted to show you that we aren't helpless little humans who need protection."

He gives me a look that communicates he intends to discuss whatever it was that just passed between us later, before looking to his boss and giving a slight nod.

I let out a sigh of relief.

CHAPTER TWENTY-FIVE

SCARLETT

THE MEMORY OF THE WOMAN WHO appeared in our front room comes to mind, along with her warning. I reach out to Lucien, touching his mind with my own.

Lucien, we need to get things under control. All we want is your help finding Megan and to help figure out what is going on with all the people going missing. That means we're going to have to figure out a way to work together.

"Damien. Step down," Lucien commands his lieutenant in a stern tone. "We don't have time for this shit. There are important matters to discuss."

"Fuck," Damien growls, tearing his eyes from Abigail's and pointing at her twin. "Just keep that bitch the fuck away from me," he warns before coming and standing at Lucien's side, his eyes going back to rest on Abigail.

"Now that we have that out of the way, maybe we can get back on track?" Lucien drawls, looking around at everyone in the room and daring us to argue. Nobody says a word. "Good. We need to figure out an arrangement all of us can live with because we are going to need one another. Humans and Naturals are both being taken, and we don't have a fucking clue who's responsible."

"What kind of arrangement, exactly?" Pamela asks with curiosity and a touch of suspicion.

"We will share intel and help each other whenever possible," Lucien replies to Pamela's question with confidence. "We'll put everyone in groups; each patrol will have a combination of our people."

I hear muttered protests from the other side of the room; the look of distrust on their faces says it all. Lucien's men clearly aren't thrilled with their boss' decision. Judging by the way Lucien's eyes flash red, he's displeased with their reaction.

He slowly turns his head, fire burning in his eyes as he stares at each of them in turn, daring them to continue. "If any of you have any objections, you know where the fucking door is." The silence in the room is palpable until he turns around and addresses my family once more. "We will meet tomorrow and figure out the patrol groups. In the meantime, there is one other issue we need to discuss."

"And what would that be?" Melissa asks, her head tilted curiously to the side.

Clearing my throat, I nervously run my hand through my hair. I wish I'd told them before they got here so I wouldn't have to deal with their reactions now.

"I should have told you sooner, but there is a meeting taking place in this room later this evening," I inform them, watching as they turn towards me. "We need to be there."

Staring at me with a puzzled expression, Emma demands, "What kind of meeting? Why do we need to be there?"

"Why didn't you tell us before now?" Ava asks, folding her arms over her chest angrily.

Lucien cuts in, answering their questions for me. "I apologize that you weren't told before today. I wanted to wait until I received confirmation from the rest of the attendees. Damien, myself, and a handful of my men will be in attendance, as well as members from both councils, and delegates or leaders from the Fae, Vampires, Shifters, Gargoyles, and Angels. The goal is to create a task force to deal with what's been going on. We need to figure out who all has gone missing and try to find the common thread so we can stop anyone else from disappearing." I'm relieved he doesn't mention how long I've known about the meeting or that I was supposed to tell them about it.

"Scarlett's right," Melissa shrugs, her voice unapologetic. "We need to attend the meeting."

Eyes narrowed, frown creasing her forehead, Pamela says to Lucien, "*If* we agree to attend, it will put us in a vulnerable position. You do realize that if they attack us, we will have no choice but to retaliate?" she warns.

"Melissa could put a confinement spell on us for protection," Abigail offers.

Looking around at everyone in the room, Melissa shakes her head and rubs her temples. "I could do that. But there's no guarantee it would work. There will be some of the post powerful Naturals alive at that table with us."

Pushing away a lock of hair that has fallen in my face, I look at Lucien. "Will any of the leaders or council members know we're witches?" I ask.

Lucien shrugs. "Though I've instructed all my men not to breathe a word of it to anyone, sadly, I can't trust each and every one of them. You'll have to try not to attract any attention."

I fight the urge to roll my eyes. Is he serious? What does he think we're going to do? Stand up and declare ourselves witches?

Damien pipes in. "Upon arrival, all weapons are to be turned over and everyone has agreed to go through an imaging scan to prove they aren't hiding anything under their clothes."

I study the faces of the women I hold most dear and can see how worried they are. We all join our mental link so we can talk privately amongst ourselves.

Melissa's right. This is a chance we must take; there's no other option. Megan is out there somewhere, alone and frightened. Lucien is our best bet in helping us find her, and I feel like we need to do something about the other humans and Naturals going missing also. I know we're all afraid, but I honestly think this is something we must do, I tell them.

Melissa, could you do a concealment spell that will hide our witches and omegas from all the attendees? Ava asks.

The problem is, it might not even work. Evelyn cuts in. *We know there will be countless extra-powerful Naturals in the meeting, and we would have no way of knowing whether it works or not until the meeting begins.*

I can't say for sure. I can easily put a spell in place, but Evelyn's right. We wouldn't know whether it's worked or not until we're in the meeting. But I guess that's just the chance we're going to have to take, Melissa answers.

We have to do this. For Megan. We are need Lucien's and the rest of the leaders' help. Without it, the outcome is unlikely to be in our favor." Pamela's agreement fills me with relief.

I see the acceptance in everyone's eyes, though perhaps resignation is a better word. We all know we have no other choice.

"We've agreed to attend the meeting," Mia and Abigail announce in unison. Standing side-by-side, holding hands, they turn their attention to all the men in the room. "But make no mistake. If anyone attacks us in any way, shape, or form, we will retaliate. And it will not end well for anyone."

SCARLETT

THE FOLLOWING EVENING

I CAN FEEL THE NERVES RADIATING from my sisters and cousins. I can't say I blame them; I'm feeling anxious too. Did we make a mistake agreeing to attend the meeting? Guess we'll find out soon enough.

Melissa placed a concealment spell around each of us, meaning we should appear as normal humans. We're all hoping it holds up against the powerful Naturals we're going to be in contact with. If not, we could be fucked.

Since last night, I've sensed something off with Melissa. I can't put my finger on what's wrong, but I know she's upset about something. I walk over to her and sit down in the chair beside hers, reaching out for her mind so we can speak without anyone overhearing us.

Are you going to tell me what's wrong? I ask. *I know you're nervous about the meeting. We all are. But there's something else going on with you. You're rattled. Why?*

I feel her trepidation through the link. Whatever's wrong, she's fighting against it. I know if I wait her out, she'll tell me what's going on.

She says nothing for several minutes. Finally, she relents. *It's just…*

My past could walk through that door. I don't know if I'm strong enough to face it, she confesses.

I'm shocked at her admission. She is one of the strongest people I know, if not *the* strongest. I don't know a lot about what happened in her past, but I know it was enough to change her. She was gone for a long time, and when she arrived home, she was completely broken. She didn't speak for months. It wasn't until she realized what was happening in her body that she came out of the dark hole she'd been hiding in. Finding the cubs not long after that had been another turning point for her. Whatever it was that she'd gone through had made her into the formidable woman she is today.

I don't see that woman right now, though. I see the woman who arrived home broken, an empty shell of the person she once was. Whatever is going on inside her head, she needs to snap out of it. The only thing I can think of is that this must have something to do with the shifters who will be attending the meeting. I know she lived with a group of them for several years.

Your past? As in... I let my thought trail off.

Yes.

Melissa. You are one of the strongest women I've ever known. If your past walks through that door, I know, with every fiber of my being, you can handle it. I reassure her.

I hope you're right. I feel her sigh next to me and grab her hand in mine, squeezing it gently. As our skin touches, a scene begins unfolding in my mind. It's so mixed up; I can't tell if I'm looking at the past, present, or future. I can see Melissa and there's danger all around her. An unknown man and woman appear, their faces in shadow. There are tears, arguments, fighting.

Before I can figure it out, the scene changes. This one is clearly in the future. I see Melissa again, with the same unknown man as before. They're laughing and kissing, and I hear giggling children and a faint voice calling out. What it's saying, I have no idea. The scene fades away and I'm left reeling.

I break our mental link and let go of her hand, grabbing my head. I give myself a moment to recover before turning towards her and whispering, "I promise you; I am right about this."

With questions in her eyes, she studies me, and I grab her hand once more. Giving her a smile, I tell her, "I promise you. Eventually, everything will be just fine."

She stares at me, eyes narrowed, trying to discern what it is I saw. "What did you see?" she whispers. I don't answer. I kiss her on the cheek before standing and rejoining the rest of our family.

I can feel her penetrating stare against my back, and I try to shake it off. I cannot tell her what I saw. I don't want anything to jeopardize the happy future I saw for her.

It is now seven-thirty. The rest of the attendees should be arriving soon as the meeting is set to begin at eight. As instructed, we didn't bring any weapons with us, and we went through the scanner before entering the room. I hope nobody objects to the security measures Lucien put in place.

SCARLETT

A LITTLE WHILE LATER

WE ALL JUMP SLIGHTLY WHEN THE wooden doors bang open and hit the walls. Lucien and Damien enter first, followed by Jaden and a handful of Lucien's men close behind. These are different men than the ones Lucien had with him earlier. The wooden doors swing shut behind them.

I realize that I recognize the men. They're the ones who were attacked. As they come further into the room, they all acknowledge me with either a smile or a nod. Although I'm a little surprised by their friendliness, I return their greetings. By the questions on my family's faces, I know they're curious as to how I know the men, but now isn't the time to explain.

As soon as Lucien entered the room, I felt his anticipation racing through our link. I reach out to him and see a flicker of reaction in his eyes just before he severs the connection completely. It's like a punch to the face. I feel like I might be sick. I've never felt anything like this before;

it's as though I've lost a piece of myself. I want to scream at him, to demand a reason why he would do this to me, to us... but I won't.

I take a deep breath, trying to calm myself. From the corner of my eye, I can see Mia frowning at me and I give her a small smile. I can't show any reaction to what just happened. I can't let him know how much he's hurt me. Two can play this game.

"Ladies. Please sit. There's enough room for everybody," Damien invites. "The others will be here shortly."

Puzzled, we look at one another; there aren't even enough chairs in the room for all my sisters to sit. Suddenly, the air in the room shifts, as though someone has placed their hands on the walls outside the room and is violently rocking it back and forth. As quickly as it started, it stops, and the room finishes expanding. It has tripled in size and the table and chairs have vanished. In their place, a massive wooden table and countless chairs appear in the center of the room. The table is big enough to fit at least forty or fifty people around it. On the other side of the room is a large, stacked stone fireplace, and next to it is a long wooden banquet table, laden with refreshments.

It looks like a feast for a banquet or even a wedding, not a bloody meeting. We try to keep our surprise from showing on our faces. The only way this was possible is with magic. Changing a room that way requires quite a bit of strength and knowledge, which leads me to several unanswered questions. I don't know whether to be impressed or frightened. I share a look with my sisters and cousins, and based on their expressions, I know they're thinking along the same lines as me. Lucien must be connected to someone of great power, someone who can wield very strong magic.

Lucien, Damien, and Jaden take their seats at the head of the table, the rest of the men remaining on their feet and spreading out behind them. My family and I slowly make our way over. Out of the corner of my eye, I catch Abigail staring blatantly at Damien.

I tried to talk to her about him earlier, but she shook her head and walked away. Something is obviously going on with her, but I haven't the foggiest idea what it is. I hope what I read as sexual tension between the two of them was actually something else. Damien and Mia started off on the wrong foot and I know Abigail getting involved with him is bound to cause issues.

Lucien locks eyes with me and motions for me to take the chair next to his. I raise my eyebrows as I take a seat as far from him as I can get, daring him to say something. I know it's petty, but he was the one who cut our link. I can see he's pissed that I ignored his request, but I don't care. I raise my chin in defiance and his eyes change color. As a man who is accustomed to people following his orders, I must be quite the challenge for him. My stomach tightens with lust. Like it or not, I cannot seem to get rid of my attraction for him. I wonder how one can be so beautiful yet so deadly at the same time.

The creaking of the large wooden doors steals my focus from Lucien, and though I should feel anxious about the meeting about to take place, I just feel relieved.

CHAPTER TWENTY-SIX

SCARLETT

YOU COULD CUT THE TENSION IN the room with a knife. There's something building in the air, like the ozone smell you can practically taste just before a storm arrives. Nobody can agree on what we should do and nobody will admit to any of their people going missing, despite the fact that we already know they have. It's bloody ridiculous, but it stems from a lack of trust. Everyone is going to have to find a way to get over it because if we can't manage to work together, we're all going to be in serious trouble.

The delegates from the councils arrived first, one for the humans and one for the Naturals. Immediately, they started fighting over who would be running the meeting and neither of them were pleased when Lucien cut them off and informed them he would be in charge of leading. They're now sitting across from me and my family in stony silence while the rest of the council members, five from each council, are sitting around them, arguing over every little thing.

If that wasn't bad enough, Aria arrived shortly after, entering the room as though it belonged to her. Now she sits next to Lucien, looking like his fucking queen, while shooting daggers at me with her eyes. At least she's keeping her mouth shut. I don't even know how I would keep control of my temper if she started mouthing off.

Lucien, the bastard, just sits there, letting her touch him. I watch as the glances at me with a smirk while running her fingertips across his hand. Fucking bitch. I know she's trying to torment me. Sadly, it's working.

If he hadn't broken our link, I could tell him what I thought of him. Instead, I'm just left to stew in my rage. If he thinks I'm going to let him touch me after this, he's in for a rude awakening.

When the shifter sovereign arrived, my family and I all felt the shift in Melissa. Sadness and anxiety rushed out of her, and I wanted to put my arms around her in comfort, but I knew she wouldn't appreciate the gesture. Not here. Not now. Jacob, the sovereign over all shifters saw Melissa as he took his seat and hasn't taken his eyes off her since. It's obvious they know each other, but I could only guess at the nature of their relationship. His handsome face looks angry, while my cousin has managed to hide any trace of emotion. The dark-haired woman sitting next to Jacob was introduced as his mate, and she's been giving my cousin the evil eye since her arrival.

The Fae arrived with all their usual fanfare. I was shocked to see that all the Fae King's guards are women, all of them jaw-droppingly beautiful. Based on the whispers from the rest of the table when they entered, they're his lovers as well as his guards. His demeanor is arrogant, and I haven't missed the way he looks at Mia. I really don't appreciate the way he's eyeing her, as though she's a tasty meal waiting to be devoured. Luckily, she hasn't seemed to notice. I can only imagine how she would react. It's bad enough to have to watch Abigail and Damien eye fuck each other. Everyone in the room can tell there's something between them. They're acting like horny teenagers.

The Vampires arrived all together, but their leader Nathan will not be attending. Jax will be filling in for him, though he didn't say why. I don't like the way the Vampires and Jaden have been eyeing each other, as though they're ready to come to blows. So far, nobody has done anything, but the vicious looks being thrown around are distracting.

The Gargoyle Elder, Reid, and a group of Angels were the last to arrive. Gargoyles look human but looks can be deceiving. The Angels, a mix of male and female, are regal and striking. They have their wings hidden from view, probably using a concealment spell which allows them to call their wings when necessary.

There are about sixty total people in the room by the time the meeting starts. My family and I have gotten a few suspicious looks, but the concealment spell seems to be working so far. There were a few people who questioned Lucien about who the hell we were, and Lucien had told them half-truths; that our sister is missing, and we turned to him for help, and about the soul keeper and soul eater who appeared to have been involved. It seems that the soul keeper and soul eater part distracted them from their suspicion of us because as soon as he finished speaking, the room erupted into chaos. It took at least half an hour to calm everyone down so we could move on.

Lucien's gaze flickers around the room until it lands on Jax. As he speaks, his eyes narrow. "Jax. Where is Nathan? Don't give me any bullshit, either. He's never missed a single one of these bloody meetings and I know the message I received wasn't from him. Tell me, what the hell are you hiding?" Lucien demands, his eyes flashing red.

Jaden, who is sitting beside Lucien, tenses, and the rest of the room breaks out into murmurs. Jax looks around the table before turning to his men and clearing his throat. His expression hardens in anger. "Nathan is missing," he announces, confirming everyone's worst fears.

The entire room goes silent. You could hear a pin drop outside.

The two delegates from either council finally seem to wake up and join the meeting as they start throwing questions at Jax faster than he can answer them. They want to know why they weren't informed, how long it's been, and every detail of every minute since Nathan went missing.

I see Lucien, Damien, and Jaden share a look and watch with bated breath as the scene in front of me continues to unfold.

"How long?" Jacob snarls, baring his teeth.

"A month. We've been looking for him every night since, but there's been no trace. It's like he just vanished," Jax answers, his voice full of frustration.

A growl of displeasure falls from Jaden's lips and his pure, unadulterated hatred for the other vampire is palpable. "Why has this been kept from me?" he demands.

"You're no longer a part of our coven, so why would I keep you in the loop on coven affairs?" Jax responds, his eyebrow arched condescendingly.

Jaden stands, his face full of uncontrolled rage. A deep growl rumbles from his throat as violence blazes in his eyes. The lights in the room flicker.

"Do not push your luck, Jax. If you keep attempting to provoke me, you will leave this room in a body bag. You know the rules. Whether I'm in the coven or not, Nathan is my blood, and I should have been informed. Tell me, Jax. Why isn't one of Nathan's blood leading the coven in his absence instead of you?"

Ripples of shock travel around the room at finding out Jaden is related to the Vampire King. The men standing around Jax shift uneasily. They know the laws of their coven and know they've been broken. On top of that, Jax has no lawful right to lead the coven, but he somehow managed to take the role anyway.

"I was elected to be in charge while Nathan is unavailable," Jax states in a cool, relaxed tone.

Jaden's voice echoes with challenge as he shouts, "There is no way in hell that someone who isn't of our blood would be elected while our King is missing!"

Jax cocks his head. "Things have clearly changed since you left, Jaden," he drawls, his voice heavy with sarcasm.

The fire burning in Jaden's eyes flares brighter, his features hardening even more as he meets Jax's mocking stare.

A hand slams against the table, hard, the loud slapping sound gaining everyone's attention. All eyes turn to my side of the table.

"Gentlemen. I think the matter of Nathan, our sister Megan, and the other humans and Naturals going missing is more urgent than the two of you having a pissing contest," Pamela says, in her most patronizing tone, eyes full of contempt. "People are missing. Megan was kidnapped and now we know that the most powerful vampire to walk the earth has vanished as well. I think most of the people at this table would agree that we need to concentrate on that issue. Whatever disagreements you two may have can be discussed later, on your own time."

"The woman is right. This isn't the time or place," Reid chastises in a gravelly voice.

Jaden turns his head as Lucien murmurs something and his mouth hardens as he listens to what his boss has to say. An expression of acute anger appears as he turns towards his nemesis. He retakes his seat and bites out, "This is far from over."

Leaning back in his chair, like he's enjoying the game, Jax retorts with amusement, "I'm looking forward to it."

There's a brief moment of silence before Gil-Galad, the Fae king, speaks with quiet authority. "The woman was right. Something is going on and we need to figure this out."

"The *woman* has a name. Pamela. Please remember it and use it from now on," Mia announces.

Gil-Galad glares at Mia, annoyance written across his refined features as their eyes lock. A smirk spreads across his face, one eyebrow lifting in challenge.

Pamela and Abigail send warnings through the link, telling Mia to behave herself. They're right. We can't afford too much attention being on us.

She tears her gaze away from his and looks down at her hands.

LUCIEN

IF THIS MEETING DOESN'T work, we are beyond fucked. We're going to have to find a way to work together. That means not keeping secrets like the one Jax has been keeping from all of us. I'm so fucking pissed off, but it's nothing compared to the rage radiating from Jaden.

Jaden has had dealings with Jax before, and apparently things haven't gone well in the past. How Jax was able to get the vote to oversee Nathan's coven is something even I'm having trouble coming to terms with. Jaden isn't the only one who doesn't trust him. He's definitely up to no good. But whatever he has planned, I intend to deal with it.

Then there's Scarlett. I felt her pain when I blocked our link, but I didn't have a choice. I knew Aria would be at the meeting and I wasn't willing to take the chance that she'd be able to pick up on our connection. I must keep Scarlett and her family safe. If that means letting Aria touch me and pretending like I still care about her, so be it. Even if it means hurting Scarlett.

I hear the clearing of a throat and I look down the table at Austin, one of the smaller region leaders. He's been nervous since he arrived and it's clear he has something he needs to tell me.

"Austin," I acknowledge him with a nod, prompting him to speak.

Clearing his throat again, he wiggles nervously in his seat. "Some people in my region have gone missing," he says in a voice so faint; I have to struggle to hear him. I barely manage to bite back a snarl. I knew I'd made a mistake when I gave him his own region; he's too weak to lead. He's neither ruthless nor powerful, two qualities necessary to be in charge. He continues in a voice slightly louder than before, "At first, I thought little of it as the people who reported them missing said they've gone missing before and shown back up after a few weeks at the most."

"What's different this time, then?" asks Damien, giving me a 'what the fuck' look.

"Since the first report, we've received twenty-five more reports of people being missing. All different ages, both male and female, some human and some Natural," he explains, looking around the room nervously and never quite meeting mine or Damien's eyes.

Fucking idiot. I gave him a part of my territory to run, and he didn't even think to keep me informed of something so important. Bloody useless fool. I want to put my hands around his neck and squeeze until his eyes pop from his head. I look over at Damien and he looks every bit as angry as I'm feeling.

I turn back to Austin. "I want a list of every single person who is missing from your region before you leave tonight," I order, watching as he gives me a shaky nod.

Turning my attention to the rest of the region leaders in my territory, I ask them, "Has anyone else had anyone disappear in the last few weeks and neglected to tell me?"

I curse, rage building inside me, as half the hands lift. I slam my fist down on the wooden table, causing the glasses to rattle. The sound of cracking wood echoes around the deathly silent room.

"Has anyone else had people go missing and not come forward?" I demand in a deceptively calm voice. My temper is a drumbeat in my skull as every territory leader from all the other regions nervously raise their hands. Jacob, Gil-Galad, Reid, Jax, and Archer all stare at the people they trusted to be in charge, the people they counted on to keep their part of the region safe. The people who were expected to report to the region leaders when something happened so that we could keep our regions safe.

"Why the fuck wasn't I notified!?" Jacob roars. "Why weren't any of us notified?" He locks eyes with each and every one of his territory leaders before he turns his attention to me, his face reflecting the same rage I feel building inside of me.

"Jacob, I'm sure I speak for everyone here when I say, I'm sorry. Please accept our apologies. We had no way of knowing how important it was," Luke says to his leader, his head bowed in shame.

"Your apology is worthless, and I don't accept it. Do you think because we've given you regions to run in our territories that you're somehow in charge? That you get to make decisions without consulting us? You bloody don't. You should consider yourselves lucky to be permitted a seat at this table. All of us want a list of every single human and Natural that has gone missing from each region by tonight. No fucking excuses," Jacob rants.

I notice his eyes flashing silver and know he's struggling to keep his wolf under control. The leaders in question squirm in their seats. Jacob's orders ringing in their ears, all of them grab pens and paper from the center of the table and start scribbling names.

"When did Megan go missing?" Jax turns his attention to Scarlett and her family, grabbing my attention as well.

"About a week ago. Megan was out with a group of friends and just vanished," Melissa replies, shifting in her seat to face him.

"And nobody's seen her since?" asks one of the council members. "Are you even telling the truth? You're sure none of you know where she is?" He scoffs, looking at them with suspicion glowing on his face.

Melissa's face tightens in anger, and I ready myself to jump in if she decides to try anything. I won't let her expose Scarlett's secret. If any of them show their powers, everyone in the room will know exactly what they are and that cannot happen.

CHAPTER TWENTY-SEVEN

MELISSA

I FEEL MY STOMACH CLENCH and tighten with anxiety. Seeing the shifters again is bringing up all my old fears and insecurities. I fight to keep control of my emotions, even as I feel myself growing increasingly uneasy under their scrutiny. I push my long silver hair behind my ear as I continue to ignore Jacob's and his mate's stares. The sight of the happy couple has been battering me since they came through the door. Knowing they're still together is breaking my heart. I should be the one sitting at his side.

I need to find a way to lock these feelings away, but the mark he gave me so long ago is throbbing due to him being in such close proximity. I'm just relieved that the concealment spell I put in place is still working.

The council member who seems to suspect us of lying is an idiot. Why the hell would we make something like this up? What could it possibly gain us to pretend that our sister is missing? He's obviously human; maybe all of them are needlessly paranoid.

"If we knew where our sister was, why would we be here? Why would we ask Lucien for his help?" I question, rolling my eyes. What a complete twat. How do these people even get elected to the council?

As though I hadn't even spoken, the council member looks around the table. "Am I the only one who thinks this doesn't ring true? I think they're hiding something." He looks back at me before continuing, "And

I demand to know what the hell it is!" His lips are puckered in annoyance as he slams his hand down against the table.

"No one is hiding anything or lying about anything," I reply in a droll tone, crossing my arms across my chest, the motion making my cleavage more pronounced. With an expression of disgust, the council member turns up his nose and looks over at Lucien.

What a rude bastard!

Lucien looks at the man with an expression of irritation on his face. "Megan was last seen in my club, which is why Scarlett came to me and asked for my help in finding her. Scarlett and her family will be remaining here as I continue searching for answers," Lucien informs everyone. We haven't discussed staying past the meeting, so I'm surprised at his announcement.

The council member's lips thin with annoyance. "Lucien. You know the council must be informed before you take any further action. I will inform them of the situation and get back to you."

Lucien snarls, causing everyone to lean back in their chairs. His eyes flash red and when he speaks, his voice is deeper and echoes around the room. "Do whatever the fuck you want, but do *not* forget to whom you are speaking to!"

The council member blanches, cowering in his seat. "I'm s-s-sorry, Lucien. I meant no offense," he stammers.

Little weasel. He has no problem treating me with disrespect, but the big bad demon reprimands him and he acts like a submissive little puppy.

LUCIEN

MY DEMON IS FIRED UP AND unwilling to go back under the surface. I cannot believe that stupid little human would dare speak to me in such a way. Who the fuck does he think he is?

I hear someone clear their throat and look around the table to see that the insubordinate territory leaders seem to have finally finished their lists and are passing them over to the region leaders. I don't bother to read the lists handed over to me. I just pass them to Jaden who glances down at them before folding them and placing them in the pocket of his black suit jacket. I will look at the names later this evening.

I feel Aria leaning into me and the sensation of her breath against my neck and her fingers stroking sensuously down my arm make me shudder in disgust. "My love. I think it's prudent you inform everyone here exactly who… and what these… ladies are," she says loudly, gaining the attention of the entire room.

Fucking. Bitch.

ARIA

I'M GOING TO TAKE THEM DOWN. They have no right to be here. I'm livid and my demon isn't having it.

I'm fueled by hatred and vengeance. I want to eviscerate every single one of the witches sitting at this table. I watch with delight as the leaders and council members look at Lucien to gauge his reaction to my words.

I can tell he's pissed. A thin smile appears on his lips. "Do you have a death wish, Aria?" he asks in a deadly whisper. A shiver runs down my spine as his demon flashes in his eyes.

Reluctantly, I bow my head in surrender. I'm glad I said it, but perhaps I should have found a way to reveal their identity without putting myself at risk. I just want him to get rid of his whore and the rest of the cunts sitting with her. I recognize the bitch covered in those freaky tattoos. The people in this room should know who they're dealing with. If only so they can deal with my problem for me.

My precious spy has given me invaluable intel. Lucien's plaything has apparently been making friends with one of Lucien's men and he hardly leaves her side, and I've already set the wheels in motion to get rid of Alex. My spy told me he's gone to visit his family and I've made sure he won't be returning.

Whore. I will teach her not to touch what belongs to me!

I lock eyes with her and let her see my hostility as I run my fingertips down Lucien's hard chest and kiss him on the cheek. "I'm sorry, my love," I whisper in his ear, my voice soft and timid. "I just can't bear the thought of you looking like a fool, which is what will happen if you allow this charade to continue."

LUCIEN

ARIA BOWS HER HEAD AND WHIMPERS when I glare at her. Her punishment will have to wait. I can feel my demon straining to be released, but I push him back. Now is not the time. I'm not the only one struggling to hold their temper, though. Damien and Jaden aren't faring much better. I can feel the tension running through them as they try not to react. Aria has put every single person in this room in danger.

Aria never does anything without a reason. I should have followed my gut and had her banned from the meeting. I should have known she wouldn't be able to keep her mouth shut.

The room is silent, still. Everyone is looking at me, trying to figure out what the hell she's talking about. The councilor finally speaks up. "Lucien? Care to explain?"

Before I can respond, Aria shoots out of her seat beside me, pointing at Scarlett and her family. "You fools!" she screeches. "Can't you sense the abomination among us?"

"What the fuck is Aria talking about, Lucien?" the council member demands, a shadow of alarm crossing his face as he stands up, the rest of the council following suit.

"You bloody fools! Those women are witches! Every last one of them. Can't you idiots feel it? Can't you sense the witch inside them!?" Aria rants.

The room is cloaked in shocked silence, and I finally have a chance to speak. "Sit the fuck down and shut your fucking mouth, Aria." I snarl. I need to get her under control before all hell breaks loose.

"No. Lucien, it's time you opened your eyes. You've obviously gone soft, believing everything that red-haired cunt tells you. I've done some investigating of my own. They're making it all up. There is no sister. They are the ones responsible for the missing humans and Naturals. It is time we find out what they're really up to."

"Do you have any proof of these allegations, Aria?" a member of the council asks. "Because until you provide proof, this is merely hearsay."

"I hate to say it, but I agree with him. We will need proof that what you're saying is true. If they are indeed witches, why have they chosen to reveal themselves now? If they've been living in secret among us all this time, why would they come out in the open?" Jax questions.

"Archer. Did you know about these witches?" Jacob's mate demands, speaking to the Angel, her haughty tone seeming to echo around the room.

Attempting to calm his mate, Jacob takes her hand into his larger one and kisses her fingers tenderly. "Marguerite, my love. None of us know if these women are really witches. However, I too would like to know whether you knew of this, Archer." Jacob looks at the Angel with eyebrows raised.

The Angel shakes his head. "You know we do not interfere."

What he says is true. Angels are forbidden from speaking of what they know. Should they issue a warning, even one that saves lives, they'll be punished. They could even lose their wings.

Slowly removing her hand from her mate's, Marguerite mutters, loudly enough for everyone to hear, "Guess that's a yes, then." She turns to glare at Melissa, Scarlett's cousin.

One of the guards standing behind Gil-Galad speaks up. "Are you a witch?"

The Fae King turns and glares at the woman and her face flushes pink as she winces, before she runs from the room.

I place my hand on Aria's arm, hoping the distraction will give me a moment to keep her quiet, but she shakes me off. "Don't you fucking touch me," she snarls. Turning to the room, she screeches, "Are you all witless? How can you not see that they are witches?!"

"Aria. Calm. The. Fuck. Down." I growl quietly. The rest of the room is looking at Aria like she's lost her damn mind, and I'm hoping I can get things under control before the situation blows up completely.

Those hopes disappear when Aria turns and looks at Scarlett. Before I can stop her, she's throwing a swirling ball of red, blue, and yellow energy straight at the witches. Damien, Jaden, and I jump from our seats.

SCARLETT

WE DON'T HAVE TIME TO REACT. I watch in horror as a ball of light flied straight towards me before slamming into my chest. It feels like a wrecking ball. The impact causes the chair I'm sitting in to fly backward, slamming into the wall behind me. I feel my head strike the stone. Fuck! My head starts to pound immediately. I shake it in an attempt to clear my vision, causing pain to ricochet around my brain. With eyes screwed up in pain, I try to take in my surroundings. Everything appears to be happening in slow motion.

Through cloudy vision, I can just barely see Aria. She's standing in the same place, and I'm almost certain I can hear her chanting. Behind her back, a whirling portal forms and as it grows and stabilizes, I watch in fascinated horror as a group of about twenty men step through it into the room. They look around the room, standing at attention, until Aria starts shouting orders in a language I've never heard before. The men charge towards us.

I try to stand, only to fall right back on my ass. Whatever the hell she hit me with was no typical energy bolt. It has physically weakened me. My witch tries to emerge, and it takes nearly all my remaining strength to push her back down. Her frustration and anger fuels my own rage. I long to let her come forward, but I know it's a terrible idea. My omega has remained blissfully silent, but I can feel her watching. Something is definitely wrong with me, though.

I force my hand to lift and touch the back of my head. Shit. There's a deep gash there and I can feel blood sliding down my temple. When I look at my hand, it's covered in sticky red blood. My omega finally jumps up and takes notice. I'm more seriously injured than I thought. Warmth travels through my body, growing nearly unbearable, before I feel the wound on my head stitch itself closed. I know if I have any other injuries, she'll take care of them.

I need to help my family. I try to stand once more, but my legs tremble, knees buckling. Biting back a cry of frustration, I collapse in my chair and watch helplessly as the scene unfolds around me.

Melissa reaches behind her back, pulling out a long gold and silver sword. How the hell did she manage to bring that in here? I saw her go through the scanner. Turning swiftly, she strides towards me, determination written across her face. In horror, I watch as a man walks up behind her, and before I can even shout a warning, she pivots on the balls of her feet, silver hair flying around her head as she swings the sword and slices the man's head clean off. My mouth drops open in awe as his head wobbles slightly before dropping to the floor.

Sensing another man charging in her direction, Melissa ignores the blood covering her face and body and, waiting until he's almost upon her, she ducks under his weapon before lashing out with her foot, kicking him in the abdomen. Once he's down, she leans forward and runs her blade through his stomach.

Pulling her blade free quickly, she twists and jumps back as another weapon whistles through the air in the exact place her head was only seconds before. Throwing her sword up in the air, she cartwheels, catching the blade as she lands in a crouch. She swipes the sword clean through his legs and his piercing scream echoes around the room as blood pours from his wounds. Standing, she continues cutting through the enemy as she makes her way towards me.

I watch as the rest of my family joins the flight, their features changing one by one to reveal the witches who share their bodies. My sisters conjure their individual daggers to defend themselves, using them to cut and stab any who would harm us.

Evelyn marches towards Melissa, fire burning in her eyes. My heart jumps to my throat as a large man reaches out to grab her from behind, tangling his hand in her multicolored hair and dragging her into his arms.

I hear her grunt as she grabs onto him, her feet sliding backwards despite her struggle. I feel helpless as I watch him tug her head back, bringing a thin black dagger up to her throat. Her screams are deafening as she manages to twist her body around until they're face to face, and almost as though her hair has caught fire, it changes color and starts to glow. Her eyes change from their deep emerald green to a brighter green with orange and red flames swirling in their center. The side of her mouth quirks as she lets of his wrist and lashes out with her fist, striking him in the face repeatedly.

His head snaps back and forth as she hits him, his nose splitting open and splattering blood all around them. With one final punch, he lets go of her hair and staggers backward. He bobbles on his feet for a moment before hitting the floor with a thud.

Evelyn grabs the black dagger from his hand and plunges it straight through his heart, twisting it until it's embedded deep inside his chest. With a grunt, she pulls it back out and slices his throat with it.

Something in the corner of my eye catches my attention and I look to see Pamela using one of the men as her shield as another tries to thrust his sword through her stomach. Beside her, Mia is stabbing her dagger into the groin of her own attacker, and he falls to the ground, a river of bright yellow blood pooling beneath his body.

Across the room, an enormous man with ash-grey skin and black soulless eyes grabs Abigail from behind. I glance around and see that nobody else has noticed she's in trouble. If I don't manage to do something, she could get severely injured. I reach down and grab the dagger I keep in an ankle holster and gather as much strength as I can muster, hurling the dagger at him. It flies straight and true, burrowing right between his shoulder blades.

I allow my witch to come forward, and she forces the blade to rotate one way, then the other, shoving it deeper inside of him. Finally, his arms let go and Abigail turns, facing the demon who had her in his grasp. Her witch is now out in full force; her black hair has turned a pale white; her eyes lit an eerie yellow. A sinister smile appears on her face as she slices the demon chest to groin, gutting him. She watches with a satisfied smirk as his innards fall to the floor at her feet. She looks at me and our eyes meet, and she gives me a nod of thanks before turning back to the fight.

I see Ava fighting in the corner of the room and notice that Evelyn has joined Melissa and they are fighting back-to-back. An endless horde of men continue to rush from the portal Aria created and the territory leaders and council members have finally joined the fray. There are several people who are apparently disloyal to their leaders, or perhaps they're just cowards, because they're gathered in the far corner of the room, trying to avoid getting pulled into the fight.

I notice my family, Lucien, Damien, and Jaden all throwing worried looks my way. I must look worse than I thought. They can't afford to concentrate on me, though. Any distraction could cost them their lives.

Opening the link to my family, I feel our minds meld together and order them to stop worrying about me, assuring them that my omega is healing my wounds. Breaking the link, I watch Mia and Abigail join forces. Chanting, they clutch each other's hands, raising them in the air. Their eyes change color, turning a dark purple as their chanting grows in intensity, causing a massive fiery black ball to appear in front of them. Even from where I'm sitting, I can feel the power reverberating through me.

Suddenly, a wave of dizziness hits me out of nowhere. What the fuck is happening? My entire body begins to tremble and the pain inside my head intensifies. I have no idea what's happening and I'm fucking terrified.

In a panic, I look around. I can't find Emma. Where is she? Out of the corner of my eye, I see Aria staring at me and when I turn to look, she smirks. Fear takes over and I black out.

SCARLETT

SIX MONTHS LATER

I WATCH THE OCEAN AS I WAIT for the sun to rise. I still cannot believe how he played me. I was such a fool to believe in him. What's the saying? *Fool me once, shame on you; fool me twice, shame on me.*

Never again. I hate him.

Is it possible to both hate and love someone at the same time? I've heard people say that there's a thin line between the two, but I never really understood it until now.

I have more than just myself to think of now. I know he's going to find me eventually, but it will take time. Still, I really need to start planning my next move.

"Scarlett. It's time," Pamela calls out to me, just as the sun breaches the horizon.

With a groan, I manage to stand from my chair and slowly make my way over to my sisters who are gathered, waiting for me, my hands gently placed upon my stomach.

EPILOGUE

MEGAN

LOCATION AND TIME UNKNOWN

A COLD BREEZE TEASES THE TENDRILS of my hair and I frown. Did I forget to close my bedroom window? I remember going out the night before and meeting up with a group of friends. Strangely though, I can't remember coming home. My room smells odd as well. I take a deep breath and try to identify the refreshing scent that reminds me of the ocean.

With a sigh, I force myself to open my eyes. What the hell? The room is completely dark and it's obvious I'm not in my own bed. If I put my hand right in front of my face, I wouldn't be able to see it. Where the hell am I?!

I can tell I'm on a bed of some sort, but the mattress under me is bloody uncomfortable; the springs stabbing me in the back. I reach out with one hand and feel a cold stone wall. Pulling myself into a sitting position, I lean back against it. Immediately upon moving, I feel a steel chain around my wrist. What the fuck is going on?

I tug at it and hear the sound of jangling metal till the silence in the room. To say I'm frightened would be an understatement, but panicking won't do me any good. I know my sisters will be looking for me. I allow that thought to calm me slightly.

They won't give up until they find me. I wonder how long I've been here. Hours? Days? It scares me that I don't know who has taken me or why. I need light so I can see where I am.

"So. You're finally awake."

The voice comes out of nowhere, making me jump. The voice is deep and rough, coming from the right of where I'm sitting.

"I was starting to think you were never going to wake up," the voice says, and I realize he's moved. It came from in front of me this time.

"You could have given me some kind of warning that I wasn't alone in here," I say, trying to keep fear out of my tone and infuse it with some semblance of false bravado.

"Pray tell. How was I supposed to do that?"

I huff, recognizing his logic. Of course he couldn't have told me while I was asleep and how would he have warned me without scaring me? But the thought of someone else being in the room with me, surrounded by darkness, creeps me out. I ignore his question. He doesn't expect an answer anyway.

Instead, I throw a litany of questions his way, hoping he knows the answer to at least one of them.

"How long have I been here? How long have *you* been here? Where is here exactly, and how the hell did I get here?"

A deep rumble of a laugh echoes off the stone walls. Not a happy laugh, though. It sounds… angry.

"If I could tell you all that, little girl, well, I wouldn't be here."

I decide to ignore the 'little girl' comment. For now. "Can you tell me anything?"

"Of course. Though you aren't going to like it," He warns me, his voice closer than before. Fuck. What does he mean by that? Should I press him or just leave it alone? Fuck. I need to know whether I want to or not.

"Please just tell me." I huff.

"You're in a holding cell of some sort. From what I've seen, there's about twenty of them on this level. I'm not sure if there are more…"

"Do you know who took us? Or why?" I interrupt.

"Yes. I've seen who is holding us. You will too, in time."

I don't like that there are so many cells. What the fuck is going on here and why are they taking people? What are they doing to them? Who the fuck is they? I realize I just spoke my thoughts aloud.

"Oh, they want Naturals and Humans alike. You're the fourth…" he trails off as though considering his next words. "Person to be put in here with me."

I really don't want to ask, but I can't help myself. I don't like where this conversation is going and I have a really bad feeling in the pit of my stomach. "What happened to the other three?" I choke out.

"Oh, they took them away when I… finally finished with them," he tells me.

A shiver travels down my spine at his words. It feels like fear, but I'm not afraid of him. At least I don't think I am. His voice is like silk and crushed velvet rolled into one. His words, 'finished with them,' reverberate in my mind. Shit. I really don't like this.

My cellmate is obviously a Natural; a dangerous one at that. I pull my legs into my chest and rest my head on my knees. Why can't I be stuck in a cell with a normal human or even another witch?

No, fate couldn't be so kind. I'm afraid I know exactly what he is, and it terrifies me. I really hope I'm not locked in a cell with a vampire.

Who would be crazy enough to abduct and hold a vampire? They're so strong that even the most powerful Naturals don't like to cross them. Plus, there's the whole blood thing. They love it, crave it even. There are humans and Naturals who enjoy giving their blood to vampires. There are even clubs that indulge that kind of kink, one of which I stupidly ended up in.

Clearing my throat, I force myself to ask. "What do you mean, when you were finished with them?"

"What do you think I mean, little girl?" The voice asks from only a few inches away. His breath smells like fresh mint as it caresses across my face and I swear I can feel his lips on my cheek. I shudder uncontrollably.

I'm neck-deek in trouble and there's no way out.

I'm totally screwed.

Printed in Great Britain
by Amazon